FINDING ANNIE

Best Wishes

Peter Maher

FINDING ANNIE

Travels with My Great Aunt -
From Tipperary to Trenton N.J.

Peter Maher

Library of Congress Control Number:		2019942740
ISBN:	Hardcover	978-1-9845-9003-9
	Softcover	978-1-9845-9002-2
	eBook	978-1-9845-9001-5

Front cover picture taken by Marge Maher on our tour,
'walking in Annie's footsteps', March 2019:
Sculpture, "The Immigrants" located at the south end of the
Eisenhower Mall in Battery Park near Castle Clinton, which served
as a processing facility for newly arrived immigrants from 1855 to
1890. Annie Elizabeth Maher passed through here in 1878.

Print information available on the last page.

Rev. date: 06/05/2019

To order additional copies of this book, contact:
Xlibris
800-056-3182
www.Xlibrispublishing.co.uk
Orders@Xlibrispublishing.co.uk
797300

Acknowledgments

JANINE HALLISEY IS a remarkable researcher specializing in Genealogy. Her contribution to the historical accuracy of this book is incalculable. She has taught me some of the skill and art of research too, a gift I treasure. However, she has also been my guide to America, New York and New Jersey in particular, and has tried to ensure that those sections relating to their country will resonate with American readers. We accepted that a man writing in a woman's voice would not necessarily be easy. She has tried to help ensure that the female roles are authentic. Finally, she has helped to proof read the manuscript and any errors that remain are all my own. It was Janine who arranged our tour of New York and New Jersey, walking in Annie's footsteps, visiting the places she frequented, houses where she worked or owned. It proved to be a moving experience. Thank you Janine.

Bill and Renee (deceased) Mann who took me on my first tentative drive through Freehold and Long Branch, New Jersey and without whom there would have been no story to tell.

Jenny Adams, **Anne Stuart** and **Lynne Walby** have given endlessly of their time helping with the analysis and proof reading of this work. They have advised on plot, on character and helped with the, seemingly endless, task of ridding the manuscript of its errors and faults.

Prof. Andrew Scull and Prof. Gilbert Honigfeld for allowing me to use their books to gain inspiration and insights into the events at Trenton Asylum between 1917 and 1935. Particularly to you Gil for arranging that our tour of N.Y. and N.J. took in the Asylum. Thank you for having the patience to engage with the bureaucracy at Trenton to gain permission to tour the grounds. I had tried repeatedly to try to gain access to any records of Annie's that might still be held there, but Trenton, and particularly the Cotton Years, remain hidden from public view.

Marge Maher, last but not least. You have put up with me for so many years tinkering away with my family tree. The actual writing started, with your encouragement, during a holiday to Puglia, Italy in May 2018, and has continued for a further 10 months since, almost every day; Marge you have been my sounding-board throughout. At each stage, you would patiently listen to my analysis of both plot and character and helped me to understand, develop and clarify both. Your help in understanding female relationships has been invaluable. None of this would have been possible without you and, as always, you have my gratitude and my love.

CONTENTS

PROLOGUE

MY NAME IS Peter Maher and as a septuagenarian I wanted to set my family in context for you, the reader, while I can.

I am three generations away from my family roots in Ireland and so as a south London boy, born and bred, they seemed very distant from me. As far as I knew I was a cockney, and a protestant, having been sent to local Church of England schools in Blackheath and Lee Green in London.

My mother always explained my height and my blue eyes as traits won from my paternal great grandfather Patrick, who was also known as John Peter Maher; "a handsome man" she declared. I was to learn that, in 1864, he had brought his family from Clonmel in Southern Tipperary, Ireland, to live and build a new life in Sheerness in Kent, U.K.

As I grew up, there was little or no contact with my father's family, and one could be forgiven for thinking that he had no aunts and uncles to speak of. I discovered later on that there were some remarkable characters among that generation, so even now I fail to understand why they were never spoken of or their achievements lauded.

In part, that was what prompted me to try to find that lost Irish family and its descendants, so that I could put their life, and mine, into some sort of context. Thus, I started researching my family tree and the discoveries along the way have changed my perspective on my life.

My first shock was to find that my Irish family was Roman Catholic, not Protestant. I found that my great grandparents had 11 children, three while still in Ireland and then a further 8 once they had emigrated. The eldest was my Great Aunt Annie Elizabeth Maher born in 1860; I could trace her to Clonmel but, aged around 4 years old, she seemed to disappear from public records just at the time that her family emigrated from Clonmel to England. I concluded that she must have died as a young child. As you will learn there were a number of childhood deaths among the 11 children in the family.

It was my brother, Christopher, who turned up the most significant clue. He found the passenger manifest of a ship docking in New York on September 30th 1906. On board was one of those eleven, Joseph

Paul Maher. In that record, he stated that he was "visiting my sister in Long Branch, New Jersey. Annie Maher, New Ocean Avenue, L.Br. N.J."

Out of almost nothing we had learned that Annie Maher was still alive, but that, and extensive local research, posed as many questions as it solved. Where had this Irish woman been for 42 years? What had she done to accumulate sufficient money to buy houses in the prestigious coastal resort of Long Branch? How and when had she come to America; what had she done since arriving and were there any other members of her family there too?

When I found her, I discovered that this remarkable woman had an amazing life and, in some respects, is a role model for many of us. This book is about her life, in all its detail and, as you will probably gather, has resulted from significant amounts of research. But, at least to begin with, I shall let Annie tell her own story.

CHAPTER 1

Origins in Ireland

I WAS BORN, Annie Elizabeth Maher, in Clonmel a small town in Southern Tipperary that seemed to coddle me in my early years. My extended family were steeped in the Catholic rituals and as the eldest child of Patrick and Alice I was baptized there, in St. Peter and St. Paul Catholic Church in Clonmel, as were my two younger brothers, surrounded by those families and wrapped in their warmth and pride. From an early age, it was clear to me that my father wanted his eldest to be a boy, and a successful boy at that; he was often cold and distant with me while warm and paternalistic towards my brothers.

We were not poor, but my father's work as a carpenter, apart from the thriving line as coffin-maker-to-the-poor, was heavily dependent on the economic circumstances that Ireland had found itself in since the potato famine.

But poverty is a relative term, and our privileged position, with our own house and my father's workshops in outbuildings where he plied his carpenter's trade, was in stark contrast to farm workers in the countryside. Their makeshift homes on small lots rented to them by moneyed landowners were often no more than hovels with large families living in one all-purpose room.

More than a million died from illness and starvation during those famine years, and more than twice that number joined the exodus from their beloved country to points across the globe; never had I expected to be included in that number.

As a young girl living happily in Clonmel all was right with my world. Even then I did feel different, as though destiny had touched me on the shoulder, without my knowing what life had in store for me; just a feeling, an anticipation, a growing excitement.

Our extended family was however affected by the troubles of the times; my Uncle John O'Brien and his new wife Anastasia had left by ship to sail to America. New York is where he landed and settled and, despite the deeply held prejudice against the Irish there, he was destined to join a family florist business that gave them new-found wealth and security. It was his support and connections some years later that were to prove significant in my life.

I heard the grown-ups talk about American cousins who lived a different life in a different world. It was the story of new opportunities that did have an impact on family conversations: to escape the poverty of the potato famine and its subsequent effects and to find a world where your efforts could be rewarded and your family nurtured. Emigration was, and remains throughout history, a compelling theme.

My Irish family's destiny, at first anyway, was to lead us to the old world, rather than the new, to our traditional foes in England. Such had been the impact of the repressive political and religious inclinations of the British; such had been the disinclination of the British establishment to support the plight of the rural poor in Ireland during the famines, that it affected even a small rural community like mine in Clonmel. And yet here we were, a family contemplating the prospect of economic migration to that very land.

It was, in part, my parents' adherence to the strict Catholic codes on childbirth, that like many other catholic families, kept them chained to poverty. By the time of our emigration to England in 1864, at 4 years of age, I was the eldest of three with another not far over the horizon. In my mother's lifetime, there would be 11 live births.

But hand in hand with birth came its twin sister, death. For my parents' generation, and future generations like my own, childhood mortality was rife; grit under the shell that spat out dead children and yet provided the encouragement to further procreation.

Later in my life it was the sounds of grinding procreation that were to set me apart from the norm, against marriage and the conjugal, dominating, ritual relationships with men, and was to launch me on a different course.

Chapter 2

First to England

BUT FIRST TO England, to the arms and the tight embrace of the military, and to training for a life in service. The news on the family network was of a stable and generous living to those Irishmen prepared to work in the docks in England. My father Patrick's skills were of course in the realm of carpentry, but he was able to sell his efforts as an effective laborer to the recently rebuilt Royal Dockyard at Sheerness, Kent on the Isle of Sheppey; Sheerness is a town that sits at the mouth of the river Medway as it flows into the Thames. The Isle of Sheppey is on the north Kent coast in the south east of England on a stretch of estuary mud that forms the southern shore of the river Thames at the confluence with the river Medway.

My father Patrick and his Irish brethren hit the perfect time in the history of the dockyards at Sheerness. The docks had been refurbished to cope with stresses at nearby Chatham Royal Docks. The anxiety about pre-emptive seaborne military attacks on the Chatham Dock, and the demands for better faster ships, led to changes in the manufacturing processes; the make-up of the workforces changed with metal working replacing wood working skills as dockyards fully harnessed the use of steam and made the conversion from constructing ships of timber to those of iron.

For the group of workers first recruited to Sheerness was the prospect of living in prefabricated wooden sheds built on an uncertain triangle of land just outside the dockyard walls. In an earlier time, for 'home improvements' they would use items that they would beg, borrow and steal from the docks, including gallons of naval blue paint. As a consequence, this growing township was known as "Bluehouses" and later "Bluetown", a suburb of Sheerness. The blue paint could not disguise the fact that these dwellings were really shacks; damp, cold and unhealthy.

Sheerness became the home town for my family. For my father especially, Bluetown was the indelibly blue-painted backdrop to his life. Even on his death certificate in March 1901 were inscribed the words: "died of a cerebral hemorrhage at 13, High Street, Bluetown, Sheppey, Kent.

In that new hometown members of the family were suffering from illness and poor diet. Patrick was the younger of my two brothers when we came across from Ireland. He had the privilege of bearing my father's name, an unusual occurrence. In our family, when the oldest male member of the family line died, then the eldest son adopted that Christian name, as a way of passing the name Patrick down the line. For example, my father had been named John Peter but, on the death of his father Patrick, John Peter became known as Patrick too.

My brother was such a delightful child, he had those childlike qualities that we all adored, but he had an other-worldliness about him too; caught in a quiet moment he would seem mature, insightful and thoughtful. Yet here he was aged only 7 years the first of my siblings to die. He died, because of the squalid conditions we were living in, from tuberculosis. His wheezing pain as he slowly slipped away pervaded the whole house, but the inevitability of his going did not make his death any easier for us.

It was hard for all of us to bear; the loss of a sibling, especially a younger sibling, lives on with you, at once sad and unsettling as you become aware of the slender grip we all have on life. For my parents it was doubly difficult, to have your own child die before you is heart-rending. They were filled with remorse and guilt, feeling responsible that in some way their bringing the family from Ireland to these conditions in Bluetown was their error of judgement. In the end, they leant on and were supported by their faith and the church people who gathered around them to cushion the loss. It was, after all, just God's will.

As is the Catholic way, Patrick's departing was followed by two new children, Thomas William, born in 1871, and then Alice Maud Elizabeth, born in 1873. Patrick remained with us in spirit, but his bed was soon occupied and the hustle and bustle with new young children around the house kept my mother busy and distracted.

I had one remaining Irish brother, James, and now two English siblings. We had lived through Patrick's T.B. and were alert to the symptoms, so it was a great shock to us when James developed a heaviness of breath and a wheezing in his chest. There was little that could be done; the advice was to move him out of his present living condition to somewhere he could get fresh air and warmth. Such a place did not exist within our orbit of influence. There were still family members in Ireland but the conditions in which they lived were not much better.

Instead we had to listen to him deteriorating. We would lie awake at night listening to him increasingly struggle for breath. My mother Alice prayed to God so often, promising her soul in exchange for the continuing life of James Maher, but He did not respond to her prayers and entreaties. James died aged only 14, just 5 years after the death of Patrick, leaving me as the only Irish-born child in the family.

The loss was even greater for my parents; this was their second child and the move to England had stolen him away from us. Such child mortality was not new to the community at that time and so there was a sort of practiced, well-rehearsed response to another child's death. Again, the priest and the community rallied around us and helped to ease our pain in prayer, and embraces, and pots of Irish stew at the doorstep to save my mother from the chores of supporting her family.

CHAPTER 3

Early Years in Service

HAD MY MOTHER not grown so overprotective and concerned about my health in the Sheerness environment, I might have stayed there and died there; instead her actions changed my life; indeed, she may have saved my life.

I was happy in the bosom of the Irish community in Sheerness; it was names and faces, accents and routines that were familiar to me and I had the family to help and to look out for.

Her plans to relocate me into employment were traumatic, but in the depth of my heart and my consciousness I understood the benefits of this move. At the time, Patrick had recently died and James's health was failing, but I was to be saved, leaving home and family at the age of only 12. It did cause tensions within the family, and it was made clear that my father did not approve.

In Sheerness, in my rare encounters outside the Irish community, I understood that my accented persona was not what would bring me advancement. In New York, for example, my cousin John's letters told us about significant prejudice against the Irish. Of course, the U.S.A. was a new nation populated largely by immigrants, and so perhaps it was the sheer size of the Irish immigrant group, many of them from poor starving rural communities, that made them the target of such treatment.

It has always seemed ironic to me that, having only recently banned slavery, the Irish were part of a new slave class, poorly paid, working often in poor conditions, in the dirtiest or most dangerous jobs in New York.

It was of course the Catholic Church that helped my mother find a place for me. On the grapevine, they knew of a Royal Naval Commander stationed in Sheerness who was looking for a residential domestic servant to work in his household. He wanted a maid to do general cleaning duties and support the care of the children.

Whatever destiny had for me, I had to be able to present myself in as sophisticated a way as I could. My language had been modified to an English accent following 8 years of living and schooling in England. Nonetheless I had to adjust my language and accent further, be conversant with the ways of my new life companions, their habits, their eccentricities, their norms, certainly if I was to reach the heights I aspired to; from rural poor to capitalist.

Commander Farrell, his wife and children shared none of my experiences or the Sheerness I knew. My father Patrick and Commander Farrell both worked in the dockyard at Sheerness but apart from their Catholicism had nothing else in common. Thus, I was introduced to their family home in Belvedere, living in servants' quarters.

Belvedere was a newly-emerging area of substantial properties built by Sir Culling Eardley in north west Kent, just south east of London. From the heights of "Lesness Heath", the ridge it sat upon, it had commanding views down to the Thames and out towards Greenwich and London.

My first experience of privacy came with this job. Though my quarters were no more than a small box-room, at least I was the only occupant. There was a fireplace with a metal grate and a floral tiled surround.

The bed was narrow and the cotton sheets and blanket tightly wound. A small dressing table with a mirror atop and a chair occupied the furthest wall. In one corner, much to my delight, was a small book case with three shelves laden with books. Mrs. Dubby, my primary school teacher, had nurtured and encouraged my reading, and this was another step forward along that path of discovery.

This was all part of an arrangement that Mrs. Dubby had forged with me. Early on in my school career she had encouraged me to read, initially no more than children's books, but over time she challenged me with more and more demanding material. "Read and Learn" was her mantra, not just for me but for all her little charges. The school had a collection of books and she initially picked out titles for me but as time went on I became an avid reader. I worked my way systematically through their treasure house of literature; authors like the Bronte sisters, Jane Austin, Charles Dickens. I was taking home 4 or 5 novels a week, but I also learned the benefits of text books and learned, for example, accountancy skills from materials published by the newly formed Institute of Accountants.

I took steps to relieve the starkness of my new home. My mother had made me a colorful patchwork quilt that soon covered the bed, and a small rag-rug, some comfort to the feet from the black-stained floorboards. I was allowed kindling for the fire and a small daily ration of coal for the winter months. Soon this stark place was a warm retreat away from the drudgery of domestic service where I could steal time to read and follow my dreams and my heroes in the novels I loved.

My working hours were long; I started at five in the morning and, worked through to eight thirty in the evening, but longer if I was needed. The children might need help and attention during the night or, if the Farrells were entertaining, which they did frequently, I would be called upon as kitchen porter to fetch and carry. Later on I was allowed to wait at table, clearing plates and cutlery or bringing items to the guests.

I had developed a daily pattern of reading and notwithstanding these early mornings and late finishes, I read for at least an hour before going to sleep. I read Sir Walter Scott, Jane Austin and Elizabeth Gaskill, all borrowed from the Farrells' library. I also loved poring over the atlas and dreaming of exotic lands. In one sense, it was calming and helped me to sleep, in another it would fill my mind with notions that would feed my imagination and dreams all night long.

My visits home were infrequent; rarely I would have a day in Sheerness. They only served to show the growing distance between me and my family. My language and accent were changing by osmosis, my deportment and style commented upon by family and neighbors; "Isn't she doing well" was my signal to try harder to learn the requirements of a household like the Farrells. In time my body took on a new shape and fullness that left me slightly embarrassed. "What a bonny young girl" was the new Sheerness assessment of my progress, and I knew what they meant.

There were several things that Mrs. Farrell seemed to find endearing about me; she could show me once and know the lesson was learned and absorbed. Another was the way that her children, particularly the younger ones, would clamor for my attention, cry when I left for Sheerness, and be waiting on the drive or at the windows when I returned. She seemed very happy with my contribution to her family household and, while she never offered explicit praise, I caught her smile or laughter when I carried out tasks for her or played with the children.

In time, Mrs. Farrell became a second mother to me; while I craved better conditions for my mother Alice, Mrs. Farrell had managed to exemplify all the hopes and aspiration I had for my real mother; she combined her love for her husband and her large and growing family, with a sophistication and social grace that brought endless visitors to her door.

I am embarrassed to say that the comparison of the Farrell household to our small blue home in Sheerness became painful to me. My mother's home was never short on love but it was cold, damp and dirty. I began to avoid staying there more than a few hours a visit.

My only problem was with the Farrells' third eldest son, Anthony, who I discovered had become fixated upon me. The Farrells' house was my haven but there is always a thorn with every rose.

We were of an age, and as we passed 16 together he tried to press his attentions on me. His elder brothers had by then joined the navy and were away, but Anthony saw himself as a bohemian artist. He apparently secretly sketched me as I went about my duties.

As I went about my cleaning duties I came across his portfolio of work carelessly set aside. I could not resist the temptation to look and sat down on a stool by the window and opened up the large folder of sketches and paintings. Its contents came as a complete surprise to me. The likeness to me of many of his figures was undoubted. He had caught the firm lines of my face and the symmetry of my facial features with the wide oval piercing-blue eyes and with narrow dark eyebrows, slightly raised in question; nose long and straight with slightly flaring nostrils. He had my physical proportions right too, with the fullness of the curves and the length of my legs, inherited I guess from my tall father.

The troubling part I found in later sketches; here he had let his imagination run riot and had me cleaning, while in a state of undress, and others lying recumbent in only my underclothing, loosened slightly to reveal expanses of bare flesh; to all intents and purposes I might have been stark naked. More troubling was the setting for these poses; it was clearly somewhere in my room with sketches of me at my dressing table brushing my long hair, the recumbent poses framed on my bed lying atop the quilt that my mother had fashioned for me. He was not a visitor to my room and I could only guess when and how he had gained access to my most private places.

I flushed with embarrassment as I began to comprehend the thoughts going through this young man's mind. I had done nothing to prompt this interest in me, except for the same courtesies that I extended to all the children, and yet I must have been responsible, carried myself in a way that had prompted his fertile mind to see more than was evident to others. He was a very kind, quietly spoken person and was always polite and courteous towards me; I would not have dreamed what shadowy thoughts lurked behind his softness towards me.

I sought Mrs. Farrell's help, without mentioning the drawings I had uncovered. I later decided that this had been a mistake on my part, in my attempt to maintain some stability in my relationships within her family. I talked instead of his upsetting my routines and disturbing me. She was a smart woman and quickly understood the actual motivations of her son and the reasons for my complaints. I expected she would understand and protect me; how naïve I was. She promised to try to dampen Anthony's enthusiasm, explaining to him that I had work to do and should not be disturbed or bothered by him.

I could tell from his reaction to me that Mrs. Farrell had done this very promptly. That same morning, we coincided in the living room as I was cleaning out the fireplace. As I bent and swept and shoveled the cinders into the brass scuttle I suddenly sensed his presence in the room. I turned and saw him with his back to the closed door. I tried to rise from my crouching position with a little dignity, brushing my hair back with my hands and straightening my pinafore, I stood before him in silence with my back to the fireplace. He stood motionless as his eyes scanned my body from head to toe, and my skin crawled as I imagined him undressing me in his mind's eye. The long motionless silence was broken as he spoke; "Mama says that, apparently, I must not disturb you while you are working; not while you are working: I'll do my best". With that he turned and was gone.

When I was in my room, I took to propping a chair against the door handle; my room was in the same area of the house as the children and was also close to the large room where Anthony was now sole occupant, as his older brothers were mostly away.

Two nights later, when I had retired and was sitting up in bed with my latest novel in my hands and only a small candle alight to aid my reading, I heard the creak of the floorboard immediately outside of my door. In a moment, Anthony entered the room (in my tiredness I had forgotten the chair against the door handle as my last line of defense); he closed the door silently behind him and leaned against it. It was shadowy in the candlelight but I could see that he wore a silk dressing gown and I could see his painting portfolio that he clutched to himself, and I witnessed the evident excitement on his face.

I didn't call out, opting instead for trying to reason with him. "I want to sketch you" he blurted out. "Be my artist's model? You are so beautiful I want to draw you again and again. Pose nude for me at your dressing table, like Ruben's Venus." My education at that point did not include Rubens but the message was transparent. Whether sketching me was his primary intent, his ambitions for this encounter were clear. He walked to the far side of the room, pulled out the chair for me to sit upon, and then in one movement had put down his portfolio and discarded his clothing. His intentions now were very evident.

When I refused to do as he asked, he became agitated and loud, sufficient to rouse some of the household and Mrs. Farrell in particular. I used the opportunity to leap from my bed and escape to the landing just as Mrs. Farrell arrived. The door was wide open and she stared in silence at the sight of her son, standing naked and vulnerable in my room. She said nothing but instead stood to one side silently, with just a gesture inviting her son to leave and return to his room. Wrapping his thin robe quickly about him, he did so with just an angry glance at me as he passed. Mrs. Farrell addressed me: "I'll talk with you in the morning", and she promptly turned her back and walked away.

I was convinced that thanks to our earlier conversations she understood my situation and would help further. I tried to tell her of my discovery of Anthony's sketches and that these apparent poses were a thing of his fantasies and imaginings and that I had never "sat" for him; she seemed disbelieving and disinterested. Nonetheless that morning it was I who was gone, leaving Anthony and the younger children in a state of shock.

Mrs. Farrell explained that I was to be dismissed from her service and return to Sheerness. When I tried to defend myself, she said: "Remember this my dear, the lord of the manor is always right. I have a position in society and my son's reputation to protect. I can't have an attractive young girl, however innocent, in the house to distract him. Because you have been so special to me I'll write a letter of recommendation and help you find a new situation." I seethed at the injustice of it but it was a lesson I never forgot. The offer that she would write a letter of reference for me to carry and that she would undertake to find a suitable alternative for me was small comfort.

Here I was, at almost 17 years, dismissed from the only job I had held. I returned to Sheppey and to my family home feeling ashamed, embarrassed and extremely angry.

CHAPTER 4

The Officers' Mess

I HAD BEEN home for just two days when a courier arrived at our doorstep. That was surprising in itself and far from the neighborhood's usual experience. Surprising too for the import of the two documents he carried with him.

The first was a handwritten covering note from Mrs. Farrell saying only, "Dear Annie, the attached is the least you deserve." And signed "Rosemary". In the five years I had spent in her service, I had never used her Christian name.

As my mother read through Rosemary's note that had been handwritten in copperplate on her personal headed stationery, she wept long and openly, interspersed with, "Oh Annie, Oh Annie".

The second was even more surprising in that it was from the Commander of the Royal Naval Garrison and was an appointment to the civilian staff at the Royal Naval Dockyards at Chatham: I was to report there at 08:00 the following Monday. I was to join the mixed military and civilian staff serving the Officers' Mess. The wage I was to receive dwarfed the wages I had received from the Farrells.

Rosemary Farrell enclosed a ten-shilling note, a paper pattern and instructions on which shopkeeper would have the correct fabric for my uniform. It was a dark blue wool, sturdy and attractive with a stiff white cotton apron that would be pinned to the front. My mother and I sewed furiously to have my dress ready. "You will only need one dress and two aprons to start, I'll send a second along in time". Mother said. While I was sewing the bodice, I made sure it fit, but not too well. I did not want to draw attention to myself and encourage the type of attention I had received at the Farrells.

This had been my first direct experience of the unwanted attentions of a male, albeit a dreamy-eyed sixteen-year-old fantasist. In this case, it seemed to have worked out well for me, driving me in a new direction and to a new range of experiences that would significantly impact on my future.

The significant size of the naval garrison at Chatham was probably only as a result of the concern about security. As a port, it was tidal and with the volume of Royal Naval shipping would often have large numbers of ships waiting at anchor in the Thames and the approaches to the Harbor. These were seen as highly vulnerable to attack from enemies approaching through the Thames estuary.

My father seemed pleased about my new appointment. He considered this a "proper job" and was keen to share his experiences of working in Royal Naval facilities, and those descriptions did help in my first few days at Chatham.

I stood outside the gates at Chatham Dockyard in awe at what I saw; huge gates with monumental stone pillars and walls at either side opening into a cavernous space.

Zero-eight-hundred-hours was clearly not the usual time for change of civilian shift when thousands of workers, like my father, would stream in and out of the yard like a tidal wave. It had been the only concession to my first day; I was to be shown to my quarters and, within an hour, would be working as part of a team to serve in the Officers' Mess.

My quarters were a bunkhouse. It was of course all female, but the room had been divided into 4 more or less equal parts, the delineating lines made by furniture and hanging curtains that could be partially drawn to offer a little privacy. Oh, how I missed my box-room. There was only one unoccupied space and this was to be my home for the coming months.

The other three occupants were all civilian workers recruited to the Mess, like me, to undertake general duties. I had little opportunity to get to know the occupants of these three berths; they did not have the long-term aspiration that I had, and saw the opportunity as a way of contributing to the family income rather than, as it did for me, offering the range of skills that I knew would be marketable in an entirely different setting.

I reported to the kitchen at zero-nine-hundred-hours. The Mess was refuge to the officer ranks from their undoubtedly tiring duties. It was on the ground floor of their accommodation block and comprised 3 main areas that they referred to as Lounge, Bar and Dining Room. The basement housed the staff whose jobs were to service the needs of the Officer Class.

I was put in the charge of a Naval Rating whose job it was to teach me the ropes. Preparing food was not my forte but acting in a kitchen porter role was more familiar to me. It was some weeks before I had direct contact with the officers' areas, carrying food to the dining room as part of the formal service: numbers varied, but 12 or more officers would be a normal expectation.

The evening dinners, mainly just officers, but sometimes with wives invited, were very formal affairs. Outside those times it was less formal, with lunchtime buffet food that had to be kept replenished and a bar staff charged with trying to keep pace with officers' drinking.

Below stairs I was just plain Annie to civilians and Naval staff alike; on the first floor, I was known as "Marr" a telling English mispronunciation of my ancient Irish family name. Not that I had much human contact with officers; it was as if I were a ghost-figure expected to know precisely what was needed at any point.

I would stand to attention with trays of drinks or canapés and move intuitively towards someone needing refreshment even though they had not asked for it.

At table I was taught, over time, the rigors of "silver service"; the skill of serving food to seated diners using no more than a fork and spoon. Entering on their left side while offering them food to choose from, occasionally being given an indication of what they wanted, sometimes not, and just pressing on with the task until some grunt or gesture signaled a sufficiency had been served.

Over time in this daily ritual, individual preferences and capacities became known. That made life easier and less prone to rebuke. Then there was the under-stairs banter about the proclivities of individuals. We discussed the behavior of the officers and how it changed as the evenings progressed and the wine flowed. I particularly enjoyed the evenings when the wives joined their husbands. We all joked how much better behaved all the officers were when the wives were present. We all enjoyed looking at the wives' gowns and hair and the glitter of their jewels.

What I had become, as this period of my life in service came to an end, was something like being a hostess in a cordon bleu Men's Club. How on earth would this fit me for anything else in life?

CHAPTER 5

Introductions to New York

MY MOTHER'S O'BRIEN family network came into call. My cousin John, from my mother's side, by then a veteran of New York, had established a family florist business.

John O'Brien had fallen on his feet and had started by working as a gardener near Green-Wood Cemetery in Brooklyn for the floral firm of James Weir and Sons. The Weirs lived on 24th Street near Fifth Avenue in Brooklyn and they had greenhouses in the neighborhood. The Weir firm supplied flowers for the Green-Wood Cemetery. By 1878, when I arrived, Uncle John O'Brien worked as a florist wholesaler and retailer, with James Weir's retail shop providing floral decorations to some of the biggest names and places in fashionable New York City.

Part of John's charm was winning the confidence of his patrons and seeking out and fulfilling, with unerring exactitude, precisely what was wanted. Gilt-edged notes would be delivered by staff with flowers for fashionable high society who would flock to him when having even a modest dinner party, perhaps only with a dozen or so guests, or when throwing a formal ball for hundreds. They would demand of the venue, "flowers by John O'Brien please". He became a sort of status symbol for the rich and famous; a very lucrative trade indeed.

It was precisely during one of those conversations, for which he was famous, with the mistress of a very significant New York household, when she said, "Oh John, I wish I had someone like you working for me all the time". He replied, "You can, I know of an outstanding girl in England, Annie …"

He regaled her with the now legendary family story about my work with the Farrell Family and in the Officers Mess at The Royal Naval Dockyard at Chatham. "I'll have her!" she exclaimed; and so my life in America would begin.

That family were the Bolmers and my new mistress Georgiana. Following an exchange of correspondence and references taken up with the Royal Navy, and a copy of my reference from Rosemary

Farrell provided, within a short time I was offered a position in that household, as Georgiana Bolmer's Lady's Maid.

The Bolmers fixed a date for my sailing to New York and a single steerage ticket booked in my name duly arrived. While, at the same time, excited and scared by the prospect of a new life in America, my final split from my family and the life I had known in Sheerness since early childhood was difficult. There were scenes of joy at home as well as tears and anguish about my leaving. The start of my journey was not too bad, sailing out of Sheerness itself. That meant that the family could come and wave me off, though to be honest, I don't like long goodbyes; I would rather be gone. To my surprise, Mrs. Farrell was there and after our farewells she pressed an envelope into my hands; "something for you when you get to America" she said. The "something" I discovered when aboard was a further $10 dollars to add to the money I had managed to save already.

The trip was in one of the new generation of iron clad steam ships and was much quicker than in sailing days. However, steerage passengers did not have cabins. Instead we traveled in one large room separated into sections by type: single men at one end of the ship, families in the middle and single women at the other end, which is where I found myself.

The berths were canvas and could be stowed away during the day. Down the middle of steerage were long tables where the passengers sat for much of the day and where they had their meals. After my periods of semi-independence and privacy I found myself with a hammock in an open room with little or no privacy. Steerage was smelly and noisy, not least because this large group of passengers had to cope with cramped conditions, rudimentary and shared sanitary provision and constant periods of sea sickness as the ship pitched and rolled its way across the North Atlantic.

I traveled light, with a single bag containing all my clothing and books. I owned two dresses, one for work and one for Sunday, and two chemises and these undergarments went next to the skin, and also served for sleeping; It had real benefits when trying to survive with little privacy in the cramped steerage facilities. My four pairs of drawers, which I wore all at once for the journey, went to the knee and they helped to stave off the cold and damp. This was supplemented by my petticoat which provided both warmth and helped to create shape in my skirt. I had a few pairs of stockings, a corset, a hat, cape, gloves and only the shoes I stood up in. My clothes were largely made in homes back in Sheerness. We purchased the fabric and my clothing was made by my mother with the help of my sisters and other family members and kindly neighbors. As long as these clothes lasted, I would always have those people with me. Indeed, clothing was meant to last and I would be able to change little details, adding clean lace to a collar and sleeves or changing the sleeve shape, in order to freshen the clothes and make them more up to date.

Nothing prepared me for the New York winter and my English home-made clothing was inadequate for the task.

I landed at Castle Garden at the Emigrant Landing Depot at the southern tip of Manhattan. Originally a fort, Castle Garden was a round cavernous building. After disembarking, we had to pass in single file before the officials, who recorded our names, nationality, age, occupation, starting point and destination, and also asked whether we had any money or not. I had funds for my trip; I had saved $10 and Mrs. Farrell had kindly given me a further $10 as a farewell present.

There were thousands of people coming off ships and all manner of thieves trying to steal the money from newly-arrived immigrants by pretending to have jobs and housing for them. John O'Brien was there, and was able to wait in an area set aside for family members, to claim me. John protected me from those scoundrels and led me out onto the Battery and into the streets of Manhattan.

I was unprepared for the hustle and bustle of New York; I had never seen so many people in one place in my life. I had been to London once but this city was busier with people rushing in every direction; it was more cosmopolitan than I remembered in London too. Apart from the swirling mass of crowds, my first impression as we walked out of Castle Garden was of street vendors; there were push carts selling food and drink everywhere.

One very popular food in New York at the time was apparently the oyster. Oyster carts, filled with ice, were plentiful. Oyster shuckers were cutting open the shells and serving the cold oysters right out of their shells — a natural plate if you will. They were also cooked and served hot; either way they seemed ubiquitous in New York.

Other push carts were selling large hot pretzels and sausages; John explained that it was because New York had a large German population. Water was not a popular drink since it was considered unsafe. There were carts selling cold coffee and tea as well as carts selling small beers or root beer. John suggested we stop and try some of these strange foods and, I must say, my first meal in New York was a memorable experience, and a pleasant change after the monotony of the food in steerage. We ate oysters, considered a delicacy in New York, but widely available and sold here off the back of carts. John O'Brien explained to me that New York Harbor was awash with oyster beds and reputed to have half the world's supply of oysters. Oysters were highly nutritious and huge in size. A poor New Yorker could eat oysters daily and the rich and elegant would be served oysters in the finest of New York restaurants.

We had left Castle Garden and walked five or six minutes to the Whitehall Street Ferry and caught a "side-wheeler" across the East River over to Atlantic Avenue in Brooklyn. The river was teeming with boats, ferries, steamships, sailing ships and skiffs. Towering over it all were two structures, one finished and one with workers clambering over the scaffolding like flies. Strangely these enormous towers were standing in the middle of the water. John must have seen me staring with my mouth agape. He explained with pride that these two towers would soon be connected by a platform to create the New York – Brooklyn Bridge. "You'll be able to walk from Brooklyn to Manhattan. By horse it will take ten minutes – no standing and waiting for a ferry".

John had arranged that the horse-drawn flower delivery cart picked us up on the Brooklyn side of the ferry for what was to be a half-hour drive to the O'Brien house on 28th Street near Fifth.

You can imagine my elation and excitement, but now I was feeling tired and dirty and needed some comforts of home.

CHAPTER 6

The O'Briens

I HAD A few days before I was expected to report to my new employer and so could take the time to spend with some of my mother's family.

The O'Briens occupied two houses side by side on 28th Street Brooklyn; cousin John and his family lodging in one and his brother, cousin Timothy, in the other.

John's family were to play an important role in my future, particularly two of his daughters Margaret and Josephine.

He had married his wife Anastasia while they were still in Clonmel, Southern Tipperary and then emigrated to New York, U.S.A. in 1863. On my arrival in 1878 they had four children, Mary aged 8, Margaret aged 7, Hannah aged 4 and Thomas born only that January. They were in that Catholic procreating loop and doubtless more children would follow.

I learned more about John and his interest in the flower business. Back in Clonmel he had been an agricultural worker and, on his arrival with his new wife Anastasia in New York, he had sought similar work. He struck lucky in finding employment with the Weir family.

The floral firm of James Weir and Sons, who had been in business since about 1850, agreed to employ John O'Brien as a "Gardener". The Weirs lived on 24th Street near Fifth Avenue in Brooklyn and they had greenhouses in the neighborhood. The Weir firm supplied flowers for the Green-Wood Cemetery. John O'Brien lived on 28th Street near Fifth, just a few blocks away. John worked initially in greenhouses growing flowers and greens for the Weir family business.

The Weirs were to become famous for their Brooklyn Greenhouses particularly one at the corner of 25th Street and Fifth Avenue, across the street from the main entrance to the Green-Wood Cemetery; the cemetery provided a captive audience and was good for business you might say. That 25th Street and Fifth Avenue corner greenhouse, while it survived, was surely destined to become an historic landmark in the city.

Manhattan was too crowded to contain any cemeteries so Green-Wood had been built in 1832 in what was then a rural setting. The City of Brooklyn grew up around the cemetery. Green-Wood was set in almost 500 acres of rolling hills. Green-Wood, like most cemeteries in the 19th century, became an oasis and a popular spot to visit. It was so popular that if you chose to visit and didn't have family buried there you bought a ticket to get in. John O'Brien wouldn't have had to buy a ticket because he was a known and trusted worker there, delivering flowers for funerals. You can only imagine my surprise at being on a bustling city street, walking through this gate for the first time and suddenly arriving in a bucolic place, with quiet tree-lined avenues, birds singing and beautiful views of Manhattan. John and I got into the routine of meeting here when our busy schedules allowed and just enjoying the stroll and chatting in this quiet rural idyll in the city.

John's interest had turned from the manual work of growing flowers to the potentially lucrative business of supplying the New York elite. While he had, by then, not learned to read and write he had a keen eye for people and for meeting their needs. Anastasia was able to do the bookwork, like ordering, accounts and advertising, that were initially beyond John, but she soon taught him those skills and he became an accomplished businessman. His key skill though was in working effectively with people of all classes, and his quiet charm managed to overcome any prejudice about his Irish heritage. By the time I arrived on the scene he was already running a highly successful business. He had managed to persuade the Weirs to supply him with fresh flowers and plants and John ended up as one of their best customers. This close connection with the Weirs allowed his business to flourish quickly.

CHAPTER 7

Meeting Georgiana Eleanor Bolmer

A BEAUTIFUL AND substantial house on East 60th Street was the home of the Bolmer family, and Georgiana Bolmer was my new mistress. She was one of the offspring of Manuel Texido Bolmer and his second wife. She was a lovely smiling young woman, about 5'5" tall with brown hair done up in elaborate braids on the top of her head. She had short curled bangs as was the fashion then. The day I met her she was wearing a white cotton day dress with a tiny waist and bustle at the back. It had a surprising touch of black lace at the cuffs and neck and a bright red flower at the waist. I had always thought the women at the Officers Mess were beautifully dressed but they couldn't compare to Miss Bolmer.

I had no idea what to expect but was surprised that she was only four years older than me at just twenty-two. What a stark contrast there was between our two lives, though ironically there were some similarities.

26 East 60th Street was to be my home for some time and my "apartment" more generous than I had ever experienced before. I ate in the kitchen with the rest of the family servants but on the top floor I had two small adjoining rooms, a sitting room and a bedroom devoted entirely to myself. My first real privacy for a while.

My primary role as maid to Georgiana, was to meet her every wish and accordingly when she needed me and pulled the bell, it would sound both in the servants' quarters and in my rooms. It was at most two floors for me to travel to her suite of rooms. As a lady's maid, I was in charge of her toilette, her hair and helping her dress. I soon came to know her extensive wardrobe intimately and would often suggest combinations of gloves, jewels and arrangements of her hair to best complement her gowns.

I treated her and her family as I had become accustomed to treating my first employers, the Farrells. Yet that focus on her needs brought me close to the center of her most intimate life. She in turn was much more open than Rosemary Farrell had been, and called me Annie in our private moments. It seemed clear to me that she intended a public and a private face, courteously formal and business-like in public settings, but more open and relaxed when we were alone or working together.

Our private face was a complicated affair too; in one way, just like Rosemary Farrell, she was a mother figure in my eyes despite the closeness of our years; perhaps that was what I wanted to find, a replacement for my own mother. However, in time the growing friendship between us would leave us feeling like loving sisters or lovers rather than mother and daughter. I understood why John O'Brien got on so well with her in their dealings over flowers for various occasions; she was easy to like.

Georgiana's was a complicated family and it took me some time to fully understand the relationships. Georgiana was one of nine siblings or half siblings; Her father's first marriage to Emma Jane Shapter ended when she died on February 3rd 1848 aged only 29, leaving two children named Gertrude and William. He then married Georgiana Buckmaster and they had 7 children; Gertrude, Manuel De Forrest, Thomas H., then Georgiana Eleanor, Clarence, Louise and finally the youngest Estelle. Most of the household saw me as a general servant but with specific duties and responsibilities to Georgiana alone.

The one person from that group who made an immediate impression on me was Manuel De Forrest Bolmer. He was eight years my senior and, as I thought, rather a quiet, cold fish who hardly acknowledged my presence in those early days. The irony did not pass me by that my experiences with an aspiring artist in Kent, while turning out to be beneficial in the end, actually had led to my being thrown out of the home and the household of my employer. De Forrest Bolmer was an aspiring artist too and the echoes with the past were strong.

I was also wary because I did not wish to give De Forrest Bolmer any clue that I found him in the least bit attractive, although I did. He wasn't a large man, maybe 5'6" with brown hair, a fair complexion and light-blue eyes that were his most arresting feature. However, this was my golden opportunity, my destiny, to engage with Georgiana Bolmer and carve out my future in the U.S.A; I would not risk everything for the sake of an imagined relationship that seemed as spontaneous as it was ridiculous.

The family, and especially De Forrest Bolmer, had apparently developed quite a reputation for bravery in the local area. It went back to a fire that had occurred in the adjacent house on East 60th Street. They had been alerted by the noise and commotion out back and had rushed out into their yard; they found flames pouring from the next-door house and Mr. Steiner, their neighbor, standing on the arch of his bay window. Despite De Forrest Bolmer's warning, "Don't jump or you will be killed, hold on and we will save you!" Before De Forrest could fetch a ladder, the poor man jumped, hitting his head on the coping of the balcony and fell, dying, into the Bolmers' yard. His skull had been fractured in a terrible manner.

That tragedy was followed by the injury to Mary McGuire, one of the female servants, who came to a window screaming for help. She too jumped and fractured both of her thigh bones and received other terrible injuries. Shortly afterwards Mr. Steiner's two daughters, Deborah and Flora came to the window calling for help. By this time De Forrest had raised the ladder to the window, and he carried Flora down to the ground. He went back, at significant risk to his own life, to save Deborah, but to his horror she protested that she would not leave without saving her mother. Even though De Forrest was trying to prevent her by grabbing hold of her clothing, nonetheless she refused to leave the burning building and both women died, overcome firstly by fumes and then burnt beyond all recognition.

The fire was a great shock to the whole community, partly because they recognized the potential danger of living in these tall buildings in the event of a fire. It was also the loss of life; members of their local community, there one moment and then snatched away by death at the next. Despite all this, when I heard the story, it piqued my interest in this unassuming, quietly-spoken artist. What other hidden depths did De Forrest Bolmer have in his armory? He didn't much enjoy the label as a local hero but, in some quiet moments, it did bring a smile to my face.

New York was a city of incredible wealth and I had landed in one of the oldest and most revered families there. The Bolmers were "old money" descended from some of the first Dutch settlers of New York. They lived lavishly but they were also committed to doing good. Many of their social activities centered around raising money for those less fortunate. While Mrs. Astor planned her large balls, and was written up in the Social Pages, the Bolmers were more circumspect.

Caroline Webster Astor and a lawyer named Ward McAllister had devised a list of New York's social elite. McAllister was rumored to have suggested that "only about 400 people in New York society" mattered, and, coincidentally, Mrs. Astor's ballroom could only accommodate about 400 guests. As a result, Mrs. Astor's 400, the social register of these worthy guests, was created. They would throw lavish and rather decadent parties populated from within their set, known variously as "The 400" or more disparagingly the "Knickerbockers", a term they hated.

This was not for the likes of the Bolmers; Georgiana and De Forrest had begun to establish a much more enlightened set, whose interests lay in the artistic and the intellectual. They were to demonstrate a conservative but well-connected life that brought many benefits. Their connections in that society were to have a long-term influence on the Bolmer family, and their love for travel and for the arts was to take them all over the world.

Mrs. Bolmer, Georgiana's mother, was a quiet woman who never liked planning events. She was happy to turn that work over to her daughter. Because of this my work as a lady's maid was augmented with the role of young Georgiana's secretary. I loved the work and we soon developed an efficient and effective working relationship together. My mistress had defined the parameters for an event, for example a dinner party for some of her father's business partners, and in the past, would have taken the whole load upon herself to bring it to fruition. Increasingly I did the hard work of contacting suppliers, helping with guest lists, invitations and menus, and organizing floral decorations with my cousin John O'Brien.

After one stunning event that had been a glittering success, we repaired to her rooms to prepare her for bed and sleep. She wanted more champagne and had secreted a bottle of the finest upstairs and ordered me to open it. Such was my history in the Officers Mess this caused me no problem, but she thrust two glasses towards me, "one for yourself".

At my age, you might have thought I would be familiar with drinking, but none of that; I could select it, open and check it, pour it and serve it but alcohol had never before that night crossed my lips.

We sat side-by-side on her divan, drank the champagne together and laughed and cried at all the highlights and the people with their gossip and odd little ways. I had held back a little on the champagne but Georgiana was quite drunk after an hour and, with her post-event exhaustion, she fell quite asleep.

I turned down her bed and managed to help her on to it. Without any ceremony, I undressed her and pulled the bedding over her naked body; her hair was splayed across the pillow and she was deeply asleep now. I stood for a while and watched this delightful young woman as she rested. It gave me pause for thought, drawing comparisons between our two lives. Georgiana was a flamboyant and intelligent person, who I felt sure was destined one day soon to be married to an eligible young man who could give her all that she wanted. Would I be part of that future?

Certainly, it seemed to me, I would have to adapt in order to succeed. I had already abandoned my mother's Irish brogue entirely and enunciated now as a well-spoken English Girl. That would not be enough though to be convincing; I was mixing with well-educated and well-read people and so while my background reading had enabled me to have informed conversations on literature and geography, I had to continue to broaden my horizons and to read avidly.

The other great hurdle was my Catholicism. While I had abandoned that faith at an earlier stage, the somewhat prejudiced circles within which Georgiana moved were Episcopalian Protestants and I had to be careful not to ruffle feathers. Instead I quietly allowed Georgiana and her set to just assume that I shared their belief and their religion. On Sunday mornings, I joined the family and staff at services at St. Thomas Church on Fifth Avenue. The Bolmers sat up front and the staff sat at the back. Church was a place to see and be seen. I didn't follow the service so much as enjoyed watching New York's elite dressed to the nines for Sunday service.

CHAPTER 8

The Arnold Family

MANY ELIGIBLE MEN flitted within the periphery of Georgiana's life, and it was not my place to pass judgment on any of them; though Georgiana would often ask, "what did you think of so-and-so then?"

The Bolmers were wealthy and that brought with it some concern that suitors might be after her money, but the opposite was true and wealthy men were less anxious about their wealth being the target of any aspiring partner if that partner had wealth of their own.

When Richard Arnold first appeared on the scene it was through his contacts with Georgiana's artist brother De Forrest. Richard Arnold and his father before him were avid art lovers and had a vast collection, built up over the years, and Richard had sought out De Forrest because of his growing reputation as a landscape artist.

He had invited De Forrest and Georgiana to his home to see for themselves some of the great works of art in his collection. It soon became clear that Richard Arnold was smitten with Georgiana and she with him. When asked, "what do you think of Richard Arnold then?" I suppressed my reservations. He was 31 years her senior and one of the wealthiest and influential men in New York City; who was I to question him or his suitability? Richard Arnold owned and operated Arnold, Constable & Co. a large department store in the "Ladies Mile" on Lower Fifth Avenue. Georgiana took me there shopping one day while we were planning a gown for a summer party. It was there that she broke the news to me that Richard had asked to marry her.

Richard Arnold was a cautious man, he insisted on a pre-nuptial agreement that essentially cut Georgiana out of his will. As reported in the New York Herald on Friday May 19th 1882:

"A Considerate Bride

"Miss Georgiana Eleanor Bolmer and Richard Arnold, both of this city, were married on Wednesday last. From an instrument recorded yesterday in the Register's office, it appears that two days before the bride, in consideration of $5,000 cash, released her husband's estate, comprising a quantity of real estate in this city, from her dower right as his wife".

In fact, it was probably a very astute move on their part. Georgiana was wealthy in her own right and had no need of Richard's money. If doubts had hung over his children's assumed inheritance throughout their married lives, one could imagine tensions building within the family about whether Georgiana was "just after his money"; at a stroke that prospect had been set aside.

He would be 57 when he married her and Georgiana only 26. Nonetheless the relationship continued and, as the day approached, she would take me into her confidence; she concluded: "Well, for my first man, you might say he was experienced. It seems sensible to me that if I am to marry then I should marry for love, marry well and marry richly".

I did broach the question of my position after her marriage and she dismissed the suggestion that there might be no room for me in her new life. "I have set down certain conditions", she explained, "and you are one of them". We set about planning her wedding gown and the many dresses she would need for their honeymoon trip. "We will need some new clothes for you as well". Shopping became a delight as Miss Bolmer, soon to be Mrs. Arnold, and her lady's maid were treated like royalty at the Arnold, Constable & Co. store.

On Wednesday May 17th 1882, a bright spring day, the two were wed at St. Thomas Church on Fifth Avenue and 53rd Street in Manhattan.

It was undoubtedly the wedding and the social event of the year and Georgiana's maid was central to the organization of the event. Whenever Richard questioned her about the detail of the planning she would respond, "don't worry, Annie has it in hand". Quite surprisingly he seemed happy with this riposte and over the weeks I felt he had developed a regard for what I brought to his wife, his wedding and his new future family arrangements. I had little understanding then of what my role in helping Georgiana to organize their wedding would have upon the attitude of his existing servants.

Now we were on the move again, this time to Richard Arnold's mansion at 1261 Fifth Avenue, the street at the heart of high society in New York.

I didn't understand the importance of Richard or his father until I found an old clipping shortly after I moved into 1261 Fifth. Richard Arnold's wealth had come from his father's lifetime of entrepreneurship and real estate ventures. Aaron Arnold had co-founded the company Arnold, Constable & Co.

Aaron Arnold's death on Saturday March 18th 1876 was an important landmark in New York Society. The Death Notice in "The New York Daily Herald" the following day read as follows:

"Aaron Arnold, Merchant

"Yesterday morning, Mr. Aaron Arnold, the senior member of the firm of Arnold, Constable & Co. expired in his residency in this city in the eighty-second year of his age.

"Mr. Arnold has for years been favorably known as a merchant of enterprise and a man of spotless integrity. In his business career, he has been successful beyond most of his fellows, and leaves, as the result of his labors, one of the largest business houses in this city.

"He was born in the Isle of White in 1794 and, while yet quite a young man, he came to America and sojourned for a time in Philadelphia. After studying the trade advantages offered by most of the cities, he concluded to begin business in New York. He and Mr. Hearn, his nephew, opened a store in Canal Street in 1827, and the concern prospered, very soon gaining the best repute among businessmen. Success excited more ambitious efforts, and the present immense business of the concern has been built up mainly due to Mr. Arnold's exertions. He took a leading part in the management of the house until the erecting of the uptown establishment, when he withdrew from active participation in the affairs of the concern, which have since been conducted by his son, Mr. Richard Arnold with Messrs. Constable and Baker.

"Mr. Arnold was some time ago attacked by pneumonia, and through his advanced age and enfeebled condition speedily sunk under the malady. He had two (twin) children, Mr. Richard Arnold and Mrs. Constable. Mr. Arnold was of a retiring disposition, and although eminently fitted to hold official trusts he always avoided the publicity they would entail. His taste for the fine arts, too, was a marked feature of his character, and he leaves one of the finest private collections of paintings in the city.

"Mr. Arnold's demise is spoken of with regret by all who knew him and his record among business people is one of an upright and Christian gentleman."

It was to this dynasty and its successors that my destiny was to be intrinsically linked for more than 25 years. Richard Arnold, though old, had latterly been the driving force behind the business and the combined wealth of Georgiana and Richard was immense.

Little Annie Elizabeth Maher, from Clonmel in Southern Tipperary and Bluetown in Sheerness, was now living on Fifth Avenue and at the focal point of this new dawn in the life of New York.

CHAPTER 9

1261 Fifth Avenue

I SLOWLY GREW accustomed to this magnificent house where Richard had lived before his marriage to Georgiana. I was introduced as Lady's Maid to Georgiana Arnold, but I was entering a household with a well-established and loyal staff and a pre-existing hierarchy. There were ten residential staff and at least a further ten who were non-resident.

The core group of servants had been there for many years and some of the ties were familial, namely the McCluskeys. Mary McCluskey was the Housekeeper, Margaret McCluskey the Chambermaid, while Lizzie McCluskey was Lady's Maid to Richard's daughter Mary. The McCluskeys were older than me at 47, 42 and 34 respectively when I joined the household. The McCluskey sisters had been with Richard since he set up house with his first wife Pauline sometime after their marriage in 1855; they were a formidable triumvirate.

Mary McCluskey, the Housekeeper, had been in charge of all the female employees of the house including all maids and scullery workers. She also often acted as a social secretary for the first Mrs. Arnold, sending out invitations, helping to arrange seating at parties, keeping track of who called and who was owed a call. She would also present menus for approval, oversee the ordering of flowers, keep track of the linen in the house and so on. Georgiana had in mind a stark shift in responsibilities. Georgiana and I had grown accustomed to my being responsible for some of those tasks and the discussion and future relationship with Mary was not going to be at all easy.

The McCluskeys had some formidable allies in the servants' quarters too. Bridget Gannon was the Cook, Mary Hughes the Laundress, and there were two further live-in general servants, Bridget Fay and Margaret Stanton. The real powerhouse below stairs was traditionally the Butler; George Laing had an Assistant Butler, Francis Egan; and finally the important role of Coachman was filled by John Kidwell.

George Laing would oversee the Footman and would be in charge of hiring extra staff if the family was having a party. He was also in charge of the family silver and china. The silver was kept in the "silver safe" which was held in a strong box sunk beneath the floorboards in his own living quarters; one door that was always kept locked. A separate room housed the china and tableware and again George Laing had the only key. He was also in charge of all wine and liquor in the house which he managed in the butler's pantry; needless to say, there was very tight control on access to that room too.

This group of ten staff, now eleven with me, lived and worked closely together. The Housekeeper and the Butler had their own offices in the lower ground floor area, and the Assistant Butler and Coachman also had quarters there. Only the female staff were allowed in the servants' quarters on the top floor; Mary McCluskey and Bridget the Cook each had their own room; Mary's two sisters shared accommodation as did the other three remaining female staff, Mary the Laundress and the two general servants Bridget and Margaret.

Georgiana had allocated me two rooms again, clearly much to the annoyance of the other staff. I had become used, at East 60th Street, to the privacy of my own accommodation, and to have a space, other than my bedroom, to live, work, sew and relax in was sheer luxury.

What potential problems this upheaval might cause was for Richard and Georgiana to deal with; all I had to do was to live in a very tense environment until I was able to bring people round, and not let it get me down. The tensest relationship was with the Butler and his assistant. I'm not sure why these men found my presence so difficult. I suppose it was that my role seemed to challenge the existing order.

In the end, Richard and Georgiana saw the significant staff individually and in private. Such was the mutual regard held between Richard and his servants that nothing was ever spoken, at least in my hearing, of my arrival and my role within the household. Initially relationships were a bit chilly, but I find it hard to be chilly with people and my natural openness and smile was soon working its magic and all was calm at 1261 Fifth Avenue.

The key figure to win over was the Housekeeper Mary McCluskey; with her onside it would be relatively straightforward to win the support of the other women on the staff.

CHAPTER 10

The Couple

RICHARD AND GEORGIANA were one of the most influential couples in New York. Their range of interests, their social and business networks, their links with politicians and religious leaders was astounding.

They partly saw their role, and not for just business purposes, to link together this range of people dedicating their huge joint wealth to doing good, and encouraging others to do good too. They were acutely aware of the privilege they enjoyed and the stark contrast with the lives of ordinary New Yorkers.

Let me share with you just one Ball in January 1883 that they threw for the glitterati of New York. It took Georgiana and myself months of planning and hard work to bring it to fruition and it was to turn the tide for my future with Richard Arnold, so successful was it.

1261 Fifth Avenue was a great place to throw a ball; it's hard to give credit to its proportions, but for example the Art Gallery housed all of the late Aaron Arnold's painting collection, as well as those Richard added to the family collection. Art was taking over our lives and formed a perfect conjunction between Georgiana's interests, her brother, the artist De Forrest Bolmer, and the long-standing focus of the Arnold family.

At that event John O'Brien did us proud. The New York Times in its February 1st edition eulogized, "The Art Gallery at the rear of the house was used for dancing, in connection with the parlors, which were handsomely decorated with flowers. Lander's orchestra, screened behind living plants and ferns, played for the dancing."

Georgiana and I worked closely to make sure her gown for the Ball was perfect. It was a white satin dress with large and very realistic silk flowers stitched diagonally across the front. She chose the color to go with the beautiful matching necklace, earrings and bracelet of pearls and diamonds that Richard had given her for a wedding gift.

When everything was cleared and the last of the guests were gone, Georgiana sought me out. We joined Richard Arnold in the family sitting room. It was he who spoke first: "Miss Maher please sit down." I perched on the edge of a sofa trying to recount anything I might have done wrong. Richard Arnold sat opposite me with Georgiana standing behind him.

"Miss Maher, Georgiana has been singing your praises for many months, and I have been able to see with my own eyes, since our wedding and beyond, the remarkable set of skills you possess; your organizational capability and your fluency and empathy with people from all walks of life. I have come to realize that you are just what is needed here at 1261 Fifth Avenue. I would like to offer you the post here of Assistant Housekeeper, with special responsibility for managing the social and formal functions we have here".

I was breathless and astonished.

"Of course, you would continue, as you have, supporting my wife Mrs. Arnold as her Lady's Maid, but in addition take on the governance of these aspects of my household and ensure that everything is done in the efficient manner as if you were doing it yourself. In short, apart from my wife, you would have the role of managing all the social functions in my household. You will work with my wife when we are resident; in our absence, you would take sole charge of our future social plans".

I was stunned into silence and the long pause prompted him to restart.

"I will talk with Mary McCluskey about this. She will welcome your support and finds these organizational matters tiresome. Needless to say, there would be a significant enhancement to your remuneration since this role carries substantial additional responsibilities".

Still disbelieving, I could utter not a word.

Georgiana interjected excitedly, "Come on Annie, will you take the job or no?" "Yes, yes I would love to do that job". There seemed to be a collective sigh of relief and then, quite to my surprise, he reached for a tray set on an occasional table near him with three champagne flutes on it.

"Let me propose a toast to you Annie Maher: 'To the future'"; we raised and chinked our classes, "To the future!" I had to fight hard to keep back my tears.

I retired to my room, still breathless at the stunning advancement and opportunity I had been given. At 33 years of age I would be helping to run the household of one of the most prestigious houses in New York. But it was more than that; I had grown to understand Georgiana's confidence in me; she knew what we might achieve together. This though was a ringing endorsement from Richard Arnold.

True to his word he did have a talk with Mary McCluskey, and afterwards with the Butler as well and, from that moment on, Mary and I were firm friends. She was only too happy to relinquish her former role in helping to lay on these occasions. As significant events appeared on the horizon, she always supported me and encouraged other staff to do so as well. We worked as a good team and the whole experience had a very positive impact on the way the Arnold household was organized and run.

Relationships with the Butler and his assistant remained frosty.

I couldn't sleep that evening and sat down to write to my mother, and the family, and to Rosemary Farrell, with the news.

CHAPTER 11

The Start of the Travels

DURING THE FOLLOWING year, everything really did begin to take shape. I had been reintroduced to the staff by Georgiana in my new role as Assistant Housekeeper and there seemed to be genuine warmth at the news. I got to know them individually, both resident and non-resident employees. Generally, they were doing a good job, but some lacked the style that working in such a household required.

I helped them to understand that often they were the presenting-face of the Arnold home when they opened the door, carried baggage, took or returned coats, brought tea or offered sandwiches; if this were not done with military precision, and in full "uniform" then it reflected badly on their masters. We did practice runs until we were like a platoon on parade; well done Officers' Mess!

That year too, Richard Arnold built a grand new extension to their store; trade was really looking good. They had an existing store on 19th Street. The new five-story building now extended all the way from Broadway to Fifth Avenue on 19th Street. The cost of the extension was in the order if $160,000, a small fortune in its day.

Everything you could imagine was available there from fabrics to ready-made clothing, oriental rugs to carriage blankets, bedding to china. It was now completely modernized with gas lighting and new steam-driven elevators. We would go there often in preparation for our future trips.

Our work together continued but Georgiana introduced a further level of interest. "Richard wants us to travel a little" she explained; "we want to see some of Europe's great cities, see sculpture and art works, and do some shopping. Would you draw up some plans for a trip next Fall and we'll see what that looks like? Be sure to include an appointment at Worth, since we will be in Paris; I'll be needing some new gowns." I was excited and readily agreed.

"While in England you must take time to see your family".

"I'm coming too?" I asked "but I thought I was to look after things here for you if you were away?"

"Richard and I have been so impressed with your work with the household we think you have them in a shape where we can close down the house and trust a skeleton staff led by George Laing and Mary McCluskey to manage things in our absence. There are no pressing social events that you have to worry about. Yes, you're coming too."

Thus it was, in 1884, I was to have the opportunity to travel home for the first time in 6 years.

The tour did involve a lot of planning but, in the end, we decided on a limited trip; more would follow later. We planned for London and Paris. We would cross the Atlantic to Paris and then cross to London, to enjoy the sights and delights of these two great cities, the galleries, museums, buildings and monuments.

We were to sail into Cherbourg and then travel by coach and train to Paris. We stayed at the George V hotel just off the Champs-Élysées; I saw that the luggage was taken to Georgiana's suite and that her cases were carefully unpacked before returning to my modest room to do much the same. When I describe this as modest, it is the largest room I have ever occupied.

I had booked for them, in advance, tickets for the Opera, a concert, and various museums and art galleries; in fact, I booked three of everything, but the least expensive for me of course; I was happy in my advertized role as "Lady's Maid to Georgiana Arnold".

Richard Arnold in his own inimitable style had made his own contacts and in particular went to the U.S. embassy to meet with the newly appointed American Ambassador (Envoy Extraordinary and Minister Plenipotentiary) Robert Milligan McLane, that famous Democrat who had represented the U.S.A. across the world. Richard and Georgiana had dreamed up, in advance, a reception for some significant business figures in France, and guests traveled from afar to meet the head of the legendary Arnold family.

Richard was reserved in such company and so that led to an invitation to Georgiana, and me, to attend. Of course, Georgiana's role was to charm both American and French guests with her usual skill; she did so with consummate ease. My role, described as "Maid to Georgiana", was to follow 5 paces behind her, ready to answer any call she made to me, but largely to blend into the background, Officers Mess style.

It was a highly effective event from all points of view, and was to add new dimensions to Richard's businesses back in New York.

Then of course there was the world of art and painting. Georgiana's brother De Forrest Bolmer was with us on the trip; he was himself an accomplished artist and widely known as such. The Arnold family's fabulous collection of paintings, started by Richard's father Aaron Arnold, was already legendary. Then, via contacts made through De Forrest Bolmer with members, new and old, of both the Hudson River Painters Schools, their shared interest grew.

The original 'Hudson River Painters' was established 30 years earlier as a prolific group of artists. They were not, as the rather derogatory name implied, parochial local painters but they traveled the world to paint, and to collaborate together. De Forrest Bolmer's art school travels took place at the time of a second wave of Hudson River artists. Like their namesakes, and De Forrest Bolmer, they traveled widely in developing their art. It was, later, to become part of my remit to organize travels for De Forrest and his artist friends, both in America and further afield.

Of particular note was the first massive exhibition by "La Société des Artistes Indépendents". This was to become an annual event, but it was important for Richard Arnold to be there, as the custodian of a fabulous art collection in New York, and also for Georgiana to be there, and to be seen to be there. We met several American painters, then domiciled in Paris, and set some scenes to be followed up in later travels.

Paris was alive with such events, such as impromptu concerts, cabaret, poetry readings: the only frustration knowing what we might have to leave out.

I was charmed by Paris, we strolled through its romantic streets soaking up the atmosphere. Georgiana and I spent a day at The House of Worth buying gowns for next season. Georgiana had a lovely figure and sophisticated tastes. She hit it off with Mr. Worth, a delightful Englishman running his own fashion house in Paris, and he waited on her himself rather than handing her off to one of his staff. He seemed to like all Americans and he famously said of them that they: "have faith, figures, and francs – faith to believe in me, figures that I can put into shape, francs to pay my bills".

Then to England, by train and boat, arriving at Brown's Hotel in Mayfair, London. There was a certain sense of irony in my choosing to book this particular luxury residence for the Arnold couple, not that a sense of irony was something that most of the Americans I knew had any understanding of.

Initially the former valet and maid to Lord and Lady Byron, James and Sarah Brown set up this hotel after they got married. I must say that, though I envied their enterprise and success, I had neither marriage nor property in mind, though either of those might change in due course.

I settled the couple into their suites: they were to occupy one whole floor of one of the 11 historic Georgian townhouses that went to make up this hotel. They were comfortable and had their week-long itinerary booked.

Included in that was the recently-opened new American Legation at 123 Victoria Street in Westminster, only a year old but already becoming an important port of call for people with interests in business, the arts or in new collaborations between the U.S.A. and England.

For me it was a train journey from London to Kent to visit with my beleaguered family and to make contact with the Belvedere household and Rosemary Farrell in particular. Finally, it would be back to Liverpool for the crossing to New York, but taking in York on the way.

CHAPTER 12

Back to Kent

IT WAS A relatively long journey to Kent, the line to Sheerness had opened in July 1860, the year I was born, but it required a connection to Sittingbourne which meant changing trains.

As I emerged from the station at Sheerness, that I had last seen 6 years earlier, the changes were very evident. It had less of a frontier-town feel to it, much more building had gone on with more shops and houses. The changes were evident in me too; I had left as a rather shy and slightly disheveled 18-year-old but now was dressed and presented for New York. While I grew accustomed to the modestly fashionable attire servants might afford, I nonetheless drew glances as I walked through the streets of Sheerness to my parents' new home.

My parents were now at No. 2 Bentham Square in Sheerness, a step up from the Bluetown home. Of course, I had written to tell my parents of my arrival and the week-long stay but, even as I stood on the threshold and knocked on the door, I was not sure what to expect.

The ghostly shadow that opened the door was my mother Alice Maher. My father was out at work in the dockyard, James and Joseph were at school, along with their older sister Alice. 15-year-old Mary was "resting in bed". My mother stood for a moment, taking me in, then stepped towards me, hugging me tight, whispering repeatedly, "Annie, it that you, is that really you?"

We went indoors and of course straight to the kitchen where she put the kettle on; in the background was that warm smell of Irish stew cooking. Isn't it strange how evocative smells can be, transporting you immediately to another time in another place? She held my hands, pulling my arms out to each side; "Just look at you; will you just look at you, fine clothes an' all". She had never lost that gentle Irish brogue that I knew so well and at times in this quiet private time it was almost as though nothing had changed.

We spent an hour sipping tea while she quizzed me about my new life in New York. Even as I told her the stories it was like make-believe to me too, but all too solid and real. When I was able, I asked about the family. She told me that Margaret was quite poorly and at my suggestion we went upstairs in this cramped 3-bedroom terraced house to see her. It was not her own private room, as I had come to expect, but she shared it with her sisters Mary and Alice. We roused her gently and she sat up to kiss and hug me. "Fancy finding me like this, in bed and all". "No, you rest if you need to" I reassured her. But no, she was up in a trice and we reassembled around the kitchen table.

I was interrogated on that same round of questions posed by my mother. My work, my employers, my "home", my interests, and again it all came pouring out.

Later in the afternoon, while still in full flow about Paris, the children arrived back from school. A chill ran down my spine as they filed into the tiny room. Mary, I remembered though she had grown. Behind her were two brown-headed little boys, the exact replicas of the brothers who had died when I was living in Sheerness. It took me a moment to realize they were not ghosts, just younger additions to the Maher family whom I had never met.

Mary, at fifteen was so grown up, and with a hunger for learning. She wanted to be a teacher she said. Next was Thomas, a bright and scrupulous little boy. "And you Thomas, what would you be?" I asked. After a thoughtful pause, "I want to run the Royal Navy" was his ambitious reply. Then Alice, who was 12, and also such a studious serious little thing, wanted to teach too, "just like Mrs. Dubby". James at 8 declared that he wanted to be just like his father and work on ships. Finally, little Joseph at 6; "I want to travel and see the world, just like you" he offered with starry eyes.

I was now a little worried about sleeping arrangements. "Don't worry, we're putting a small bed in the girls' room so you can sleep in the room with Alice, Margaret and Mary; a tight squeeze but I'm sure you will all get along fine". Then a pause: "we got that bed for baby William, but God bless him, he hardly survived to use it".

The impact of that simple statement was profound. It sank like a sword into the side of a wounded animal, and left just stillness and a sticky silence in its aftermath.

The children were full of questions. I think they really liked having a proper big sister, one they hardly knew except for my letters to my mother. They seemed to know my life backwards and were full of the stories they told at school. "Oh, you must come back to school", pleaded Mary, "Mrs. Dubby is still there and is now my teacher, she dearly wants to see you again."

Then-just after a quarter past six, a key in the front door heralded the arrival from work of my father. He was a tall man, well over 6ft but now bowed slightly with the stress of his heavy manual labor. He stood full in the kitchen doorway and just gazed at me. The room had fallen silent as if waiting to find what mood would greet us.

It was then that I remembered the anticipation in this, oh so simple act, not of putting the key in the lock, but rather the act of closing the door itself. Sometimes it would be just a gentle click as the door was pressed home. If it was a crashing sound that sent the windows in the house rattling in their frames, then it was ominous news. I would scuttle away like a crab, defensive and anxious to hide, upstairs preferably where it would take more of an effort to reach me.

"Alice", he finally spoke, "I had quite forgotten". On this occasion the door had closed quietly and the Irish brogue was soft and quiet. He came across and kissed me on the top of the head. "I'll wash and then we must eat; everything ready?" He need not ask; mother had the stew slowly cooking only shortly after he left for work that morning, and in any case she did not answer, as if in rebuke.

Why was I not surprised that he had forgotten the details of my visit? Of course, he knew I was coming, but the lack of interest was not new.

Ever since my early childhood his disappointment in me was clear, I was not a boy nor, apparently, successful.

Even now he took little interest in my life or my success. As the evening progressed, if prompted, he might force out a response, "really", or "that's good dear" but he hardly took in the subject let alone understood what his most appropriate response might be. In his mind, marriage and children were the only option for a girl and so he showed little interest in my career or travels. Not only was he disappointed in my gender, he felt that I had failed to achieve what I was born to do, marry and give him grandchildren.

By nine o'clock the children and he were in bed, and I was back with my mother across the stained wooden kitchen table. In this setting and with the first question she asked, "Is there a special man-friend?" I was surprised by the vehemence of my response.

My retort, "And why would I need a man!" was too emphatic and too loud.

It did prompt a discussion about her life with Patrick, about the tragic loss of life in our family, and our shared concerns about Margaret. She declared that she felt physically exhausted and that she found childbirth and bringing up children to be a huge physical and emotional strain.

She also owned up to Patrick's lack of engagement with the family, except the money he brought in, and how all the daily chores were left to her. The Red Lion pub in Bluetown was his haunt when he wanted to escape the house, household chores and the family, which was often. She explained that he could be quite demanding after he'd had four or five pints; not just on her, she went on. I let that comment go, not sure how or if to follow that line of conversation.

"Thank you my dearest for your kind and regular letters and the money you send me. I don't tell your father less it finds its way to the Red Lion". The amount I sent home was not much, but was a gesture I had adopted when I first went away to work in Belvedere; there seemed no reason to stop now that my work was in New York.

By the end of that first evening, the plans for me were almost set. Essentially, almost all of the family wanted to show me off, to friends, family, teachers, clergy, neighbors. I had this endless whirl of visits and endless tea and sandwiches trying to live up to the stories that had been told of me. Of course, that was no great effort since my progress in those years had been rapid. However, I did not want to disrespect Georgiana and so played down or did not mention all of the personal aspects of that relationship; to the Kent family, she was just my "employer".

I took the children to school that second morning, and of course we arrived early. I left the children in the playground and went in search of Mrs. Dubby. Shortly after arriving in Sheppey as a five-year-old I was enrolled at the school. A rather plump lady, short in stature, she seemed calmly resigned to having another pupil in her class to supplement the 44 children already there.

Seats were in serried ranks, at desks that had the china ink pot embedded in the top next to grooves to hold pen and pencil. For several years, I was elevated to the role of "Ink Well Monitor"; in the closing moments of the day I would set off around the classroom with a wooden tray. Into that I would carefully place each ink well. Mrs. Dubby had two ink wells at the teacher's desk, one with black-blue ink and the other red. I would dutifully fill each well from the large glass jars of ink kept in the cupboard behind Mrs. Dubby's desk, taking greatest care not to spill a drop.

Mrs. Dubby was like a hoarding squirrel and would gather a whole range of materials from a wide range of sources, books, pictures, displays in glass-covered cases of leaves, feathers, butterflies, beautifully colored rocks, fabrics; her classroom was an Aladdin's cave of learning. She was my teacher and my mentor, she taught me a love for reading and enquiry and showed me how to "Read and Learn".

Books had become part of my life and were significant in developing my mind, my creativity and my systematic approach to life.

As I quietly entered my old classroom, I was swept back in time; nothing had changed from the sanctum that I remembered. A small bowed figure sat at the teacher's desk, surrounded by stacks of children's work plus her infamous mark book that recorded every detail of each child's progress.

She looked up as I closed the door. "Mrs. Dubby" I said. A flash of recognition and she seemed to fly from her desk towards me. "Annie Maher" she cried, "how good to see you". She clasped my shoulders and held me at arm's length. "My how you have grown up; a proper lady in all your smart clothes."

I spent only 20 minutes in her company, sharing details of my life and progress; she was intrigued by the high life in New York and the stories of my work there; "I'm not surprised, not surprised at all", she intoned. Then after the school hand bell was rung, the children from each class lined up in height-order, boys in one line, girls in another. The silence was so profound it was disturbed only by the call of a curlew.

The looks on the faces of my siblings as I emerged, with Mrs. Dubby, onto the playground to bring the children in, was one of sheer excitement and pride. As the class filed in, Mrs. Dubby held me again at arm's length. "You have always learned well my dear, but now you have really excelled yourself."

"It was you who taught me Mrs. Dubby and without you I think I would have a different life, indeed be a different person".

"Well, you know what I always say my dear, 'Read and learn, read and learn'. It's not just things, it's about people and relationships. You can never have enough learning so you keep at it my girl and make us all proud.

"I will, I will" I promised her as our knitted fingers reluctantly freed themselves from their clasp and I walked away and she towards her classroom. "Goodbye and thank you Mrs. Dubby" I called as she disappeared into her classroom's outside door. Words could not express enough of the gratitude nor the debt that I owed this hugely influential woman who held the lives of frail young children, like mine, in her palms.

What Mrs. Dubby taught me carried with me through life and seemed to attract people's attention in each place I stopped.

Then there was the trip to Belvedere: I had been invited for afternoon tea with Rosemary Farrell. She seemed so pleased to see me, and even saying to me on the doorstep when I greeted her as Mrs. Farrell, "Rosemary my dear, you must call me Rosemary."

She seemed thrilled at my success since my ignominious and unjust dismissal from her service. There was no mention at all of Anthony or his ambitions for me as an artist's model. I tried to thank her for her kind words, her reference and for her pulling strings to arrange for my employment at the Officers Mess in Chatham, but she would have none of it.

What was of particular interest to her was my employment in New York and the family that I now worked for. She wanted to know all about the Bolmer and Arnold families and was intrigued by the variety and scope of both their interests and my work. She asked how I found working for Georgiana. I was perhaps a little unguarded in my descriptions of our work together and in my enthusiasm for Georgiana's personal style.

"You have been very lucky" Rosemary shared in confidential tones. "this woman has a lot to teach you and a lot to give you, not least this special friendship that she has offered. Treasure it and keep it like a first love. Come to enjoy your time together with her; there are so few rare moments for women to express sincere and tender feelings one for the other. Don't be afraid of that closeness, emotional and physical, and don't hold back your feelings and emotions. Platonic love is a gift that women are given and it should be treasured like a special flower. Men seem to have no equivalent, concerned I suppose that it might reflect badly on their manhood.

"I had such an opportunity once, and wasted it, to my everlasting shame. It was only when you came to work here that I found those sorts of feelings again; it was quite a surprise to me and not something I felt I could give in to, given my earlier experiences. You try to thank me for what I did for you, and yet I felt the need to thank you for reinvigorating my life, and I still feel great shame in having treated you as I did".

That conversation had great significance for me. I felt in some ways liberated by what Rosemary had shared.

We enjoyed another hour or so together before I had to travel back to Sheppey. As we stood at the front door, at Rosemary's instigation, we hugged each other and she kissed me on both cheeks. None of this had the formality of our last meeting; and I was intrigued and decided to write asking if Rosemary would share with me her "wasted opportunity". As if through telepathy she asked, "Will you do me one favor, will you write to me as often as you have time?"

On my last morning, I got up deliberately early so that I would see my father before I left and to care for him as I used to. He ate a simple breakfast of toasted bread and the strong tea I had made for him, not even forgetting the two heaped teaspoons of sugar that I remembered he liked. I had made up his snap tin too; great wedges of fresh bread I had bought from the bakery shop even before he was awake, and then with the rare treat of butter and the great chunks of cheddar cheese he liked, and finally two fresh green apples bought that morning too. I was not seeking thanks, he wouldn't even look in his tin, but I knew that at least he would think of me when he did so around midday.

We spent what might be our last few minutes together in silence. "Well" he said as he eased his great frame from the chair. He threw on the coat that had been on the back, pulled on his ratting hat, picked up his snap tin, and made for the door. Almost as an afterthought he looked over his shoulder and said, "Have a safe journey Annie".

"Father!" I called out in command rather than in farewell. It stopped him in his tracks, one hand on the open front door. I stood in the hallway and we both just stared at each other, trancelike. "Look after Mother and Margaret", I instructed. He just stood for a moment, looked, and then was out and gone.

The only physical contact I had with my father in that week was a kiss on the top of the head on the first day; since then, rarely a glance and so few words.

By the end of that week, as I made my way back to Sheerness railway station I was quite exhausted. I went to the station, alone, partly because I think that my mother and Margaret would have found the walk too much, but partly because I feared the farewell and the certain knowledge that I might not see at least some of these people ever again. The front doorstep farewell was quick, a hug, some kisses, and then the false promise that I would not leave it so long before I returned.

Then, like my father, gone. Even though my quick pace had already sped me towards the station, my mother's wail of anguish that followed after me down the street was haunting and indeed lived with me for years. The echoes of sadness and tears throughout my lifetime seemed to have been an unwelcome companion and very present at that parting.

I later learned that, after I left for New York, Rosemary Farrell had taken to visiting mother on occasion. She would arrive with a white baker's cake box, neatly tied in ribbon, with special treats for the whole family; those visits to my Sheerness home and our long correspondence over many years were important both to her and to me.

CHAPTER 13

Return to New York

THE JOURNEY TO London was difficult; I felt tightly wound, heavily over-anxious, sad and tearful; I was more or less composed after a seemingly endless journey across this capital city. As my journey progressed it seemed less and less like a country where I belonged.

Yet of course it was not; Ireland was my home country, southern Tipperary my home county and Clonmel the seat of everything that was important to me. But oh Ireland, how many times, like Disciple Peter, would I deny you?

Back at Brown's Hotel I left a message at reception to arrange to meet with Georgiana. We had to confirm the rest of our itinerary and our journey to York and on to Liverpool, and then catching the ship to New York scheduled to arrive there on November 3rd 1884.

We met in my room, reserved for one night, and Georgiana read from my face what a week I had lived through. "What happened?" she asked. "Don't ask" I pleaded, "I'll just cry". "Come here" she said softly, holding out her arms to me. We came together in an embrace and she just held me ever so gently. "There will be time when we get back to New York". Georgiana spoke softly in my ear. I replied affirmatively, "It will take a little time; I don't yet understand myself what horrors I discovered in this one visit; we'll wait until New York".

With that I changed the subject, now brisk and business-like. The London trip had been a great success, with a combination of artistic and business networking with key figures on the London scene.

Next up was the trip to the old city of York; it sounded right to me, old York to New York, and I knew they would be intrigued by the old walled city. So it proved, as we walked the quaint narrow streets and The Shambles, and visited the stunning York Minster.

After York, the long 105-mile journey across country to Liverpool, down to the docks and then embarkation, was very tiring. Richard and Georgiana had a state room, mine was a very modest little cabin, but it gave me some time for privacy and reflection. We were to get some relaxation on board the ship; it had been an emotional time for me and at times exhausting.

As we sailed into New York, it did genuinely feel as though I was coming home. I felt at ease in this place and as though I could achieve whatever I wanted and that anything was possible. With those farewells in Sheerness I knew that I was leaving England far behind me and with little expectation that I would see my parents or siblings ever again.

It took a few days after our return to New York before Georgiana and I had a chance to talk. She had a lazy morning and I had taken her a breakfast tray to her room. We bolstered up her pillows and she sat up with the tray on her knees and happily ate the light breakfast and fruit juice.

I was busy bustling about the room picking up hair pins and tidying her dressing table when she said "Tell me then". With Rosemary's advice still clear in my mind, I started. I began to describe the sense of hopelessness in the house. Margaret and mother both so badly drained, barely coping. The younger children with learned self-sufficiency surviving O.K. but what would they do, how would they manage without their mother? What if another of them fell ill? And then to my father, his life, his avoidance of any family responsibilities, his drinking, his demanding ways. What had mother meant by that throwaway line, "demanding, not just on me"? There were echoes in my past that I could not put words to.

I had talked of my mother's "overprotectiveness" of me being the factor that led her to find me residential employment when I was twelve years old. But it was something in that coldness and the stare between my father and me, before he left for work that last morning, that troubled me. Was there something in this of him? Were there things he knew, that he was keeping from me?

Then I told her of the unusual afternoon-tea with Rosemary and her analysis of female relationships, and of her advice to me.

Georgiana had just listened quietly, not saying anything or interrupting. She set her tray aside and knelt next to me where I had come to rest sitting on the side of her bed. She pulled me toward her with my head resting between her breasts. She stroked my ears and that lock of hair gently with her fingers and kissed the top of my head as my father had done, but with a lingering lightness of touch. "There, there", she said, "we will fathom it out someday. Your Georgiana will take care of you, never fear, and let no one else harm you". She moved my head so that I looked upwards towards her and she kissed me.

CHAPTER 14

Death Stalks

IT MAY BE that, as we get older, it might seem as though death were stalking us like a carrion crow; certainly, in my case, the last few years had seemed like an onslaught from which I might never recover! I was used to being in control, arbiter of my own destiny. Death was the one exception and when it came knocking you understood how vulnerable you were.

The primary emotions were guilt and anger; guilt that there was something I might have done, some other path I might have taken that would have led to a different outcome. Anger, not with myself but with the deceased. Why, why die, why now?! No matter how in-control I felt, death reminded me that my grip on life was only a passing self-indulgence.

In 1880 it had been William who died, only a babe in arms; sad for me but another blow for my mother.

In 1881, my brother John passed at the age of 15; two sons, two brothers in the space of a year. I hardly knew William, and for much of John's life I had been working away, and so a stranger to him too. My mother now had lost 4 children and in her letters to me you could hear, feel and read the heartache.

Having been able to return home in 1884, I did have the chance to witness the deteriorating health of some family members. Margaret looked so poorly, and my mother seemed skeletal and sallow skinned. But that brief time together was no refuge for my fears and anxieties, and made the leaving more difficult and the subsequent absence more troubling to live with.

In August 1885, the final two straws, Margaret died of tuberculosis, the same illness that had taken her two brothers before her. It must have been such a blow to mother. In October that same year news arrived of my mother's further failing health and then, only a few days later, she had died too.

It was Georgiana who brought the telegram to my room. I was in my living quarters when she arrived at the door and suggested I sit down.

She gave me the unopened telegram, fringed in black, and I shook like a leaf. I was to discover how traumatizing the death of a parent can be. All of those feelings of guilt and anger came flooding back and I wailed like a banshee.

The words in the telegram were brief and to the point and from my father, adding to my feelings of guilt and culpability. "Mother died Tuesday STOP Funeral next Thursday STOP No Flowers STOP". Nothing else he said.

Georgiana came to me and cradled my head against her. I was weeping and shaking uncontrollably, slowly she stroked me and calmed me. "Wait here", she ordered, returning minutes later with a large whiskey glass filled with golden light-brown liquid; the first time I had tasted spirits and the first sip took my breath away and made me choke. I took refuge in the elixir and, as I drained the last drop, I felt strangely in control again: but no, as I tried to stand it was only Georgiana's firm hands that kept me from falling.

We stood again in a tragic embrace, Georgiana stroking my face and whispering conciliatory words into my ear. "Come with me and lie down for a while". She led me to my bedroom and, sitting me on my bed, slipped the shoes from my feet. "Come on, head on pillow". As I curled up, fetal position, still sobbing gently, Georgiana had lain down behind me, on this perilously narrow bed for two, holding me close. Again, she simply held me tightly and her honey-soft words eased my inner tensions. There we lay until I fell sound asleep.

Looking back at my mother's death, the anger was much more potent, universal and yet specific than I had expected. How can one blame Catholicism for this poor woman's demise? Downtrodden and brainwashed into believing that her only skill and purpose was for procreation; that it was her duty in some way to counter the impacts of childhood mortality, by creating further life only for that to founder on the rocks of death: she believed it her God-bidden duty!

I did of course blame my father Patrick, my one request of him being to look after Margaret and my mother; he failed in both respects. It was he who went along with all this, in the same way that it was her duty, so was it his to continue to seek moral and religious justification for his very existence, by procreating at least annually, to meet his Lord's bidding, when in fact the starkness of his noisy grunting and grinding, heard by all in the house, was the beginning, the middle and the end of it all. Why had he not been strong enough to resist, to desist? Why are some men such weak creatures?

It was the end of her, my mother; it was not just the births, but the deaths too, that squeezed her out like a husk of dried lemon until there was nothing, nothing left. What could I, what should I, have done?

Alice was 14 years younger than him but would need that youth and energy to survive the stresses of life in North Kent married to a man like Patrick Maher.

Her Catholicism and the catholic church in Sheppey, St. Henry and St. Elizabeth, kept her going through some difficult times. It was of course not just the premature deaths of half her children, but the grinding poverty of supporting her large family, that took a toll upon her.

The church was the custodian of our family life story, keeping as it did, often in Latin, all of our ecclesiastical landmarks, births, christenings, marriages and deaths. The same was true in Clonmel where we had come from: St. Peter and St. Paul and to St. Mary's before that, had harbored our history and guided our lives. It was now to these colossal and dusty record books that the lives of my siblings, and now my mother, were to be consigned for generations.

And then there was the Irish community in Sheppey, people like my mother who had left their homeland to find a better life. These were the very people, steeped in the same culture, who would offer support and solace as life and death and illness took its toll on her and her children. As her life went on, at least she was able to see some small improvements in the family circumstances.

I have always believed that it was the loss of 17-year-old Margaret in August 1885 that contributed to Alice's final decline. Less than three months later in October, Alice joined that roll call of early deaths aged only 47. Alice left 6 remaining children and a disengaged husband for whom she had provided the structure and stability that had allowed him to function in the way that he did.

Patrick was remarried two years after Alice's death to Mary O'Connor on Christmas Day 1887. He was 63 years old and Mary was 46. They declared, on their marriage certificate, their ages to be 42 and 38; maybe they just felt young at heart. They had no children.

Chapter 15

"Nellie" Georgiana Eleanor Arnold

OF COURSE, I had early notice of Nellie's arrival, about 7 months to be precise. Georgiana was so excited, it had been three years since their marriage and Georgiana had worried about age and virility, Richard was now 59. Her account was that Richard was a quiet shy man, avoided exaggerated behavior, and was somewhat constrained in his displays of passion: "Brief bouts of frenetic activity and little satisfaction" was the way she described it.

But we had months to prepare. The first task was to find the best gynecologist in New York; at the time, Joseph Brettauer. This was an emerging medical specialism and Mr. Brettauer oversaw the whole period of the pregnancy and the birth. The home birth was organized with military precision, as you might expect of me.

It was Joseph Brettauer who confirmed the pregnancy. Georgiana had kept it a secret from Richard until she was certain. He seemed excited by the prospect of a new child; fatherhood of course was not new to him, he had two daughters and a son from his first marriage.

That's not to say that he got involved in the details that would need to be in place once the new-born arrived. We had a nursery prepared, redecorated and equipped, all the bedding, diapers and clothes in place along with all the rest of the paraphernalia needed for the arrival. In an adjoining room was a space set aside for the, still to be appointed, resident nanny.

Although we didn't know for certain that the baby would be a "her", Georgiana declared "one of those feelings" and she felt certain. I took it upon myself to sew a beautiful christening robe for the baby in beautiful white lace with a matching cap. I made sure to line the entire gown with smooth white satin so it would be soft against the baby's skin. I envisioned the gown being worn again and again as the Arnold family grew.

Richard's existing children were all in their mid to late twenties and were cool at the prospect of a new half-sibling. This would be the only challenge that Georgiana would make on the siblings' inheritance; Richard, at the time of the pre-nuptial agreement had written in an equal share in his estate for all his children, from his first and his second marriage.

When the big day arrived in a flurry of breaking waters and contractions, all went well. It was a relatively short labor. The midwife and Joseph Brettauer were in attendance and the excited staff team was on hand with towels and hot water. "Georgiana Eleanor Arnold", "Nellie", was born on Friday September 21st 1885.

The baby girl, Georgiana Eleanor, arrived quietly, like her father, and a girl as her mother had predicted. It was his choice to give the new baby her mother's names Georgiana Eleanor, saying that his wife had been a delight since she came into his life, and he knew the baby daughter would be the same. In effect, she was known by our pet name, "Nellie", for all of her life.

Later that same day there was laughter and merriment both upstairs and downstairs as Richard Arnold instructed that the whole household should wet the baby's head with champagne.

Georgiana had been sleeping in her own room for several weeks and I visited her there after her exhausting day. Though she was tired and uncomfortable she wanted to show the baby her own room next door. We went together with the little mite into that bright sunny room, and having shown her the musical box that played a lullaby, her crib with its pink trimmings and new linen, Georgiana laid the baby down in her crib where Nellie fell fast asleep. Georgiana put her arm around my waist and rested her head on my shoulder. I quipped as I looked around at the pinkness, "lucky it was a girl after all!" We laughed; Georgiana stroked my face and said, "Thanks Annie, I couldn't have done all this without you".

We had employed a Nanny for the baby and she was due to start the following Monday, so we had the whole weekend to get to know and play with our new arrival. By the time Monday arrived it would be back to work as usual.

New arrivals in my good catholic family were not always as happy an occasion as this one had been for Georgiana. She seemed so fulfilled by the experience and was more relaxed than even I had known her to be.

To be fair to him Richard Arnold took great care with his new daughter and seemed much in love with her.

The Nanny we had hired was Adele MacCullough; she was 18 years of age and set to play an important role in all our lives

CHAPTER 16

Adele Marie MacCullough

ADELE WAS BORN in May 1871 and was only sixteen when I hired her as a nurse. In fact, she had lied about her age on application saying she was eighteen, and we didn't know until much later.

She had been raised by her father John MacCullough, but had escaped from that environment as soon as she was able. I heard echoes of my own upbringing when I interviewed her.

It was her beauty that was the first, and abiding, memory of her. She had flowing auburn hair that reached far down her back. Her complexion was very light and her facial features delicate. She was slight at just over five feet tall. She had other attributes that any woman would be pleased with. Which is why I didn't question her age, she told me she was 18 years old and from her presentation there seemed little reason to question that.

I had decided early on that Adele would do well in this post, her love for children was evident and she had such a softly spoken and gentle way with her. More though it was a matter of chemistry, and I knew that if the chemistry was right between Adele and me, it stood a good chance of being alright between Georgiana and Adele.

I had introduced her to Georgiana, whose opinion on who cared for her baby was paramount. I left them to chat retuning after fifteen minutes. Afterwards I took Adele to the door and explained that we would write to her once a decision had been made as to which of the six girls interviewed would be offered the post.

I went back to Georgiana and enquired, "So what did you think?" "Oh, she will do very nicely, very nicely indeed. You've excelled yourself in finding this one Annie, well done."

Adele's entry to the household was unremarkable. We had arranged a room next to the nursery with an adjoining door so that she could always be close to the baby.

Over the coming weeks, I got to know Adele well. While not explaining why, she divulged that she had escaped from Ohio to New

York. A cousin already lived here so she had a bolthole to make for. It was to that address that we wrote offering her the post.

A small-town girl from Ohio could be forgiven for being overawed by the Manhattan scene she found herself a part of but Adele took to it well.

I talked to her about the routines and standards that I needed from her to reflect the nature of this particular household. She achieved these standards with only rare correction. The baby had taken to her in the same way we all had. She got on with the job.

In time, I was able to determine more about this young girl. She had left her studies early though she wanted to work with children. Her real ambition was to be a teacher and so this start as a nanny was one step on that road; I had decided that I should support her in whatever way I could. It was my opportunity to share some of my learning, not just in the varied employment I had, but in the acquired skills in culture and the arts. She was a quick learner and in a short time was showing levels of sophistication that were a credit to her.

Georgiana took to her quickly. They spent time together with Nellie, who was such a delightful and contented child, and much of the noise emanating from Georgiana's room or from the nursery was the sound of laughter.

The relationship between Georgiana and Adele developed and was a much more direct and physical one than I enjoyed at that time with either of them. They were often close and would nonchalantly touch as if they had done this all their life; this was a nanny and her mistress and while seeming natural and right, nonetheless broke every protocol that this society expected. On one occasion, for example, I went to her room to discuss some event or other with Georgiana. The baby was lying on the bed, wrapped in a shawl, gurgling. Adele was sitting at the dressing table looking into the mirror, as Georgiana brushed the full length of her auburn hair with sweeping strokes of a brush.

They both looked up as I entered the room without knocking; "Annie, what do you think of this?" asked Georgiana. She was holding up to me this great swatch of Adele's hair. I couldn't think how to answer. To be honest I was more than a little jealous; here were the two women I loved most, clearly at ease and enjoying each other's company. It was then that I came to accept Adele's rapid entry into our friendship group.

CHAPTER 17

The Death of Richard Arnold

LIFE HAD GONE on smoothly since our tour of Europe and all seemed well.

Until the last week of March 1886 when Richard, totally out of character, failed to rise from his bed on the Thursday morning. He had fever-like symptoms and seemed very hot to the touch. He refused medical help saying that it would quickly pass. He slept for much of the day and the following night.

We called in his physician who knew him well. He prescribed some salts to be taken in water and was confident that whatever was ailing him would soon pass.

By the Sunday, he had not eaten for 3 days but began to be violently sick and had severe diarrhea. Georgiana was becoming quite frantic with worry and called the M.D. back in. To no avail and with no obvious diagnosis, over the whole of the coming week his condition worsened daily and by the second Sunday he was slipping in and out of consciousness and was quite delirious.

The whole atmosphere in the house had changed to one of heightened anxiety, if not panic, and on the Sunday I suggested to Georgiana that we call in his three older children to see him. They were mightily distressed to see their father in this state, but did their best to comfort Georgiana.

By the following Tuesday, April 7th, I called them in again. Richard was unconscious and in a coma-like state. The three of them stayed the rest of the day with him.

In the early hours of Wednesday April 8th, Richard died, slipping away from us as quietly as he did everything. He was at least peaceful and not in pain at the end. Georgiana was at his bedside holding his hand as he died; I stood guard duty by the door.

The howl of pain, like a wounded animal, that emanated from Georgiana at the moment of his death was frightening. "Richard,

Richard!" she screamed as if trying to bring him back to us. I sent for the M.D. and he confirmed death, though could offer no diagnosis or explanation other than "a complication of disorders".

It was like the mirror image of the time of my mother's death the previous year. Slowly I managed to ease Georgiana away to her own room, and 1 arranged that the mortician attend to deal with Richard's body and take him to the funeral home.

She was inconsolable, and I just sat silently with her on her bed, holding her close while her body was racked by spasms and howls of anguish and seemingly endless tears.

I went to the cabinet where I knew she held a small stock of alcohol, and poured a stiff scotch for her. She clutched it and drank slowly, much as I had when she extended me the same comfort on the death of my mother. Afterwards I slipped off her shoes and, laying her down onto the sumptuous bedding, crept in behind her and embraced her. She stroked my arm in return, "Thank you Annie, thank you" was all she said.

The funeral that I organized for Richard was to be, as he would have wanted, a quiet affair. The Funeral Service took place at St. Thomas's Church where he was a regular member. The church was full to the brim with floral tributes to Richard, many of them done by my cousin John O'Brien. John had obviously taken great care to be sure they were magnificent, knowing how close I was to the Arnold family. On the day, it seemed that the whole of New York turned out to witness the event. As the cortege passed through those streets people were lined up from 1020 Fifth Avenue to the church, which was itself full to bursting with crowds spilling out onto the street, not the quiet affair that Richard would have wanted.

At a subsequent private burial Richard was laid to rest in the Arnold Family Mausoleum at Green-Wood Cemetery in Brooklyn. I was in such a great state of stress worrying about Georgiana that I barely noticed the beautiful surroundings and the gracious little Greek Temple that served as a memorial to this great New York family.

After the ceremony and burial, invited guests repaired to the house where, in the picture gallery, we had laid on refreshment and drinks. Georgiana, and Richard's three eldest children, formed a reception line offering the usual courtesy of thanking people for attending and listening to the repetitive eulogies about his life and work.

There were no speeches, Richard would not have wanted that, and gradually the people dispersed.

At one point Georgiana seemed overwhelmed and I took her up to her rooms where she might have privacy. The enormity of her loss was just beginning to dawn on her; "What shall we do, what shall we do?" she intoned. "This will pass, I promise you. We have Nellie to think of and to look after. You know whatever is required you will do it, and I will be there every step of the way to help and support you". "Oh Annie; however, did I manage before you". She held me tightly in an iron-like embrace: just held me, and held me.

Richard's last child was only just 7 months old at the time of his death and Nellie would never know her father, except by reputation.

CHAPTER 18

Sister Mary and Sister Dorothea

IT WAS IN 1887, three years after our mother's death, that my sister Mary wrote to say that she was coming to the U.S.A.. She was nine years my junior and now still only 17 years old. I had met her last on my trip to Sheerness when she declared she wanted to be a teacher. She was a quiet, reflective and intelligent girl and I was not sure how she would fare in the rough and tumble of a New York school.

I did have some sense of how fruitful that future would be for her and what a key role she would play in my life. It was all agreed and young Mary took the tortuous trip from Glasgow via Larne to New York, almost as I had done ten years earlier. She arrived on April 21st 1887 aboard the S.S. State of Pennsylvania.

John O'Brien agreed to come with me to collect her and to help with her baggage. As he had done almost 10 years earlier for me, he had arranged for the horse-drawn delivery cart to meet us, now though with the opening of the Brooklyn Bridge we did not have to use the ferry but instead were to be able to travel in style across this new feature on the New York skyline, the tallest structure in New York.

Receiving family members were allowed to stay near the brokerage office while their kith and kin were processed. Mary looked exhausted when she emerged from the queues of passengers waiting to verify their credentials; she was so happy to see a familiar face. I introduced her to our cousin John, and we set off on foot to where the delivery cart was waiting. Again, as I had done, we stopped off at some of the food and drink vending carts and had some delicious oysters and introduced Mary to the first of the American traditions welcomed by so many travelers to New York.

She was given a rapturous reception, as I had been, at the O'Brien household. Since my arrival, the family had grown from three children to six; they now ranged from eighteen through to six and Thomas (aged 10), Josephine (aged 7) and Andrew (aged 6) were the names added to the list.

The children loved Mary instantaneously and clamored around her to hear details of her life in England and her long journey to New York.

Their mother intervened to insist on a little peace for their cousin so that she could begin her recovery. Mary was able to wash some of the grime from her body that accumulates during such a long journey and then over tea with the O'Brien family we discovered that she did not have long to stay with us, just two or three days until she was to take the next stop along her future pathway.

Young Mary had used her catholic connections back in Sheerness to obtain a place in a religious teaching order. In April 1887, Mary became a novitiate of St. Dominic at St. Mary's of the Springs Convent; she was to begin a teaching career that was her vocation, expressed at a very early age. She was to be known as Sister Dorothea (Maher). Springs Convent was based in Ohio and that was Mary's next port of call. Mary was ordained on May 29th 1888 in Zanesville Ohio in the Order of St. Dominic at St. Mary's of the Springs.

Inevitably as we talked with John and Anastasia O'Brien, the conversation turned to a discussion about religion. Unlike me, Mary had sustained her faith throughout her lifetime. She talked enthusiastically about her work back in Sheerness. Mrs. Dubby had taken her under her wing and suggested that Mary might volunteer to work in the school. She did and spent much of her time working with other children in the classroom, listening to them as they learned to read, or as Mrs. Dubby would have put it, "read to learn." From this experience, Mary had concluded that she should devote her whole life to her God and to the Catholic church. This stood in stark contrast to my own beliefs.

I had abandoned Catholicism at quite an early point in my life, because I thought it damaged lives, and I had never really mentioned my Catholic background to Georgiana; not that she had ever pressed me on it. Instead I let it be assumed that my faith was in the Church of England. Georgiana, like much of the elite society in New York and beyond, had adopted the Episcopalian church. Based firmly around the Anglican Church of England notions, Georgiana had a very strong connection and I had just let it be assumed that this too was my church of choice. This was one of the few times that I had misled Georgiana and, I must say, right now I had started to regret the deception. However, my strident, critical views on religion would not have been particularly welcomed, so it had become just an area of my life that had remained determinedly private.

Of course, Mary and Georgiana would have agreed that, while there was a history of tensions between their two churches, their intent was to do good for others furthering their faith and, no matter what route they undertook to achieve this, it served the common good of peoples and of society. Sadly, they wouldn't get the opportunity to meet, not while I continued my subterfuge of being an Episcopalian. How would

I explain a Catholic sister to Georgiana? I am sure, had they met, they would have gotten along like a house on fire and I would have been able to just sit back and enjoy my sister's chatter with this kindred spirit that was Georgiana.

Talking of our good intentions towards others, our thoughts and conversation turned too on the remainder of our family back in Sheerness. Since mother died and now Mary had come to the U.S.A., my father was left with only four of his children. However, to all our surprise he had remarried and to a much younger woman, 18 years his junior; not that age seemed important to them since on their marriage registration certificate they had both chosen to declare themselves younger than they actually were. They had selected Christmas Day for the ceremony and Mary O'Connor became the new Mrs. Maher. From my sister Mary's description of her step-mother she was a welcome and refreshing change within that household.

They had left Bentham Square and returned to Bluetown, now residing at 13, The High Street. It seemed typical of my father that he refused any attempt to gentrify himself or his residence and returned instead to the heart of the Sheerness docklands.

By all accounts Mary O'Connor coped well with him and provided Thomas, Alice, James and Joseph, aged now seventeen, fifteen, twelve and ten respectively, some stability and routine that had been sadly missing since our mother's death. Thomas had joined father working in the dockyard but was intent on joining the Royal Navy as soon as he was able. Alice, on the other hand, had followed what was becoming a family tradition and was helping out at the school, very much in the way that Mary had. Here was another of the Maher girls who had been supported by the redoubtable Mrs. Dubby. Both of our younger brothers were still there as schoolchildren and so she was able to keep a watchful eye on them.

The most important lesson I learned in my time with Mary was the extent to which she reflected my own determination and grit; she was not only an intelligent, sensitive and hard-working person, she had a steel that ran through her and gave her hidden strengths and would make her capable of great things. Once Mary had made up her mind, she had the strength of will to carry it through, all by herself if necessary.

I returned to the O'Briens one more time to visit with Mary before she submitted herself to the training she was to be given, to both take up holy orders and to achieve her lifetime's ambition as a teacher. Again, watching Mary's encounters with the O'Brien children it was self-evident that this was a true vocation she had chosen to follow and that her skills in shaping bright minds was a true credit to our Mrs. Dubby, who had been such an influential figure in all our lives.

CHAPTER 19

837 Madison Avenue

RICHARD'S WILL INCLUDED a provision that allowed Georgiana to live in their shared home on Fifth Avenue in the event of his death. However, the house was part of his estate left to the children of his first wife, and Georgiana was keen to settle the matter so that they could, if they wished, dispose of the house and agree probate on the estate. The house actually sat vacant for years. They shared a concern that there might be allegations that Georgiana had only married Richard, a much older man, in the expectation that he would die before her and leave his wealth to her. Of course, that was the motivation for their much-publicized pre-nuptial agreement which effectively cut Georgiana out of his will. Nonetheless, her living in the house might have perpetuated that myth.

What was assured, and Richard laid great stress on this, was that if there were any children from his marriage with Georgiana, then those children would be properly taken care of in his bequests. There was of course only one child from the union, Nellie, and she was left the sum of $1,000,000 to be accessible to her upon reaching majority; in the interim Georgiana would be able to draw down interest on that sum, to support the child.

The hunt for an alternative home did not take long to find; that home was known as "the Sternberger House". The wealthy merchant Mayer Sternberger commissioned the firm of Thom & Wilson to design him a home at 837 Madison Avenue between 69th and 70th Streets. The architects produced a five-story, Queen Anne style mansion. The red brick made it look very sumptuous and the internal aspects mirrored this opulence.

It was however to be Georgiana's own house and as it was not on the monumental scale of the Fifth Avenue mansion, it was going to be much more manageable and require fewer staff to maintain it. The house was also much closer to Georgiana's brother, De Forrest who was now living at East 60th Street. In fact, he became a regular visitor at 837 Madison Avenue.

Georgiana's first decision was to appoint me as Housekeeper. For the first time, I had full sway on matters relating to the way the house was run and the deployment of staff. My first task was to appoint some reliable people; Adele was an essential person, caring for Nellie as she did. A good Cook was a prerequisite for a successful household; preparation of food for staff and household was a given, but invited guests could only be fed on the best quality ingredients prepared to the highest standard. This was the job I gave to Mary Murphy, who like me had come from England. She had arrived three years earlier than me and had worked in the kitchens of some of the finest houses in New York. While 15 years my senior, we got on like sisters and she was so good at her job; guests would rarely refuse an invitation to eat here, partly because of Mary's skills. Mary introduced me to Anna Keenan who was equally at home in the kitchen helping Mary as she was in the dining room, expertly serving guests. I was able to bring her along further by teaching some of the skills I had learned in The Officers' Mess We were of an age and similarly got along very well. My final full-time appointment was for a Laundress and I chose Elisabeth Eagan who, like Anna Keenan, was the same age as me and like me she came from Ireland but had worked with Mary before.

There would of course be some part-time appointments, a Butler or manservant, given that it was an exclusively female household, who was needed largely when we had male guests, to attend to their needs. The yard was too small for stables and Georgiana's horses and carriages were stabled out; a coachman was just 'on call' from there if needed and we usually could give 24 hours' notice at least. He would just arrive at the appointed time ready for the departure.

Georgiana accepted my advice on some essential remodeling and redecoration needed to make it fit our purposes, however the interiors were all of her own design and she sourced materials and furnishings of the highest quality, with many of them influenced by our travels.

The ground floor was to be the servants' working area and their access door below the stoop staircase was the servants and delivery entrance, separate from the main house entrance. While the rooms below stairs had comparatively low ceilings, there was a lot of space that could accommodate most of what was needed, a new kitchen, large enough to serve as an eating place for staff, offices, various storage facilities, linen, and wine for example.

The yard housed the laundry room where the washing would be done and then hung inside that room, rather than have the unsightly line of drying laundry cluttering the yard, open to everyone, particularly upstairs guests, to see intimate items. There was an outside dry privy that staff would use and where chamber pots were emptied as required. It was away from the house at the furthest point in the yard for obvious reasons.

On the second floor were the public rooms; the single dominant feature was the grand staircase, which led from a large square foyer. It was a grand design with intricate carvings and made a strong statement to those entering the house, the first twelve stairs led to a landing and then it turned left up five steps and left again, as if coming back on itself, in a further flight of twelve steps to the next floor.

At the top to the right of the stairs, doors opened onto the drawing room, which was used when large numbers of guests were visiting. It had a large corner fireplace that was always prepared and had a basket of logs to one side. The sitting room was more intimate with armchairs and a chaise arranged on a beautiful Persian rug around another fireplace. Then there was the library where Georgiana and I worked together on the household management and the organization of events and where Adele, undertaking a wider range of tasks, would open correspondence and answer letters.

On the third and fourth floors were the bedrooms for guests and visitors. They were very opulently furnished. Georgiana's room had a large French-style four-poster bed, and all had sitting areas, dressing tables and wardrobes or fixed closets. The dressing room that gave off from Georgiana's room had full length mirrors that could be moved to give an all-round view. Closets were fitted into the wall and gave her the copious space she needed to house her dress collection, with banks of drawers for other clothing and one whole closet for shoes.

Adele and I were in the attic rooms with the rest of the servants but between our rooms was a sitting room that we both shared with access for both bedrooms. It meant we could spend time together and relax in the quieter moments, usually in the evening. Behind the grand staircase, hidden from view, was another, narrow set of stairs that ascended from basement to attic. This was for the staff and had a small landing on each floor with a door that led to rooms at each level. It meant that staff could magically appear wherever they were wanted in the house.

This house, the first home that she owned, was a triumph of design and style.

CHAPTER 20

For the Sake of Nellie

FOLLOWING THE DEATH of her husband, Richard Arnold, it took some time for Georgiana to recover and I worked tirelessly with her brother De Forrest Bolmer to bring her away from her grief.

Our focus was on her responsibilities to her daughter and that provided a potent motivation to keep her going. It was not just the maternal responsibilities she had but also that in Nellie was her lasting contact with Richard. She had clearly loved him deeply and his loss to her was a deep personal tragedy.

Later, as she was showing real signs of brightness, we began to focus on a new big trip to Europe. We would plan a more extensive venture than just our Paris/London trip with Richard. De Forrest had really wanted to see Paris again; he had studied there in 1877 and would bring some new insights into the tour, However, this time we would take in Italy and even further afield; De Forrest harbored a real desire for a return visit to Cairo and to paint again the pyramids at Giza which he had last painted on a trip back in 1883; we agreed to incorporate both. De Forrest encouraged a goodly number of his colleagues to set aside some time in early summer, in 1890, to join us. We began to enthuse with Georgiana about the great enjoyment we would all have from this extra special trip. Most of all, we agreed, it would be taking Nellie with us that would make all the difference. She would be five years old by the time of the planned trip.

Nellie, though really too young to understand the plans, became quite excited as the trip came nearer and you could often hear her talking with her mother and with Adele about what she might expect to see. I felt slightly guilty that again I was to be treated to a place on this tour I was planning but poor Adele would be left behind, but nearer the time De Forrest came up with some interesting ideas about that.

As that planning went on we had some memorable domestic trips. De Forrest advertized in the N.Y. Herald on September 4th 1888: "Wanted – on ocean, furnished cottage with stable. Address Mr. De Forrest Bolmer, 26 East 60th." It was thus De Forrest discovered the Wright family that owned a property in Elberon New Jersey called "Wright Cottage" near to Long Branch. It was at 535 Ocean Avenue in Long Branch and was on the ocean-front, sitting on the eastern Atlantic Seaboard south of New York. Howard Wright was known to Georgiana as a supplier to Richard's store in New York. "Wright Cottage" was to figure in the Bolmer and Arnold families' future.

Elberon was a district created by perhaps the most successful property developer from the mid 1800s, Lewis B. Brown. He conjured the name Elberon using his initials and last name. In 1866, he acquired a mile and a quarter of ocean-front property south of West End; then the following year with two other large landowners he laid out and constructed Ocean Avenue in the deserted section and landscaped a park in the same region. The first sale of land there was to Howard Wright at $1,250 per acre. Property prices rose from that figure, and Brown quickly disposed of his holdings at a huge profit. So, Wright's Cottage was born.

The Wrights, like a lot of other Long Branch property owners, only used it rarely, as an escape from New York, Particularly in the long summer days when the heat in the city was so oppressive, it was just wonderful to escape to the long sandy beaches and the cooling sea-breezes of this delightful place. It was a property that was let out to other reputable families for vacations, and otherwise sat vacant.

I had concluded, when first I set foot in Long Branch, that one day I would try to afford to buy property there. A land boom was in full swing. Outsiders came in to make huge profits on the quick sale of plots of land. Divisions that sold for $500 one summer brought as much as $5,000 a year later. I had concluded that I should buy real estate on the northern side of Long Branch. Though only a short distance from Elberon, it had not attracted the big property speculators and so prices were comparatively low, but I would have to be quick.

Long Branch itself had become increasingly popular with the elite group, who were attracted to build large properties along the long flat stretch of beach bordering Ocean Avenue. Many of the houses, or should I say mansions, were disproportionately large and very ornate. There seemed to be a competition as to who could build the most unusual structures. There were mansions modeled on French chateaux, some on Rhine castles; with this wealthy group of people showing off their travels to far-flung parts, now reflected in their summer holiday homes.

Howard Wright had told De Forrest that "Wright Cottage" was available for the season and so De Forrest and I persuaded Georgiana that this was just what 4-year-old Nellie needed to take her mind off the gloom following the loss of her father and to get some fresh air into her lungs.

Five of us went away for a month during 1889; De Forrest would spend his days walking and painting fabulous seascapes; Adele was with us to care for Nellie and they had so much fun on the beach. With so much fresh air, sunshine and swimming off the beach the two of them looked so fit and healthy, not just from the sun but also from the offshore breezes that sometimes blew quite strongly here.

Initially Georgiana would just sleep, not rising from her bed until early evening; my view was that if she could sleep then that was what her body needed, so we kept quiet when we were in the house during the day, though largely the other four of us were out and about. Adele and Nellie would be playing on the beach and swimming in the sea and the surf, while I would go with De Forrest on his walks and, when he set up his easel, I would just sit quietly in the background content to watch him working and exploring his creativity; it was a very relaxing time. The process of caring for Georgiana in her grief had drawn De Forrest and me much closer together.

De Forrest Bolmer was the first man I had felt close to in my life. Of course, there was no physical relationship there and my greatest fear was ever compromising my position in Georgiana's household. I sat and watched him work, and his companionship seemed so natural to me, and he too seemed content with my company.

Georgiana was now increasingly at ease and outward going. It had been many months since we had watched her smile and heard her laughter. It was just such a refreshing change for us to understand that we had won our Georgiana back from the depths of despair to near normality.

Our stay coincided with an impressive arts festival in Elberon. All of a sudden. from a quiet seaside resort, the place was inundated with weekend guests and there was a whole series of performances and events taking place. Just a little reluctantly Georgiana agreed to accompany De Forrest to the Casino. "Of course, I will have to dress in full mourning, Annie, pull out the black moiré dress and I will wear the black steel and jet necklace". At the Casino that evening there was a performance of the play, "Who is Who; or, All in a Fog" put on by the Elberon Club. This was followed by a second play, "Sugar and Cream". The write up in the New York Times the following day was full of praise.

I could begin to relax about Georgiana; it had worried me that she had suddenly seemed so fragile, on the death of Richard, and so prone to bouts of deep depression. Now though, she seemed much like her old self, a rich, attractive young widow, and there seemed to be no concern for the future; she had taken on a new lease of life and for the first time in many months was smiling and laughing again and making plans.

It was an increasingly good time for the three of us too. Georgiana, Adele and I would leave De Forrest in charge of Nellie and the house during the long, warm summer evenings and would walk endlessly on the beach. We would take large towels with us and would just sit on the sand and chat about everything and nothing, enjoying the peace and solitude as the night closed in.

By the time our month at the seaside was over, it was not just Georgiana and Nellie who were feeling better, I felt that I had deepened my relationship with two important people; Adele was always easy to like, but over these few short weeks we had grown closer together. Georgiana frequently expressed her gratitude to me for helping her over Richard's loss; the depth of our relationship was now unrivalled.

Georgiana had met Howard Wright at the Casino and invited him over for tea. She and Richard had known the Wright family from New York and this lucky coincidence was to place Elberon and Long Branch at the center of our lives. The Wrights had left Long Branch and started spending their summers in Lakewood, a little further south, so when Georgiana made them an offer for Wright's Cottage they were delighted to accept. That move placed us at the center of Elberon and Long Branch society. We were surrounded by wealthy and influential people; Ulysses S. Grant the former U.S. President, before he died, had his cottage four houses south of us. Next door but one was another familiar figure, Isaac Vail Brokaw who was, like Richard, an entrepreneurial clothing merchant. Next door the other way was his brother William. The house before U.S. Grant's belonged to the famous publisher of The Philadelphia Public Ledger, George William Childs. Colonel William Barbour, was Founder and President of the Linen Thread Company, Inc., a thread manufacturing enterprise having much business on both sides of the Atlantic. The Colonel had bought several plots together, next door to Wright's Cottage, and had built four houses on it, one of which he sold to William Brokaw, Isaac's brother.

I am ashamed to admit that I took all this in my stride. I was rubbing shoulders with some historic figures, the rich and the famous, as though I was born to it. Perhaps I should have been.

The concentration of fame, celebrity and money brought its downsides too. Residents hired a private police force at night at a cost of $10 a month. While we were there we began to understand why it was needed. Loud noises during the night awoke the household, and we could hear shouting and screaming from the direction of the W.B. Brokaw cottage. De Forrest responded then to a loud knocking on the door; two of the private policemen said that our cottage had been burgled and they suspected that the burglar might still be on the scene. They searched and disturbed the burglar who ran into the downstairs bathroom and locked himself in. By the time the police forced the door, the burglar had escaped through the window and was gone.

The New York Sun report on 26th July the following day showed some of the tensions that had grown up between "locals" or "village people" and this summer holidaying rich class of transient residents.

"Burglars at Elberon"

"Long Branch July 25th – There is going to be an immediate boom in the private night patrol business here unless all present signs are misleading. Every season cottage owners have an opportunity to enjoy private police protection at night. The charge is $10 a month. That ensures a vigilant watch by means of the half hour signal system. There has always been a disposition on the part of even the wealthiest of the summer residents either to dispense with this safeguard or to get something cheaper. The village people, who are jealous of home industries, are in an ill-concealed glee today because some of their most gruesome predictions have come true.

"William B. Brokaw, the New York clothier, owns a cottage on Ocean Avenue, at the corner of Adams Street, Elberon. Two of his near neighbors are William Barbour, the Peterson linen thread manufacturer, and Mrs. Arnold, widow of Mr. Arnold of Arnold, Constable & Co.

The cottages of all three were made the mark for a cleverly arranged house-breaking scheme at 4 o'clock this morning. At that hour, Mr. Brokaw was awakened by a slight noise. Opening his eyes, he was somewhat perturbed to discover a masked man flashing a dark lantern in his face. Mr. Brokaw acted quickly and vigorously. He shouted, "Police! Murder! Help!" and he shouted so loudly and for so long that the man with the mask and the lantern departed without ceremony.

"The outcry aroused all the neighbors. There was a flurry such as the somber quiet of Elberon hasn't experienced in a decade. By and by there was a hasty inspection, not only of the Brokaw cottage, but of the others in the vicinity. It was then found that Mrs. Arnold's and Mr. Barbour's residences had also been visited, though in each case the burglars had departed without booty, Mr. Brokaw's cries having warned them of the danger. At the Arnold cottage, a capture was almost made. The burglar was tracked to the bathroom, but he locked the door after him and got away through the window.

"The regular police of the Elberon route consists of one man. His patrol is at least two miles long and he doesn't seem to have been around when the burglaries were attempted last night."

We all agreed immediately that doubling of patrols and costs, and $20 a month seemed a small price to pay for peace of mind; we had enjoyed a little excitement that night, albeit a little close for comfort, but it did not put us off Elberon or Long Branch at all. We four girls and De Forrest had a huge hug before we left for the station to return to New York, content that after a month away we all felt very much refreshed and ready to face life again.

De Forrest, on the other hand, had been more difficult to fathom; he was never very demonstrative, but we had spent so much comfortable time together, it was the case that now we did not need to speak to know what each other was thinking, or feeling. Certainly, after our return to New York, we continued our planning for the 1890 adventure with renewed energy; it would be good to spend more time with him.

CHAPTER 21

Halifax Nova Scotia

OUR NEXT MINI trip was to Halifax Nova Scotia in early fall. Georgiana had grown very close to The Rev. Frederick Courtney in his time as pastor at St. Thomas' Church, N.Y. He had subsequently been promoted to be The Lord Bishop of Nova Scotia from 1888, via appointments in Chicago and Boston and, after the death of Richard, invited Georgiana to visit him and his wife in Canada. Thus, a new trip was planned.

Georgiana expressed a wish that just she and I would go on this visit, especially since it was only for a few days. The journey was long though; we traveled by train from New York to Saint John, then crossed the Bay of Fundy by steamboat to Annapolis Royal, then rode the recently completed Windsor and Annapolis Railway to Halifax.

Frederick and his wife Caroline were there at the station to greet us and we traveled in his carriage to their home. I felt so privileged to be part of this group; given my failing faith I had no expectation ever to be in such close company with a Bishop. But I understood instantly why Georgiana liked him so much; he was a gentle person and so disarmingly kind that he seemed instantly like an old friend. Even on that carriage ride he put me at my ease by talking about his time in Kent. He was English and had attended King's College London. His first post had been at Hadlow, Kent, starting in 1864, the very year that the Mahers arrived close to there too. Hadlow is near Tonbridge, in the same Medway valley whose River Medway lets out at the estuary close to Sheerness less than 20 miles away.

Much of the weekend was devoted to long conversations between the Bishop and Georgiana, and much of this was about how she was handling the death of Richard. I spent most of my time sightseeing and Caroline devoted a whole day to showing me round. One memorable visit was to a new photography studio that I stumbled across. More out of interest than anything we went inside to take a look. Caroline persuaded me to have a photograph taken and sure enough I had a private sitting and then three copies of the photograph ordered to be printed up.

When I got the prints only a couple of days later, I sat down immediately and sent a copy to my family in Sheerness and a long letter telling them about our travels and our plans for the future. I did the same in a letter to Rosemary Farrell.

At the end of our trip, Georgiana invited Frederick and his wife to New York and suggested she would throw a ball in their honor. Many of Georgiana's church friends would be very interested in renewing his acquaintance, certainly those who knew him during his period of tenure which lasted until 1880. I was called in to talk through some of the detail of the proposal for, as Georgiana explained, "this young lady will be in charge of all the arrangements".

Of course, with his Bishop's duties it was hard to plan too far in advance but in the end he agreed that he would visit as soon as he was able; as things turned out it was eventually not until 1895 that we saw him in New York again.

Richard had died in 1886 and it was a full two years before Georgiana had overcome her grief and sorrow. These trips and the planning for Europe were among the key elements to that recovery, but most of all she had her faith and she had her friends around her; I counted myself as one of that number.

Like all children Nellie had been too young to take in what happened; children are so resilient and, despite calamity all around them, are soon laughing and smiling again. It is a salutary lesson that, even with the death of a parent, children do forget. Nellie commented to me at one time: "Do you know Annie, I can't really remember anything about my father, I don't even remember what he looked like". No matter how indelibly we think that we write in a child's book of life, our impact can be very superficial and only temporary. I know Richard would have been saddened to understand that.

CHAPTER 22

Travelers on the Ocean

OUR OUTWARD JOURNEY to Europe saw us set off on May 15th 1890. It was one of the most challenging pieces of organization I had ever accomplished. As news of our proposed trip was known both in the arts and church communities, and more widely, more and more people wanted to join us.

Of course, we had De Forrest Bolmer, since he helped to organize it, and with him a whole entourage of fellow artists, writers and poets. We were to be gone for 5 months, not returning to New York until late October; we docked eventually on the 20th from Liverpool. Of course, that length of trip did not suit everyone, so we had a core group of people with others coming and going at different points in our Grand Tour.

The New York Times reported our departure with a long list of luminaries sailing with us. They included a neighbor of ours at 219 Madison Avenue; that was J P Morgan, who traveled with us to London. He was a follower of the Episcopalian church and would frequently meet with Georgiana at church meetings. However, while he was considered by some to be one of the most influential leaders of the church, he was also known as a cut-throat businessman. J P Morgan was a banker and a financier. His specialism was in merging companies with common interests to form some of the largest conglomerates in the U.S.A. like General Electric and A.T.&T. He was one of the wealthiest men in the country, but not the most popular. One other person of note was W.C. Whitney who had just retired as Secretary of State for the Navy.

Among the artists in De Forrest's group was the Irish American artist Edward Gay who accompanied us all the way across Europe to Egypt and James Renwick Brevoort who had based himself in Florence, Italy for almost eight years. His first-hand knowledge of that country, and his artistic connections there, were to prove invaluable. Winslow Homer had been keen to join the trip not least because of his love of the sea and seascapes. He would set his easel up on the deck and paint some amazing images of the sea that captured the wind, the sense of power in the waves, of the perilous journey, of passing ships; he was in his element.

We landed at Cherbourg and from thence to Paris. Nellie had, after an initial period of sea sickness, managed the journey well, though like all of us was relieved to have feet on terra firma again.

As we had on our last sea journey together, De Forrest and I became almost inseparable, spending many hours together on deck leaning on the rail, watching the stars and the horizon and talking incessantly, though I must say we were not disturbed in any way by the companionable silences. This growing friendship blossomed further as our journey went on. He was very complimentary about my organizational skills and thought the itinerary I had put in place met his needs precisely.

Paris was a delight, as ever, and we spent our time mixing with artists of all kinds and of course very long meals of typically French cuisine, with a lot of chatter and a lot of wine. We spent considerable time in The Louvre; it had such a large collection it would take a lifetime to know it properly. Mostly the study was much more detailed and precise. Easels and sketching pads came out and there was rapt attention on the faces of De Forrest and his friends.

I was encouraged when Georgiana had me book an appointment at the House of Worth. The fact that she was interested in clothing and fashion again told me she was on the mend. She bought some exquisite gowns and day dresses.

From Paris, we went south to Milan, itself a magical city. La Scala was a joy and we saw both opera and ballet there. Nellie particularly loved the dancing and she declared that she had found her true ambition, to be a ballet dancer.

From Milan, East to Verona and its magnificent amphitheater. Then east again to Venice staying at the very grand Hotel Danieli. De Forrest loved it here and painted the Grand Canal with all its colors, the reflections of the water and the fleets of gondolas. Afterwards it was south to Rome. We had visited here last time we came to Europe with Richard. An historic city where there is almost too much to see.

We seemed to spend much of our time in the Antico Caffè Greco on Via Condotti; the Caffè had been open since 1870 and had made its name as a haunt for artists. With such a bevy of painters, poets and writers with us we quickly drew the attention of others. Lack of money was no barrier to a skilled artist; the walls were covered with paintings and sketches taken in exchange for a meal or bottle of wine.

Nellie loved her time there, we would often take up the whole of one end of the Caffè Greco and there was a constant flow of cake and pastries. As I sat there on the plush red seating I often wondered who else might have sat in this same place, Byron, Liszt, Hans Christian Andersen, Ibsen, Wagner; its historic and current patrons were legend.

It was then back on the water as we crossed to Turkey before making our way to Alexandria and thus on to Cairo in Egypt.

The Shepheard Hotel had become a focal point where its famous terrace, set with wicker chairs and tables, commanded a lofty and shaded view of the comings and goings on Ibrahim Pasha Street below. It was the playground for international aristocracy where every person of social standing made it a must to have tea; to see and be seen. Our group at that time was down to twelve, but nonetheless we cut quite a dash as we took tea on the terrace.

Several of the artists wanted to paint some of the best known sights in this historic land. The pyramids at Giza was De Forrest's favorite and he agreed that I might accompany him on that trip. Giza was just a little way out of Cairo but had become a tourist destination, so that as soon as we arrived in our carriage, we were surrounded by groups of young boys anxious to sell us their trinkets, or just hold us by the hand. Right at the edge of the desert, this spectacular ancient site was a wonder to behold; De Forrest had set up his easel and was painting and sketching in no time. As the day progressed, he moved from sketching to producing one finished picture, though he made some minor alterations once back at the hotel. This was to be the one he brought home with him to hang in his own house, so pleased was he with the result. I had been part of that and happy to sit and watch, under the shade of a tree, as he practiced his craft.

From Cairo to Alexandria and thus by ship back to New York by way of Gibraltar. We arrived home quite exhausted but elated by our travels and the variety of the experiences we had while we were away. It had been about providing an experience for Nellie, who had loved almost every minute of the trip; she had been in intelligent adult company for over five months and, though still very young, you could see the impact on her vocabulary and the wide range of conversations she would hold with various of our companions. As soon as we arrived home she fell into Adele's arms and they went hand in hand up the stairs to her room to reacquaint herself with her surroundings.

As for De Forrest Bolmer, he had enjoyed a wonderful and creative time. I have never seen him so enthusiastic as he thanked me for organizing the whole trip. We had spent so much time together during the trip, shared so many experiences, and I had watched him in his most creative moments as he painted, that I felt there was an even stronger bond between us. The death of Richard Arnold had brought me closer still to Georgiana and to her brother De Forrest Bolmer.

De Forrest created an exhibition, over the weeks following our return, mainly of his works from his European and North African adventure. He arranged a private viewing for his friends on March 7th but Georgiana and I went for a preview on the Friday before, and were astonished by the range of his work on display. It was quite a formidable collection and he wanted to share it with all his friends but it was then opened to the public from Monday March 9th 1891. Of course, he wanted to enhance his reputation, and bank balance, by selling his work and so the private viewing was even reported in the newspapers. "The Brooklyn Daily Eagle" printed an account on Sunday March 8th 1891.

"De Forrest Bolmer received his friends in the Tenth Street studio building yesterday after a long absence. He returns with a considerable quantity of plunder in sketches and studies – enough to cover one wall of his studio – and several finished pictures, among them a view of the Roman Campagna at twilight, with the dome of St Peter's in the distance revealed in silhouette across the desolate marsh against a pale and faintly cloudy sky; a mass of rocky spires in the Engadine flushed with the pink light of a setting sun; bits from Asiatic Turkey and the Nile region and a large picture of Ben A'an from Loch Katrine, its peaked top thrust up amid a wreath of clouds and its side lighted by a wandering sun gleam piercing through the Scotch mist, while a bird almost touches the sleeping surface of the lake in front. Mr. Bolmer paid his way through Europe by selling pictures."

I knew of course that one picture, that of the Pyramids of Giza, was not for sale and not on display, but instead hung on his wall at home.

CHAPTER 23

Childhood Mortality

THEY CALL IT "child mortality" and I should know, having had so many of my younger siblings die prematurely. The difference here was that Nellie had never been deprived of any comfort, encountered any unhealthy or disease-prone situations where she might have suffered a loss of health, unlike my brothers. Instead she died of influenza. She was one of over a million people worldwide killed by the flu in the course of this global tragedy that went on intermittently for several years.

In December 1889 in St. Petersburg the first case of death caused by flu was recorded. What was different for the world was that this was to become a pandemic that, within 4 months, had affected virtually every country in the Northern Hemisphere; by December 1890 the spread of the illness seemed to have stopped, but in March 1891 it recurred and deaths began again.

Georgiana and I had intense discussions about how to keep the household protected from this deadly strain. It was not, after all, just the young and the sickly who were most vulnerable; members of staff, should they fall ill, might soon infect others and the whole household could come down with it.

We took sensible precautions, drawing our social horns in a little so as not to bring large numbers of people together. We made as few excursions, for example to the shops or the theater, as we could, again trying to minimize the risk. When the 'flu hit our little Nellie, we had no idea where it came from or who or what she had been in touch with that might have been infected; as it was it hit her like a hammer blow. Adele was mortified and rather panicked by the situation; she felt, unjustly, utterly convinced it was all her fault.

Nellie seemed right as rain one minute and the next was carrying a high fever, complained of a sore throat, dizziness, and was quickly bedbound. She seemed to lose all the strength in her little body and could not even hold her head up to drink water. By the second day she was delirious, shouting and calling out, perspiration covered her body and she was shivering and shaking though she was so hot.

Georgiana was beside herself as was Adele; I did not think they were handling the situation well. Their extreme anxiety was affecting their behavior and, in turn, seemed to make Nellie worse; I guess she was sensing the tension even in her semi-comatose state. Of course, we had called in a pediatrician to help, but that just raised the anxiety level by another notch when he told us it was a waiting game. If the fever broke, she had a good chance of pulling through.

The fever did not break and Nellie did not pull through; Nellie died on Friday April 3rd 1891.

In the days that followed, the house was just full of sadness, and Georgiana was beside herself. She had now lost both Richard and Nellie and sank again into the depths of her misery. I managed the funeral arrangements, and according to Georgiana's wishes, she was buried in a white coffin; "for innocence" she explained. We held a small "family only" service in church and had no wake afterwards, again because the fear of this pandemic was high in people's concerns.

When we got back to the house, Georgiana did what she always did when the world became too much for her, she took to her bed for three days and just slept. It was a different matter with Adele; she was near hysteria, feeling this very strong sense of guilt as well as grief. She couldn't bring herself to sleep in her room next to the nursery because of its proximity to all the memories of Nellie. Instead she came and slept in my bed with me.

In those next few days and nights I did what I could to console her and would often resort to just holding her and hugging her as she cried. In some ways, I found that physical comfort reassuring for me as well as for her. The warmth of her body next to mine and the closeness of our forms as we nestled together in the otherwise lonely darkness, I found soporific and would wake suddenly trying to work out where I was, only to cuddle down again as I remembered. Georgiana's relationship with Adele had been much more physical than I had experienced with this beautiful young woman, just twenty years old. It just seemed to me very natural that we should live out our friendship in this physical way, as well as in our daily routines.

It was my emphasis on meeting Georgiana's needs that slowly brought Adele back to a more usual form of normality. We had a duty and responsibility, as well as an obligation as friends, to do everything in our power to help her away from her undoubted misery.

Over time, with care and affection, we began that process though, as with the loss of Richard, it would take her a long time to recover her equilibrium. I was there to manage the house and the staff and to fend off the avalanche of well-meaning sympathy that was cascading towards her. "I'm too weak Annie," she would plead, "I can't cope with visitors at the moment". Of course, I managed those rebuttals with tact, courtesy and politeness. I made sure that she was given the space that she needed.

Naturally it was Manuel De Forrest Bolmer who was one exception to this practice. He would visit whenever he could and would sit with Georgiana and hold her hand, not necessarily talking to her, but just being there. When she was asleep, or just resting, De Forrest and I would take tea in Georgiana's lounge and would enjoy that same companionable time together that we had on the tours and the Long Branch holiday.

CHAPTER 24

Georgiana Hartman

IT WAS EIGHT years since Nellie had died and the trauma of her sudden and tragic departure took its toll on all of us. Adele had been kept on, despite Nellies death. She undertook secretarial tasks for both me and Georgiana. Of course, Georgiana had been devastated and, after this further loss in her life, she took time to recover. It had been followed by the death of her brother, the Reverend William Brevoort Bolmer.

Part of that recovery was by devoting herself to her church and to good works. She had a number of charitable organizations that she worked with but the most prominent of all was certainly the New York Hospital for Sick Babies at 637 Lexington Avenue. This charitable organization was trying to help the large number of sickly babies who were suffering because of the insanitary conditions in the New York tenement homes in which they lived. Her interest had been rekindled following the death of Nellie; she wanted to support the children of New York. I felt that with every visit she made, every fund raiser she organized, every donation she personally made, that Nellie was there on her shoulder.

The hospital in New York would treat the babies and then they went on to the summer home of the Babies Hospital. This comprised of a dwelling and land, a gift of Dr. and Mrs. Thaw, of Oceanic, New Jersey. It amounted to two and three-quarter acres and had views across to Navasink River. The main house contained three wards with a total of 28 beds and there was also a reception cottage containing eight beds.

Babies were transferred three times a week by steamer and were kept for as long as their condition required. The fresh sea air was in marked contrast to the air quality in the districts from which they had come, and it wasn't long before they had a fresh look to their cheeks and their symptoms began to abate.

I was struck by the importance of this work and reminded of my own home back in Sheerness; I had lost three siblings to tuberculosis, a condition suffered by many of these very young children. In a different time and in a different place, with someone as devoted at Georgiana to support them, my own siblings might have survived.

Georgiana was on the Board of the Babies Hospital and worked tirelessly to help raise money. Benefactors were able to sponsor a bed at a cost of $1,000 a year; she herself devoted considerable funds of her own, at one time building a whole new ward for these deprived babies. Many of the social events that we laid on were explicitly to raise funds for this very good cause.

She now attended church on a daily basis and found the support and companionship there very reassuring and healing. It was there during this period when she got to know Rev. Charles Harvey Hartman. He was rector of St. John's Episcopal Church in Dover, New Jersey. Hartman's church was 31 miles west of New York City. Charles H. Hartman lived in the rectory in Dover with his mother Anna Gertrude Hartman. Anna ran the household there and indeed all of the furniture was hers. The duties of an Episcopalian rector were to meet the needs of his congregation and, in the absence of a wife, someone was needed to ensure that all of the Rector's parish obligations were met. That person was Anna Gertrude.

Harvey and Georgiana worked together on a number of charitable projects and her input was a perfect match to his ecclesiastical mission in Dover. She would occasionally visit Dover and seemed very at home in his congregation. Georgiana had no cause to worry if she was away at weekends because she knew that I had everything cared for back in New York. It did mean we spent less time together, but she was still a weekday resident and we managed this two-center relationship with our usual ease.

It was on one of these trips home that she broke the news to me of the proposed marriage. It came as no surprise to me. Georgiana had found in Harvey Hartman another gentle man with a strong commitment to family, church and community. What I could not imagine was Georgiana retreating, albeit only 31 miles, to live the life of a rector's wife in a rectory with her mother-in-law permanently in residence; however, this is what Harvey Hartman proposed.

She took time to explain to me what she had finally agreed to, and to some degree I was a little reassured. Georgiana would remain in New York for the most part, but she and Harvey would split their time between Madison Avenue and Dover. Georgiana was adamant that she would never move her home to Dover or take up permanent residence there. Anna Gertrude Hartman would continue her role as keeper of the Rectory and would manage the house during Harvey's periods of absence. At weekends, it was proposed, the newly married couple would travel to Dover on Friday evenings and remain there until the following Monday before returning to Madison Avenue.

The wedding, on Wednesday April 5th 1899, took place at St. Thomas' Church in Manhattan with the reception at home in Madison Avenue; it was to be a low-key affair with just close family and friends attending. One of the nicest touches was that Rev. Frederick Courtney, the Bishop of Halifax, was to come all the way from Halifax, with his wife Caroline, to conduct the wedding service. It was good to get back with them after my visit to Halifax with Georgiana and our discovery of our shared geography in the south east of England.

As you would expect, the service and the reception afterwards went off without any hitch, and Georgiana looked happier than I had seen her for some time. Her unusual and unconventional choice of wedding dress was modeled on those that we had seen on our travels, particularly to eastern Europe. It was a long, straight cotton garment which had then been beautifully embroidered with wool at the base, down the length of the sleeves and around the neckline. It was different from anything else I had seen in the current fashions but it had a simplicity and elegance that was fitting for such a low-key occasion.

As the day's events unfolded, the sense of a change in the wind was very strong to me; it was not just the impending new millennium, but something of more immediate importance to me and my way of life. Georgiana was to live her weekends in Dover and it seemed to me that she might eventually consider whether she still needed such an extravagant base in New York.

It wasn't that I had not thought about, and planned for, this eventuality, but now it seemed so close, so imminent, and the prospect frightened me. New York had become home for me and Georgiana's Madison Avenue house was my domain. I had worked hard to master the efficient and effective running of No. 837, and had trained my team to deliver a consistently high performance of their duties. I could see that my team would be broken up and cast like flotsam to the four winds. All of my friends and colleagues would be gone, Georgiana would be gone and I would be alone.

My fears were unfounded and, as the weeks and months drew on, we fell into a routine of squeezing all of Georgiana's New York commitments into the week days, allowing her the freedom to spend the weekends in Dover and to play the Rector's Wife. However, there were inevitably some clashes of diary when Georgiana had to be in New York when she would forgo her stay at Dover.

I am not sure that Harvey Hartman ever felt really at home in Madison Avenue; he was clearly infatuated with Georgiana, but she only rarely shared her bed with him, allocating him instead his own suite of rooms. It was an unusual relationship with Georgiana the more dominant figure of the two.

Having met Harvey's mother on several occasions, I did wonder if Georgiana played the role as surrogate to create, through marriage, the same sort of relationship that Harvey had with his mother. He had lived all of his life with his mother ever-present, and she represented a very forceful factor in his life and his work in the church.

Notwithstanding the reassurance about my future security that I gained through observing this marriage, it did prompt me to begin to set up my property portfolio that I had heard Richard talk about. I set out to achieve my ambition to be classified as a property owner.

CHAPTER 25

A Home of My Own

GEORGIANA WAS NOW more settled but had repeatedly said that she had no intention of moving to Dover to live permanently with her new husband.

I could see that maintaining two households was an extravagance, but Georgiana insisted that she would not dispose of 837 Madison Avenue; it personified her independence and her freedom to continue with her work in New York of supporting others less fortunate than herself. Had her life taken a different course then it would have signaled the end both to my work and to my home. I thought it a wise precaution to seek supplementary accommodation as a matter of some urgency.

I had spent a lifetime living in other people's homes; it hadn't crossed my mind that, one day, I might own a home of my own. Some of the properties I had lived in were very modest, others very grand in style, but they all had one thing in common; they were a statement about their owners.

I had always been interested in a conversation that I overheard when Richard was talking about real estate. He was making the point that leaving your money in the bank was not a sensible option. There was considerable benefit in making your money work for you and the best investments were in property and land. I heard him disclose that, notwithstanding the substantial sums raised by his New York businesses, by far the greater return came from 'trading' in real estate.

His father, Aaron, had bought ten lots of development land on East 81st Street, between Fifth Avenue and Madison: They were to become prime real estate and one of the most expensive areas in Manhattan. It had become a policy of Richard's company that they use a large proportion of their surplus earnings to invest in land development. The family owned several buildings in the area of Upper Fifth Avenue and they were fortunate to commission the prominent Griffith Thomas to mastermind many of those developments.

Griffith Thomas undertook the work on the ten lots in 1878, two years after Aaron Arnold died. The lots had been left to Richard and his sister Henrietta. He created a row of four-story-high brownstones which Richard and Henrietta then sold on as individual houses, making a lot of money for all concerned. In addition, Thomas was commissioned by Richard to design a private residence on the south-west corner of Madison Avenue and 84th Street, and another at the north-east corner of Fifth Avenue and 83rd Street.

Progressively I had accumulated quite a significant sum and perhaps this was the time when I should make that money work for me and buy myself a home of my own. My lessons under Richard's guidance, I could see, were critical to my future. I would, when I could afford it, buy not just houses but land too; it was a way of ensuring my financial future.

Though my parents had never owned their own home, merely rented it from a landlord, my mother had always tried to improve the houses they lived in. She never managed to find accommodation sufficient to comfortably accommodate the size of the family; though she had 11 children, in all there were never more than 7 living at home at any one time. But, as their house in Bentham Square in Sheppey went to show, it was possible to live in a 3-bedroom house with that many offspring, with the only downside being a certain lack of privacy.

Commander Farrell, his wife and children shared their family home in Belvedere, a newly-emerging area of substantial properties. The children and young adults still shared rooms but, for the first time in my experience, there was accommodation for servants' quarters; in this case only three, including me in my own box room. The concept of accommodation above and beyond the needs of the family and servants was new to me. I had been used to a "living room" serving precisely that purpose in my family's routines. If we were not in our shared bedroom, at home in Bentham Square, then the only other places were the privacy of the outside toilet facility, or the living room where we lived, ate, cooked and abluted; The Farrells had other spaces called variously: the kitchen, the dining room, the withdrawing room, the lounge. The lounge was used exclusively for entertaining guests on high days and holidays. These spaces had to accommodate all of the entertaining that was part of the lifestyle; groups of friends, neighbors, work colleagues, and so on, and thus meeting the expectations of a family well placed in society and business.

The grand houses and mansions of New York, where I served my apprenticeship, were an even more emphatic statement of the same principle. My first port of call was to 26 East 60th Street, New York, which was impressive in size and in the amount of accommodation, big enough to accommodate large numbers of siblings. I think I counted 14 offspring of one parentage or another, but it also provided the base for a social and business life that supported the multimillion-dollar budget required to keep a household of such a size. Of course, the more children there were, the more servants were required to service their needs.

Then there was 1261 Fifth Avenue; larger and grander still. Not only did this mansion have to accommodate the family and a small army of staff but had, for example, to accommodate a private art collection reportedly unparalleled in size in the whole of New York at the time. The scale of the social demand required sufficient space to entertain social gatherings of up to 400 people.

Georgiana's more modestly-sized but opulent home at 837 Madison Avenue was a welcome relief for both of us. It took away some of the pressures on the diminished household, but had the spare capacity for Georgiana, on occasions, to feel confident to host significant gatherings of her family, her social group, her religious community and, her growing favorite, the artists, sculptors and writers with De Forrest Bolmer at the heart of that group. Such was his reputation amongst that group of contemporary artists that it was becoming known as 'the De Forrest set'.

Part of what prompted my interest in having a space of my own, as I approached 40 years of age, was the realization that certain lifestyles were not available to me; I needed to reassess my priorities.

No husband for me, and so no children of my own. No family to accommodate, spread as they were across at least two continents. My friendship circle was very restricted and revolved around my employer and work colleagues. I persisted with the myth of an affiliation to the Episcopalian church, rather than Catholicism, but these were not people I felt at ease with or wanted to include in any friendship group. There was De Forrest Bolmer, whom I had been attracted to from the start, but any deep friendship with him was discounted because it threatened my livelihood.

Why then did I need to worry about my own accommodation? Well it was the realization that I may not work for Georgiana for ever. I had to have a contingency in place in case that situation came to a head.

By the turn of the century I had accumulated a significant amount of capital. I had worked for Georgiana for over 22 years and, in that time, had very little motivation to spend from my wages. I was housed free, I fed from the kitchen, I had a clothing allowance with an expectation of how someone of my rank within the household would dress. On the many trips I made with Georgiana across the U.S.A. and to other parts of the world, all my travel and expenses were paid, and I was even bought luggage and new clothing that fitted my position. In addition to that Georgiana would suddenly appear with something she had seen or picked up at the Department Store that she thought particularly fitting. As a consequence, I had quite a large wardrobe, albeit a little on the dour and somber side. Having said that, the occasional gifts that she gave me were often more flamboyant clothing than I would wear in my day-to-day routines. Most importantly, in the bank I had over $30,000; that was a serious amount of money.

Reflecting back on my life I had always been "from the servants' quarters", that is, of the serving class; having my own home would bring an independence and freedom, seldom thought of and seemingly unimportant; but having served the needs of several wealthy families, I now felt the need to elevate myself from the position of servant to become beyond the limitations of those serving classes. It seemed to me that the society I wished to frequent was one where being a property owner would make a statement about me which would elevate me beyond the confines of the servants' quarters and give me a more significant role in society.

It was the excitement and relaxation that was to be had at Long Branch that first put that idea into my head. It was Adele who made the suggestion of going together in a search for something for me to buy. There was a boarding house and inn, Barnwell Cottage, that was used as a convenient place to stay by working people from New York City. Adele did get occasional time off and would travel by train to Long Branch and had stumbled upon Mrs. Catherine Barnwell's cottage, this boarding house and tavern, just a short walk away from the railway station. She now knew Mrs. Barnwell quite well, and her manager Annie Hall, and she turned to them to see if they could find something affordable and close to the sea.

Georgiana's Dover weekend breaks offered me the opportunity to visit Long Branch and to meet and make friends with some of my potential neighbors. It was during a weekend trip to Long Branch for Adele and me, with an overnight stay at Barnwell Cottage, when I first met Catherine and Annie. They greeted not just Adele but me too with smiles and kindness, making us feel very much at home. We sat and chatted in their kitchen with great helpings of cake.

Catherine and Annie were curious about how I could have accumulated sufficient funds to even think about purchasing a property. Adele and I had to explain the benefits, and there were some, of being in service, particularly to some wealthy families like the Bolmers or the Arnolds. Firstly, with such wealth, the families paid above the norm for their servants; this was to secure the services of highly-rated staff and, as importantly, to retain them in their employ for long periods. I had worked now for Georgiana for almost 22 years. Secondly, the residential staff like me and Adele had no substantial outgoings to drain our savings. Accommodation and meals were included, as were our work clothes, in the form of a uniform and, trips away at virtually no cost to me. My income, over the 22 years since I first set foot in America, had been banked and barely touched, with the exception of money I had sent back to mother in Kent. Adele's savings, since she joined the staff later and had a lower salary than me, were less but still sufficient for her to be comfortable. Now they understood.

Then we got to the matter of somewhere to buy. They seemed a little embarrassed but got around to their suggestion, "Would you like to be our next-door-neighbor?" To our surprise, we learned that the next-door house had come onto the market for sale and they had arranged that we visit the following morning. I wasn't going to wait until then, my curiosity was so strong. I just had to take a look around the outside.

The house was at 158 Simpson Street on the west side of the street near Troutman Avenue, separated from Barnwell Cottage only by an unoccupied building lot. It was not what I had become accustomed to although it was convenient to the railway station; Long Branch station was only a few hundred yards from the house. Neither was there a "sea view", it stood a block away from the shoreline and between 158 and the sea were other houses and the Gaskin Ice Plant.

The house itself sat on a large plot; both the house and the yard were quite neglected. But it looked interesting; it was a wooden-framed building, 3 stories high with a porch around 2 sides. It faced east, toward the ocean and, sitting on rockers or gliders on the porch, even without a sea view, could probably become a common evening activity. I would have to install screening to the porch to keep out the seasonal mosquitos! The property had an outhouse in the back yard which I thought I might turn into a studio.

The most important criterion for me was what would the house have to say about me? You might, literally, say it was on the wrong side of the tracks, but certainly if I was going to consider something more along the lines of Elberon, then I would not be able to afford it. Here people would say: a forty-year-old, single woman, clearly of substantial means and a solid figure of society. With a little paint, with good-quality interiors and furnishing and some time spent in the yard, it clearly defined, "a professional woman of substance".

I had now to wait until Saturday morning to see if the interiors met my expectations.

Over breakfast I was to learn of a second surprise; Catherine and Annie had arranged for us to visit not just the property next door but also a property at 463 James Street. Adele had, on a previous visit, talked about buying herself that house and had been to look around it. "I had been so bursting to tell you" she said, "and these two ..." gesturing towards Catherine and Annie, "... almost gave it away last night". The four of us collapsed in laughter at the kindly deception; I now had two house calls to make and was so excited.

Adele explained that James Street was just a few blocks away from where we sat and ran parallel to, and about two blocks back from, the shoreline. She didn't at that stage go into great detail, but explained that she would get it very cheaply because it was quite small and a little rundown, but in a lovely street. I just couldn't believe that Adele and I might be near-neighbors even after all our time in New York; all that would wait until later and our trip next door.

158 Simpson Street was opened for us by the local realtor, and the four of us excitedly tumbled inside. It was all a bit drab and dusty having been left empty for some while, but it had a warmth about it that I took to immediately. There was a large hallway with staircase rising to the second floor, turning left onto a landing and then left again. On the first floor there was a large eat-in kitchen, a lounge and a living room; off the kitchen was a laundry room. On the second floor three bedrooms all with large windows that looked out over the porch roof; I immediately knew that the front room would be my bedroom.

The next surprise was the doorway off the second-floor landing which opened to reveal a steep staircase going up into a third-floor attic space but one where windows had been positioned on the gable ends to allow light to flood in. It was one very large space with no partitioning walls at all; I began to dream about how I might use this space.

The house had not been wired for electricity at that time and I would need to convert the smallest bedroom into a modern bathroom (I was used to such luxuries having lived with Georgiana for so long) but overall the house was lovely. It was positioned to catch all the breezes off the ocean and through the window I heard the waves crashing against the beach. "I'll have to let you know", was my passing comment to the realtor; I didn't want to give too much clue as to how positive I felt about 158 Simpson Street, an address that seemed to just trip off the tongue. The details provided by the realtor declared that the house was in the ownership of Elizabeth McGee and her husband. The legal papers were very precise in terms of defining the land belonging to the house.

Then back to Barnwell's where Catherine and Annie made the four of us drinks; though I had seldom used alcohol, I must say that this potion was very welcome and had my head spinning. Catherine referred to it as "the local brew" and I discovered later that there were a number of locals who distilled and sold privately flagons of the clear liquid that kept me, that afternoon, feeling warm and a little bit naughty.

We were in the kitchen, around the table. Three faces looked at me in silent anticipation. "Well", I said, "how do you feel about having a new neighbor?" The thrill and excitement were palpable, and there where whoops of joy and peals of laughter and hugs all round. It was so unlike me to take such an important decision without proper consideration, without even seeing any alternatives. But this house was an important statement about me, about where I had come from and what the future held for me.

158 Simpson Street would be my new home and Long Branch my new community. At least that was my intention, but it was one thing making the decision and another agreeing the sale, the price and getting the paperwork in order. In the end, I closed the deal to purchase my new home on August 8th 1900 for the bargain sum of $2,500. In addition, I made my first purchase of land. Immediately next to 158 Simpson Street was a vacant lot that had never been developed. It was actually larger than the one with the house on it. I had no idea if I would ever use this as a development site. My first inclination was just to incorporate the land into an enlarged yard around No. 158; time would tell.

In the afternoon, it was off to see Adele's proposed new home at 463 James Street. It was just as she had described it to me, in need of a little attention, but I could visualize her living a long and happy life there. She talked excitedly about her plans and of employing the services of a local man who would start some simple renovations, repairing roof and gutters and painting the exterior and the picket fence that ran along the front of the garden. Inside it was sufficient for her needs, with two bedrooms on the second floor, kitchen and living room downstairs. She would convert the living room into a classroom where she would practice her new art. She had advertized her services as a teacher and that was to prove very successful.

463 James Street was a warm and welcoming environment, and only a short walk away from Simpson Street. I had a very good feeling about both houses and a new life based in Long Branch. With Adele, here in Long Branch with me, perhaps I would not be as alone as I had feared.

CHAPTER 26

The Passing of a Generation

BACK IN SHEPPEY in Kent, Monday morning on April 29th 1901 was a beautiful early summer day. My 25-year-old younger brother, James, who had followed the family tradition into the shipyard business and was now a fully-apprenticed shipwright, was up early. He, our younger brother Joseph and our father, did not leave the house until 06:30 on a normal working day, but he had been in the vegetable garden to help nurture the small vegetable plants he had planted only a week earlier. They were just starting to sprout and push their tentative way into the sunlight. However, this morning they needed water and the occasional piece of grass plucked from the ground. He found this very therapeutic and it gave him an interest away from the shipyard.

Back in the kitchen he poured the boiling water into the teapot that stood beside three large mugs on the table. He listened intently for the familiar noise of our father and brother preparing for work. There was silence.

He went up the stairs to father's bedroom. He was anxious not to wake his stepmother, Mary, and so tentatively leaned into the room and shook his father by the shoulder. There was an immediate groan of someone waking from a deep sleep. "We need to be gone in 20 minutes", he whispered, and got a grunt in reply.

Joseph, in the next room, was a heavy sleeper and sometimes a bit reluctant to get up, especially on a Monday morning. James shook him hard and gave him the 20-minute warning too. Joseph was an engine fitter and his shift started at 7 a.m. as well.

Hardly had James made his way back onto the staircase than he heard the sound of our father falling to the floor; the vibration that seemed to shake the walls and floorboards stopped him in his tracks. Mary screamed. By that time, Joseph was at James's side, but it took the two grown men to push hard against the bedroom door to open it; Father had fallen in front of it and was preventing the door from opening fully.

Once inside, the gurgling noise coming from father's throat was sufficient to panic James slightly. He tried to coax some semblance of normality from father, but eventually he and Joseph had to lift the bulk of this huge-framed man, bodily back onto the bed. "Call the doctor, call the doctor" James repeated the instruction to Joseph. Moments later Joseph, having pulled on clothing, ran from the house and down the street. The doctor lived two streets away and probably would not welcome this early call.

Within 10 minutes he was back with Dr. Waters and the two raced up the stairs to find Patrick John Peter Maher curled on the bed like a fetal ball. Still the gurgling noises persisted and spittle was running from between the man's clenched gums and down his chin. Mary was sitting at his side stroking his temple, but she stood to allow Dr. Waters access to his patient.

"It's a stroke" he pronounced almost immediately, "and a serious one I fear". The three men managed to maneuver Patrick onto his back and they pulled the sheet and blanket up to his chin. Patrick's face was distorted. The doctor was holding him by the hand so that he could take his pulse. In a sudden spasm, Patrick went rigid and his back arched, his mouth blowing bubbles between his tightly closed lips. His face color changed to blue and the veins on his temples stood out in stark relief to his pallid complexion. With a judder, all of the tension in his body went and he slumped back onto the bed. He was silent: he was gone.

James picked up a copy of the death certificate later that same day and went to the Sheppey Registry Office in the late afternoon to formally register the death, in the sub-district of Minster. It was the end of that direct link to Clonmel, Southern Tipperary and Ireland. Patrick had died from a cerebral hemorrhage and thankfully his departure had been quick. He would not have coped with a lifetime of invalidity. I guess the false claim that this 76-year-old man was only 59 was about his need to continue working and may have had an impact on the Royal Naval Dockyard's willingness to pay a widow's pension to Mary.

Joseph stayed at home to comfort Mary and to make arrangements with the funeral director to collect the body. They had little time they could take off work and so arranged for the funeral to take place on Thursday May 2nd 1901.

I was in New York, working with Georgiana, when the telegram arrived. I found myself deeply upset by the news. Georgiana had been through the same experience in 1896 with the loss of her father and, similar to my new situation, her mother too had died earlier, in 1892, so she was very sympathetic and understanding.

It marked the closure of a number of things in my life. I was now the last surviving Irish-born person in the immediate family and it filled me with a sense of loneliness and isolation. My mother, Alice, had died in 1885 almost 16 years earlier and so was spared this loss, but I felt for Mary though I had never met her. She had apparently cared for my remaining siblings with every kindness and devotion, according to Joseph's accounts.

Deep within me was the irreconcilable animosity I held for my father; I know it was sheer resentment on a number of levels. I resented his failure to play a proper and effective role within the family and for the care of all his children. I resented his stubbornness in not welcoming change and improvement in our family circumstances. I was deeply resentful of his treatment of me, his failure to acknowledge me as a worthy descendant or to value anything I did or anything I achieved; nothing was ever good enough. His coldness towards me left me feeling fearful as a child and had haunted me throughout my adult life. It was, I thought, his treatment of women generally that was so shameful. He had two wives that he treated like vassals, and four daughters, three he drove away and the last to an early grave. I felt his rigid adherence to his Catholicism and all the values that surrounded that, without understanding the impacts of that legacy on his growing family, still continued to astonish me. Yet I was deeply sad and would miss his being alive.

There was no way that I could return for the funeral but I wrote to Mary offering my deep sympathy and regret at her husband's passing. Then, I am sad to admit, life in the household came quickly back to normal and, with the exception of a tear that Thursday, it was as if the waters of life had closed around him and that he had never existed. A family generation had come to an end.

CHAPTER 27

Open House in Long Branch

I WAS, AT this point, just a visitor to my new home and community, spending weekdays in New York and only the occasional weekend in Long Branch.

Georgiana, having bought Wright Cottage, was spending more and more time in Elberon. I think she saw it as a positive place where she had recovered from her grief and felt safe; she welcomed the quiet and the fresh air and the relaxation. Her routine was to spend a month in the summer there, and Harvey would join her instead of, as was his normal routine, transferring to Georgiana's New York home. I think he too was refreshed by the relaxed environment that was Elberon and away from his duties in Dover. Even so he was obligated to return to Dover, his congregation and his mother, most weekends and would leave us for those periods.

The other regular visitor was De Forrest Bolmer, sometimes on his own and sometimes with other members of his artists set; they would plan time away to steep themselves in the seascapes and the creative inspiration. It would bring such joy to Georgiana having such uncomplicated company to Wright's Cottage. They were perhaps seen by some local residents as slightly bohemian, but the chatter in the evenings, the poetry readings, the exchange about the best views for painting, all made for a highly-charged, creative and exciting atmosphere.

I was part of these events and would often make the travel arrangements for De Forrest and his friends. It was quite flattering to be allowed to join in those conversations and the banter; I think I took some of De Forrest's friends by surprise by my knowledge of art and artists I had, after all, traveled Europe and beyond to learn these things; then there was of course my reading: "read and learn, my dear; read and learn", echoed in my mind.

Georgiana, as soon as I told her of my home in Long Branch, was keen to visit. "I want to see it Annie, I want to see", she would intone excitedly. Despite all of her protestations, I insisted that it would not be my home until I had done some essential maintenance and repair work on it. I kept her at bay until the summer of 1901. She and De Forrest were due in Elberon and I issued a formal invitation to a "house warming"; I extended the invitation to any of De Forrest's artist friends who wanted to come with him.

Had I but known it sooner, I had this pool of itinerant labor on my doorstep. It was Con Gaskin, a neighbor, who ran the nearby fishing operation, who introduced me to the idea. "Many of my seasonal fishermen have a lot of other skills; their aim is to earn as much money as they can so that they can return home with sufficient money at the season's close, to allow their families a little respite from the bread-line that they normally trod. They would be really happy to act as craftsmen and laborers for you while you do up your house." There were periods of down-time when the fishing had to stop; the tides were wrong or the weather not suitable; they could use this time to earn a little more money.

It was agreed that I should write up a schedule of work and that Con would negotiate with his men: who should undertake which tasks and at what cost.

I split the work into three parts in my original manifest, internal, external and yard. The exterior woodwork had not been painted in a number of years and needed the old paintwork stripping off, repairing and rubbing down, then priming, undercoating and several top coats applied. The roof needed some attention too; there were a few tiles missing or displaced, ideally the whole roof needed stripping off and re-laid. Then I wanted a screen built around the veranda to keep out biting insects during the evenings.

The yard had been much neglected and had deteriorated to just a patch of scorched and browned grass. I had a vision of lush green grass and a garden with old English rose bushes, but was not sure that the climate and the seaside location made that a suitable choice. Of course, I wanted the traditional wicket fence, painted in brilliant white, to show off the house and yard and to make a statement about the owner.

Internally, the condition was not bad but it needed a complete redecoration. I had gained some clear ideas, under Georgiana's tutelage, of what would make it a really luxurious home for me. It was about the quality of hangings and wall coverings. But first things first, the structure and decoration of the fabric was the first priority.

I was surprised at the quote that Con brought to me. He thought I was about to try to beat the price down, but it was so low and saved me from the problem of seeking out separate workmen for each of the pieces of work, that I felt embarrassed to argue. Of course, I did expect that Con would have added a commission on top of the original cost, but I felt happy having persuaded him to reduce the cost by ten percent, and then round the number down to the nearest hundred dollars.

The work was to be apportioned, at first, into teams and I agreed to pay each team twenty percent in advance but then no more until completion. The start was almost immediate. I found my Saturday sleep disturbed that very weekend by the noise of activity in the yard; peering bleary-eyed from the window, I could see three men busily at work stripping the grass areas.

I went downstairs and put the kettle on, and no sooner had I done that when a loud knock on the door revealed another four men with tool boxes and ladders prepared for the outside timberwork. My opening remark, "You must have heard the kettle go on", was rather lost in culture and language. These were Scandinavians and unused to my English ways.

By the end of that first day the exterior aspects of the property had been dramatically changed. The gardening team had cleared the old lawn, had laid in paths to the front gate and around the perimeter of the house, and a further path which allowed access to the outbuildings; it was already taking shape. The outside team had stripped off the paintwork from half of the house; one of their number had in his kitbag a Nyberg Blowtorch which he brought with him from Sweden which, unlike its American counterparts, ran off kerosene rather than gasoline. Every layer of paint on that part of the house had been burned and scraped off.

My final team arrived that same morning and was headed by a lovely and helpful man, Alfarr. At home in Sweden, like my father, he had been a carpenter. He asked if he could build a completely new kitchen, restructure the staircases, and create different areas in the large, open attic space. Of course, I was happy and he promised that within 24 hours he would come back to me with design proposals. I had not known that Scandinavia had its own style of wood carving but, in all his proposed works, Alfarr had built in typical flat plane carvings in panels on the furniture and staircase. These would bring a lightness and interest to his use of wood.

And so it began and within one month the house was unrecognizable. My teams of men had managed to elevate it to be one of the best-looking properties in the area. The quality of the workmanship was first rate. In the meantime, I had been working with Annie and Catherine from next door, and Adele, to run up the soft furnishings using fabrics that I had bought from Richard's department store in New York.

All was set for the open house event I had planned for Georgiana and De Forrest's set of friends and artists and so it was in July 1901 that I acted as host, in my own home, to two special people I had to thank for everything.

Georgiana had already been at Elberon for two weeks; I was in 837 Madison Avenue during the weekdays overseeing a complete clean of the house while Georgiana was away. It was on that second weekend, after the house clean was done, that I decamped to Long Branch on the Friday ready for the event the following day.

Dearest Adele and Annie and Catherine from Barnwell Cottage helped me to prepare. It was to be afternoon tea and the Barnwell kitchen had been erupting in great cooking smells for several days. We were catering for Georgiana, De Forrest and four of his artist friends. Georgiana and De Forrest arrived first in Georgiana's car at the appointed time of 2 o'clock.

I was so happy to see the delight in their faces as they entered through the newly-painted front gate and up the new pathway to the front door. I had been waiting for them on the porch, such was my anxiety, but I need not have feared. They stopped for a while in the yard that was beginning to show the benefits of work done by my first team. "My, this looks splendid", De Forrest said as he admired the freshly repaired and painted wooden exterior.

We went inside and, before they would stop for refreshment, they wanted to visit the whole house. Of course, it was in tip-top condition. Alfarr had done an outstanding job and his craftsmanship showed in the bespoke furniture he had fitted in the kitchen and the newly-refurbished staircase where he had completed some intricate carvings on the balustrade. De Forrest showed great interest in Alfarr's carvings which he declared to be "works of art".

It gave me such joy to witness the warmth of their approval, Georgiana paying particular attention to the hand-crafted soft furnishings. The staircase to the topmost room had been transformed by Alfarr; gone was the enclosed staircase entered through a small doorway; instead he had ripped all of this out and had created a second, wide staircase along that same wall with handrail and balusters to match those he had created on the main staircase. At the top of the new stairway he created a small landing and lobby with double doors leading into the room.

De Forrest seemed overcome by the attic room and the quality of light that streamed into it through the gable windows. "Oh, this is my studio!" he exclaimed. "Each time I come to Long Branch I want to use this as a splendid workshop for my art work". He spent time pacing the space, gazing through the windows and soaking up the atmosphere of the room. "You could even put a bed over here and I can sleep-over when the creative mood takes me!" I didn't know if he was being serious.

We were no sooner back downstairs than De Forrest's four friends arrived. They had kindly bought me flowers and each had brought an original painting of places in and around Long Branch for me to hang on the walls. I was delighted and could not contain my pleasure. De Forrest came back from the car with his own gift of a painting; "Not exactly Long Branch" he announced as he passed the package to me, "but something we will both remember". I ripped off the paper impatiently to reveal an oil painting on canvas of the Pyramids at Giza. It was the one he had done of that magnificent archaeological site during our epic trip. I had been there in Egypt with him on the day he started work on this picture and, after it was finished, I described it to him as "breath-taking". It was the very painting that he had reserved to hang in his own home: I was overwhelmed.

I felt really comfortable in the company of these men. When I had worked with De Forrest on the itinerary of our European tour back in 1890, I had spent several days with him at his studio. He had a large space at 51 West 10th Street. The building had been built to house artists' studios and it had large windows to let in the light. All the artists' studios were arranged around a central double-height communal exhibition hall, with a large glass ceiling and plenty of gas lighting. De Forrest had exhibited his pictures from our European tour there after we returned from the 1890s trip.

The studios were almost silent during the months of high summer as sweltering artists would take refuge in the mountains or at the coast, but at other times it was a hotbed of creativity with artists coming and going, of conversation and sharing of artistic experiences; for me it was a real pleasure and an eye-opener to a different world; De Forrest Bolmer's world.

It was here that De Forrest worked with artists like Edward Gay, Winslow Homer, Carlton Chapman, Douglass Adams, and Renwick Brevoort, all of whom had studios at the 10th Street Studio building. What surprised and pleased me greatly was the number of female artists. I had come to believe that if women were artists then it was just a hobby or pastime to take them away briefly from their domestic responsibilities. Here I was in this cauldron of creativity with female artists like Grace Gray Taylor, Emily Novra, Alice Calhoun and Agnes Abbatt. I thought of all the downtrodden women I had known eking out a miserable domestic existence with no space in their drab lives for any spark of creativity. I vowed then to find a channel of my own; perhaps writing; perhaps a novel.

To save me repeating the viewing, De Forrest kindly showed his artist friends around while Georgiana and I went to the kitchen to put together the afternoon tea. It gave Georgiana the opportunity to share her thoughts with me. "Come here", she commanded, holding out her arms. We embraced and she held me close for a seemingly endless moment of affection. "Annie, I can't tell you how happy I am for you"; she spoke in my ear without breaking the embrace. "I have been worried, with all the tragedy we have been through together, what would become of you if anything happened to me?" I tried to protest, but she then held me at arm's length. "I want you to know that, should anything happen to me, I will make sure you are safe and comfortable".

I could not contemplate anything happening to Georgiana but after the death of her husband and daughter it was understandable that she should be having those thoughts. She was right that we had suffered a whole series of tragedies in the more than 20 years since we had first met. In that time, I had been a faithful servant and trusted employee. But that was my privilege, to serve her as best I could. I had no expectation of her feeling obliged to care for me after her death.

At a deeper level, we had been close right from the very start back in 1878; it was just one of those remarkable and yet spontaneous reactions when two people come together, as we had, an immediate spark that both recognize, and kindle into flame. And so it was this shared flame, this shared light that remained with us throughout our time together. It was a closeness and affection for each other, which largely we kept private, that underpinned everything we did together.

I did not understand and did not want to contemplate what Georgiana had said, I just could not envisage a life without her here with me. I went about my business, making tea, preparing the plates of food and, with Georgiana's help, when De Forrest and his friends returned downstairs, a splendid buffet had been arranged on the large table in the dining room.

It was a very comfortable time and the conversation flowed easily. Everyone loved the house and what I had accomplished with it in a few months. They were fascinated by the stories of the fishermen, these itinerant workers from Scandinavia, who had toiled for me so willingly and who had achieved so much. De Forrest wanted to know if, on his next visit, I could arrange for him to meet with this remarkable group of men, and perhaps see them plying their fishing trade; in particular, he was very keen to meet Alfarr. His next visit? There was to be a next visit then?

CHAPTER 28

Pound Fishing

IT MIGHT SEEM odd to highlight one industry in describing the rise and fall in the fortunes of an area like Long Branch. This was to be my home after Madison Avenue and after Georgiana, thus it was important to me to have an understanding of the area.

The fishing endeavor in Long Branch was one of the sources of local excitement though it must have seemed very alien to any visitor. The neighborhood had changed considerably. Two doors down from where I lived was a house that rented accommodation to fishermen, mostly transients from Norway and Sweden. They came in for the pound fishing season and, like their Irish counterparts, would return home to bring much needed cash to their families and communities.

Long Branch, away from the seclusion of the more select districts, was echoing with the noise of the seaborne trade and full of these itinerant men who toiled hard and, after work, played hard. You could easily see why Long Branch had developed a reputation as a source of illegal spirits. The only pastime for the busy fishing trade workers was to eat in the local café and to drink, often at strange times of the day when the tides were not conducive to fishing. There was an increasing evidence of prostitution, and houses, posing as something different, were where some of that trade was carried on.

Just across the street from my home was the Gaskin household. The father was Conover, "Con" to his friends, his wife Charlotta, and children Floyd, Myrtle and Theodore. Behind their house was the "Con Gaskin Cold Storage and Ice Plant". Con (or Conover) Gaskin was a "pound fisherman gang-master" who built the ice plant. This was very modern at the time; before it came into being, ice had to be harvested from frozen rivers and stored over the winter. He needed refrigeration to store the fish he caught so he went into the ice business as well.

It was Con's patch and he had rights over the sea and the foreshore. The pound, a circular trap-net hung on seventeen poles, was set a little way off the shore, perhaps half a mile. They caught every form of fish that swam into their trap. There was then a barrier or "weir" with poles set every seventy-five feet. As fish swam towards it they would turn back out to sea and straight into the pound.

The pound nets were lifted periodically, perhaps three or four times a tide, by this gang of hardy European fishermen under the instruction of Con Gaskin. The nets would be dragged from the pound by the boats and then hauled up the beach using ropes, pulleys and dray horses for emptying. It created a cacophony of noise and nosy visitors who all wanted to watch. The wooden skiffs, made of cedar and oak, were over 30ft long and would be laid up along the beach like mackerel, when the tide or conditions were wrong for fishing. When the fish were rising, these sturdy men would carry their boats to the water's edge and launch them towards the nets.

And that's where Con Gaskin's cold storage plant came in. In the fishing season, it would be filled with ice. The fish would be packed into boxes between layers of fresh crushed ice and then either transported to the railway station, if a train was due, or left in the cold store until one came in. Annual catches in excess of 200 tons were not uncommon, mackerel, tuna and whiting netting a sizeable income when they came fresh to market and, of course, New York only fifty miles away was the biggest market of them all.

My other life in a different part of Long Branch, Elberon, had been very different. Largely sophisticated and genteel with famous figures and politicians rubbing shoulders with each other and with the Arnold party, including me. There were distractions and pastimes, horse racing, theater, a casino; most notable though were the mansions built all along the foreshore which vied with each other for prestige.

My new home was in a much less salubrious part of town, though none the less inviting for that. It did lack the grandeur and sophistication, and was much more focused on the genuine interchange between real people. It was to prove a magnet for De Forrest Bolmer and his artist friends as they looked for ways to extend the scope of their art.

This part of the Long Branch shore was a rather problematic area at times and well beyond the experience of De Forrest and his friends. It was cosmopolitan with, it seemed, every race and color represented. Everything a man might want was available here, at the right price. At times it was busy and industrious, at others boisterous, noisy and with the basest traits of humankind on display.

The shoreline was for many years the shop-front of the pound fishing industry, with wet-fish on sale from marble slabs, cafés serving dishes of locally-caught fish and shops selling fishing paraphernalia.

There was a 'wild-west' feel to this part of Long Branch and it was an exciting place to be.

Other worldwide pressures meant that labor became scarce and the fishing activity slowly declined. The shoreline was eventually to be gentrified and given over to holiday-makers and tourists.

CHAPTER 29

A Love of the Arts

I HAD TO wait only two more weeks before De Forrest reappeared at my front door in Ocean Avenue. He had with him his great friend Edward Gay and Edward's wife Martha. I was unused to people just turning up at the door unannounced but was happy with this surprise since it brought De Forrest back to me.

Edward was, like me, from an Irish background born in Dublin at the height of the potato famine, moving with his family to America in 1859 when just 11 years old. I listened to the stories of his past without acknowledging the similarities in our experience. Edward was older than me at 64. It was not the first time we had spoken since Edward was one of the company that traveled with Georgiana, De Forrest and me to Europe and North Africa.

Like De Forrest, Edward Gay was a landscape artist and would work on huge canvases or even wall murals. He had studied art in Albany having, even as a child, impressed two members of the Hudson River School of Art, two Scottish immigrants, James and William Hart.

At De Forrest's suggestion, I showed Edward and Martha up to the top floor of the house. They too were very impressed by the carpentry and carving skills on display on the staircase and were clearly taken aback but delighted as they entered the large room with its copious space and decked in its brilliant sunlight. De Forrest was at our shoulder as we made our way upstairs and now found it difficult to contain his enthusiasm. He took Edward to the extremes of the gable ends to show him the views from the window; "And it will be perfect", I heard him saying to Edward, "we have the space and the light; just what we were looking for."

Downstairs, as the four of us sat in the kitchen again, De Forrest went on to explain what had got him so excited. "You know I am here every summer and how important a time it is for me to relax and rediscover my love of art and painting. I wondered if we could prevail upon you to allow us to use your attic studio for a few days, perhaps a week, so that Edward and I, with a couple of friends from New York, might work together, and collaborate on some new skills and techniques we have been discussing. We have been sharing the facilities at the fabulous

Bryant Park Studios, and in particular working on collaboration across our group in the formulation and presentation of our work".

Of course, I was delighted to extend the hospitality of my house to De Forrest and as many of his friends as he wanted and a tentative date was agreed a fortnight ahead. Afterwards Edward explained to me that they were currently staying at Wright's Cottage in Elberon but that he had become aware of the rarefied social environment there and that his interest had been invigorated when he had first visited me in Long Branch. "It's such a cosmopolitan atmosphere here, with different races and creeds, occupations and activities. I just wanted to experiment and capture some images of the locality".

I understood his rationale and would help in whatever way I could. I promised De Forrest to see if my carpenter and sculptor Alfarr was available at some point during their planned visit. In fact, as soon as they left, I went and sought him out. He was flattered that there was so much interest in his work by these well-known American artists and promised he would make himself available to meet with them. He seemed quite excited in sharing an art form from his mother-land and promised to bring with him some other examples of his carvings.

It was late summer in 1901; there had been a long heatwave in early July, but now the temperatures were more forgiving. Nonetheless, by the time De Forrest and his friends had unloaded all of their baggage and equipment from the car and carried it up two flights of stairs, the windows had been thrown open and they were grateful for a glass of homemade lemonade. Con Gaskin had been kind enough to supply some ice and this addition gave just a hint of luxury.

As well as De Forrest and Edward, two of the artists he brought with him on his last visit had returned. One was Winslow Homer who often painted maritime themes on his canvases. In reminding me of the earlier visit, De Forrest explained that part of their aim for these sessions was to try to capture the essence of the sea at Long Branch. Winslow had painted in the area before and one of those was entitled, "Long Branch, New Jersey" undertaken in 1868; his ability to capture the essence of the power and threatening nature of the sea was illustrated in his earlier works like "The Life Line" and "Fog Warning (Halibut Fishing)". We had discussed these at length on his earlier visit and while I had not seen them for myself, the descriptions offered by his artist friends and critics spoke volumes.

The second artist, also one who had visited me with De Forrest some weeks earlier, was James Renwick Brevoort. De Forrest had known him since his childhood as they were distant cousins and both born and brought up in Yonkers. James had been very much influenced by the style of the Hudson River Painters, indeed had been encouraged and sponsored by some of them. Once he had returned from Italy in 1880, he had left many of those influences behind. In some ways in this latter period in his career, he was experimenting again with color and mood.

They left the house mid-afternoon to explore the locality and did not return until mid-evening. I had laid out a cold buffet meal for them, so it didn't matter what time they returned. I had also been to visit Alfarr again and he had agreed to come across the following evening at about supper time to talk with De Forrest. Winslow was also keen to meet Alfarr; one of his particular interests was wood engraving and he had been fascinated by the quality of the carvings on my staircase in particular.

They settled down to an evening of excited conversation and discussions about the things they had seen, washed down with some of Annie Hall's local brew. There was no need for them to sleep on camp beds in the studio, that had been De Forrest's original suggestion. I showed them the rooms available that could easily accommodate four artists, before taking to my bed feeling very tired.

The following days took on a joy and a rhythm all of their own; these four artists were up early each morning, breakfasted and then working in the studio or out with sketch pads, easels and paints. They seemed to collect a wealth of material and inspiration from our surroundings. I confirmed with De Forrest that, on the occasions when he would paint alone, it would not disturb him if I should accompany him. Thus it was that on several days we could be found together, he intent with his focus and concentration on the scene he was trying to depict while I sat quietly in the background just watching. It was such a great pleasure for me just to be near him, at his side and being part of his life. At some point, he would stop and we would eat the picnic meal I had prepared for us. It seemed so natural, so domesticated.

At our meal on the second evening we were joined by Alfarr and the chemistry that quickly developed between him and the artists was remarkable. During our meal, he showed them some examples of carvings that he had done which were very much in a Scandinavian tradition. One was a box; on the lid a scroll design was intricately-carved, rather like those he had used on the staircase. Another was a horse, known as a dala horse, which had its bridle and saddle painted in delightful bright colors. My favorites were a whole family of roughly carved small figurines; they showed couples embracing and dancing to the music of an accordionist and a separate squeeze box player. There were figures showing people going about their everyday business, a hod-carrier, a farm worker, an old woman with a headscarf carrying a basket. Finally, there were wooden spoons with the most intricately carved handles, again with a scroll design.

That led the five of them to go to the staircase and pick out the design features where Alfarr had used some of these classical techniques in the decorative panels. He pointed out the miniature scenes showing small figures carved as a tableau or individually, almost invisibly adorning a newel post or balustrade. Winslow was fascinated and was anxious to take Alfarr to their studio and to show him some of his etchings made using intricate wood block carvings that he had fashioned. The similarities in carving style and technique were fascinating to both of them. The evening just disappeared; the four of them were up in the studio chatting and exploring the Long Branch art work; Alfarr, being more of a "local" was in a position to offer suggestions and comments on their endeavors.

As their week in residence in my Ocean Avenue home came to a close these four men were exhausted and euphoric about their week's activity and output; James described their time as "inspirational". It was not just the close of their week, but also the end of their Elberon break. Only De Forrest was staying over to lock up Wright's Cottage before he was off back to New York. I persuaded him that he might stay for a further night with me and that I would cook a meal for him.

As we sat in the kitchen while our fish stew simmered on the stove, De Forrest was full of thanks and praise. "Annie Maher", he started, "you are just such a remarkable woman". I turned my face away to disguise my blushes. "Don't make light of it," he instructed, "your generosity in giving over your house to four waifs to play in for a week has been so greatly appreciated by everyone." I tried to explain that it was my delight to do so, but got cut off. "What we had aspired to for these few days was to have moments of inspiration, perhaps reinvigoration, from our stay here and those aspirations have been greatly exceeded. We could only do that because of the atmosphere that you have created in this beautiful house. Our stay here has allowed us to explore different settings, learn new skills, and investigate ways of collaborative working that were new to all of us."

"I understand" he continued, "why my sister thinks so highly of you. I have seen for myself, observed over the years, your organizational skills making the improbable seem second nature; The way that you orchestrate events with just a light touch, taking an entourage of eccentric people around the globe as if they were on a Sunday stroll along the boardwalk. Most impressive, on display this week, is the way that you relax into a group of significant artists and converse with them as if you were one of them. Your understanding of our art is just breath-taking and yet challenging of assumptions we make through our own developing expertise. You are truly a remarkable woman."

I had nothing further I could say; I served up his supper and we spent the rest of the evening chatting about our recollections, not just of our Long Branch week, but also of our other times together. De Forrest wanted to make a prompt start the following morning and so I ushered him to bed while I just cleared the table and washed pans and plates and cutlery.

In the morning, after the lightest of breakfasts, De Forrest loaded the car and got himself prepared to travel. We stood at the front porch and, for the first time, he opened his arms and pulled me towards him. I relaxed into that embrace and felt at the same moment joyful and tearful. "Thank you again for your kindness and your hospitality" he said. "You are a remarkable lady" he repeated. I smiled weakly, "it's for the love of the Arts" I said, even more weakly, and sent him off down the path and waved him goodbye. I knew, and I think he suspected, there was more at play here than just a love of the Arts.

CHAPTER 30

Dover New Jersey

GEORGIANA FIRST BECAME ill on May 1st 1903, which was a Friday; she felt ill almost immediately after arriving at Dover, New Jersey and she apparently got worse and worse as the weekend progressed.

She had gone to Dover for a short stay to attend a church function with Harvey that weekend. She would come to Dover at weekends quite frequently, however she still kept 837 Madison Avenue as her main abode. Given that the Dover rectory was more modest, I lived and worked still at Madison Avenue as Caretaker when she was not in residence, reverting to be her personal assistant when she came up to New York each week. On occasion, when she wanted something specific from me at weekends, I would travel up to Dover and usually stay just for the day. There was a small box-room that I would use if for any reason I had to stop over.

It was very early on Monday May 4th when I got a telegram from Harvey Hartman, asking if I would go up to Dover and help him to cope with Georgiana's failing health; Harvey had sent Georgiana's chauffeur-driven car to collect me that morning and I was by Georgiana's bedside by 10 a.m. The look of relief on Harvey's face was a picture, he clearly did not cope well with illness. His mother had been dispensing care over the weekend but, at that stage, she had not called a physician. Based on my initial assessment I told Harvey I thought that a mistake.

The doctor arrived promptly that afternoon and made a thorough examination. He diagnosed influenza and said that we were to keep her in bed, give her some acetaminophen as an analgesic he had prescribed, to relieve the symptoms of pain and to try to lower her fever. "Make sure that she has a thorough rest". We were to try to break her fever by, despite her protestations, keeping her room and her bed warm. The fireplace had a roaring fire which we kept going 24 hours a day, and we heated her bed using copper bed warmers. I have this lasting image of her with bedding tucked all around her, only her face in an upward pose peeping out, and awash with profuse perspiration.

By the following Friday there seemed to have been an improvement, and she was able to sit up and take a little soup, the first food she had taken for seven days. Harvey seemed pleased and would take turns with me to just sit with her, holding her hand and talking with her.

However, she was preoccupied with writing a new will and so I arranged for her New York and Harvey's Dover lawyers to visit. When Wednesday May 13th 1903 arrived, the lawyers came at the appointed time and were entertained by Georgiana in her bedroom. Her health had remained fairly static in the period, though her temperature was still high and her breathing was labored.

After that, her Last Will and Testament complete, just as Harvey had feared, she seemed to give up and go into a decline. She became very agitated about her Last Will and Testament and whether she had made all the right provisions. During Thursday I encouraged her to write down the changes she wanted and this was duly passed to the lawyers and an appointment made for Monday May 18th 1903 when they would return and sign off a codicil.

By Friday we were sufficiently concerned to call in the doctor again. His revised diagnosis was that Georgiana's condition had worsened and that she now had pneumonia. All we could do over the weekend was to keep her comfortable.

I had alerted her friends and family about her deteriorating situation and a number of those came to see her. Amongst her siblings, De Forrest Bolmer spent several hours at her bedside, and as he left he could only summon a weak smile to me.

On Monday 18th, we had prepared Georgiana for her ordeal with the legal teams. We had her washed and in new nightwear, sitting upright within a cocoon of pillows. She and Harvey spent about an hour with the solicitors and I understood that Georgiana was now satisfied that her last will and testament was as good as it was going to get. She and the witnesses had signed it off.

I took a back seat during the afternoon because Georgiana's husband and close family were around her bed. As the day wore on she became more peaceful and slipped in and out of sleep. It was as though her struggle for life had ended and that she waited only for the inevitable.

Georgiana died at 4:30 that afternoon. Aged only 46.

Georgiana had expressed the wish to me that she did not want to be buried in Green-Wood, but instead in Woodlawn Cemetery in the Bronx. However, she did not want to be separated from her daughter, Nellie, and gave me the legal documents that she had drawn up when she had made her will, instructing me to have Nellie's body exhumed and buried along with hers.

As was her wish, we took her body back to New York on Tuesday May 19th where she was to lay in rest in the large reception room at 837 Madison Avenue. Harvey and De Forrest were there all the way through to her funeral day on Thursday May 21st. The whole of New York seemed shocked by Georgiana's death and a large number of friends, colleagues and dignitaries came to the house to pay their respects.

The Death announcement in the "New York Tribune: on May 20th 1903 read:

> HARTMAN - at Dover N.J. on May 18th 1903 Mrs.
> G. Harvey Hartman, beloved wife of Rev. C. Harvey
> Hartman, rector of St. John's Church, Dover, N.J.
> Funeral from her late residence, No. 837 Madison Ave.
> on Thursday May 21st at 1 p.m. Service at St. Thomas's
> Church, at 2 p.m. Internment Private.

For me, it was a heartrending time; I had lost not just my mistress but my closest friend. I determined that I could manage it and arrange for her funeral as she would have wanted and to do it in such a way as would have made her proud of me.

The funeral was to take place at St. Thomas' church, which was the local church she attended when in New York and which had marked all the key milestones in her life, marriages and funerals, even her own.

As he had done at her wedding, the Bishop of Nova Scotia, her friend and supporter, The Right Reverend Frederick Courtney, officiated assisted by her Rector Rev. Earnest M. Stires. It was a beautiful and memorable service and it was De Forrest Bolmer who gave a eulogy from the pulpit. The church was crowded with yet more people standing outside in the early summer sunshine, as De Forrest got to his feet and walked forward.

The whole emphasis of De Forrest's talk was about his sister's devotion to other people, her kindness and thoughtfulness, her charitable work, especially her founding and supporting the Babies' Hospital at Lexington and 55th. He talked of her love of the arts and of travel and told some stories of our journeys to Europe and beyond. He emphasized how strongly she was devoted to her church and gave thanks to her husband Rev. Harvey Hartman for helping to make her final three years such happy ones. He thanked too Frederick Courtney, and explained his longstanding connection with Georgiana. There was not a dry eye in the church. Finally, and full of emotion, he talked about how much Georgiana would be missed by all those she undertook charitable work with, but most importantly by members of her family and the group of staff who worked so diligently and closely with her. I thought my heart would break, I stifled a sob, but could not stop the tears from welling up in my eyes and rolling down my cheeks.

After the service, Georgiana's coffin was loaded onto a specially-hired train and, accompanied by her family and two of her staff, she was taken to Woodlawn for burial.

But this was not the end; De Forrest, myself and Adele were the only people present when the reinternment of Nellie's body took place in a private ceremony some three months after Georgiana's death. Nellie had been interred with her father at Green-Wood in Brooklyn in the Arnold/Constable family plot. But Nellie and Georgiana were now at rest together, Nellie's small white coffin had been brought from Green-Wood and now lay next to Georgiana's at Woodlawn. After a deeply touching ceremony De Forrest, Adele and I went out for lunch and shared again some of the great times we had had together.

Georgiana's death was more than just the loss of an employer; I saw Georgiana as more than that, as a friend, as a confidante, as a sister and a mother figure and as so much more than I can express in words.

She was my family and, apart from Adele, had been the only person left that I could implicitly trust.

Then of course there was the need to adapt to new circumstances; I would no longer be running an important household, having contact with a wide range of important people, and planning and running significant events. My team at Madison Avenue would quickly dissipate and then I would be truly alone.

It was not that I didn't have an alternative. Over three years and more, I had slowly built up a base for myself in Long Branch, so I had a place of my own to go to, and people that I knew, liked and trusted. None of this, though, provided me with the level of reassurance about the future that I dearly craved. I lacked solid support, secure and unwavering, of the sort that Georgiana had given.

The only person I knew that could offer that level of comfort was De Forrest Bolmer. He had been a central part of my life almost since the first day I had been introduced to the Bolmer family, 25 years earlier. We were very close, based partly on all of the creative moments we had spent together, but there was no physical relationship, just at times a yearning in me.

He had watched me cope with some challenging circumstances and, in turn, I had followed, and in some cases enabled, his artistic career; I had watched his creative process as he worked on memorable landscapes in several parts of the world. I suppose that in my heart I still cradled the image of him as the hero, saving neighbors from the house fire next door. Had he said, perhaps after our meal together, having buried two of our dearest people at Woodland Cemetery, "Annie, will you marry me?" I think I know how I would have responded.

I did know, and deeply regretted, that De Forrest Bolmer was not prone to such acts of spontaneous affection. He was a quiet unassuming guy on the outside, and would never embarrass himself, or me, by asking the question. I knew though, from the time we had spent together, that there was a love for me in his heart. And my real regret, given that De Forrest could not bring himself to utter the question, was that neither could I, and that we would carry our unrequited love to the grave.

CHAPTER 31

From Servant to Mistress of my own Destiny

I WENT ON to buy other properties in Long Branch. It was a matter of turning my stockpile of cash in the bank into an asset that was likely to grow and leave me in comfort in my dotage. I eventually persuaded myself that there was a financially independent person inside me aching to escape.

I was eventually to have a portfolio of property and land in Long Branch: 158 Simpson later renamed as 208 New Ocean Avenue; only one house but a different address after the road name was changed; 93 Seaview Avenue; 206 New Ocean Avenue, next door to my original house where I had bought the empty lot and now had a house built to my specification; two adjacent houses, 35 Lippincott and a second at the rear of the same lot; then there was 15 Cleveland Avenue plus a house on Oceanport Avenue, West Long Branch.

My piece of land at 208 New Ocean Avenue was to become a new business venture. I had found a reputable local building company while I was staying with Georgiana at Elberon. They were Shock and Fleming and their work at that time was in building some of the large mansions in Elberon populated by society's elite. It was somewhat of a social coup to have them building me a new house.

Adele and I would laugh at this turn of events in my life. We were staying together on the night of the 1905 census. The space on the census return for "occupation", where I would traditionally have put, variously, "servant" or "housekeeper", instead and largely for amusement I described my status as "capitalist".

I bought a very serviceable house on Lippincott Avenue in Long Branch. It was closer to downtown and I was able to rent it out. Lippincott was not my favorite house but it was a good investment; it was squeezed like an afterthought lot, but it was large with rooms on three floors and was wood cladded; and these overlapping planks were painted in a sort of mushroom color. The main roof was mirrored by ground floor thrust-extensions on two sides which had sloping roofs of a similar pitch.

I was able to do the work necessary for Georgiana while she was in the New York house. When she was in Dover, or when she and her new husband traveled to Europe, I was free to tend to my affairs in Long Branch. I rented out my properties and was able to make even more money for myself.

I did make one, purely speculative, purchase of another plot of land at the rear of my house in Lippincott that I thought I might one day build upon. This plot of land was named in the deeds as Section 4, block 10, Lot 11. I paid $2,500 for it, as much as my Simpson Street home had cost, and it was a clear sign of how land and property were rapidly escalating all along this coastline, just as Richard had predicted. I gave thanks to Richard Arnold, who seemed to be watching over me and my investments, for his sage advice.

CHAPTER 32

Joseph Paul Maher

JOSEPH PAUL MAHER traveled to New York aboard the S.S. Celtic, leaving Liverpool on September 21st 1906 and arriving in New York on September 29th 1906. At the age of 28 it was his first trip to the U.S.A. and it would be the first time that he had seen me, his sister Annie, since my return visit to Sheerness in 1884, almost 22 years earlier.

Joseph was required to complete the details about himself and his journey for entry into the ship's passenger manifest. He described himself simply; A single male, aged 28 and an Engineer by profession. He was able to read and write and gave his nationality as coming from Great Britain, to be more precise from Sheerness in Kent. He was headed for Long Branch in New Jersey though he had not yet bought his ticket to complete the journey after New York. He had paid for his own passage and had the princely sum of $400 in his pocket. He declared that this was his first journey to the United States of America. He explained that he was to visit his sister in Long Branch New Jersey. He had never been in prison, resident in an alms-house or an asylum; he was not a polygamist or an anarchist. He was 5'9" tall, his health was good and he was not deformed in any way. Joseph's complexion was fair, he had brown hair and blue eyes and the index finger on his left hand was bent as the result of an accident. His place of birth was Sheerness in Kent in England.

On the journey, he had met a delightful American couple. Dr. Henry Cotton and his wife Della. They were travelling back to the U.S.A. after Dr. Cotton's three-year postgraduate study in Germany where he had been working with eminent professors in his field. The original coincidence which had prolonged their discourse beyond what might normally have been expected, was because Dr. Cotton was to work in a hospital in Trenton, which is near Long Branch, New Jersey near where I lived.

Joseph talked to Henry, they were on first name terms quite quickly, about his reason for going to Long Branch. "I have not seen my sister since I was a child; she left to begin a very successful career in New York and only returned home once. After the death of her employer she moved to Long Branch because she loved the area so much."

Dr. Cotton explained about his background; "I have spent the last few weeks explaining to others in my profession, including in England and Scotland, my new ideas about the treatment of insanity. What I am currently exploring is the possibility that insanity is about infection. There are sources of infection throughout our bodies and usually they are contained and managed by our bodily systems. However, where those infections cross into the brain, the infection can have a devastating impact on the mind. My contention is that by dealing with "focal infection" rather than treating the symptoms of "madness" we can cure the vast majority of patients".

The three of them had fascinating conversations during the long journey and Joseph was invited to visit. He thanked them warmly, and promised to get in touch. Dr. Cotton presented as a very knowledgeable, skilled and well-respected clinician, and it filled the listener with confidence.

And thus to New York and Long Branch.

I opened the door while squealing his name and was just so excited to see him. I grabbed his hand and pulled him into the house to meet Annie and Catherine. I thrust him into the living room where a recumbent Annie Hall draped herself in an armchair like a discarded garment. Her glass was almost empty but hung at a precarious angle in her hand, the remnants of the clear liquid dripping gently onto the floor.

I invited Annie Hall to meet my little brother Joseph Paul Maher who was just 6 years old when we last met; I explained to her that when I asked that little boy Joseph what he wanted to do, he said, "I want to travel the world like you". Well here he was all these years later, traveling the world just to see me.

Annie Hall extended a hand and coyly said, "how splendid to make your acquaintance Joseph Paul Maher". There was the briefest of handshakes.

Catherine had dozed off and was snoring gently in an armchair. "And that" said Annie Hall, "is my dear friend and cohabitee, Catherine".

I offered to show Joseph to his room and allow him to freshen up, and with that I went towards my brother's two large cases. With two such big heavy cases I wondered how long he planned to stay. I carried the lighter case and he followed on up the stairs with the second one.

When he re-emerged, he tracked me down to the kitchen where I offered him food and drink. "What I would really love is some toasted bread, and a nice cup of tea; that would be good, if you have it." Of course, I had it, and commented that he sounded so proper and so English; 'a nice cup of tea' I mimicked. We toasted the bread on toasting forks over the open fire and it helped create a warm homely atmosphere.

As I chatted to him he asked "Where are Annie and Catherine?" I explained about Barnwell Cottage that Annie and Catherine ran as a boarding house and bar. When they expected guests, such as this evening, they had to open up and get everything ready. Annie had started as Catherine's Manager but they had become such close friends now that they lived and ran the business together.

We sat at the kitchen table with a large pot of tea. I prompted him to tell me of his plans; "I'm at an interesting phase of my life" he explained. "Since leaving school I had been working at the dockyard alongside father; I seemed to have an affinity with engines and so served a five-year apprenticeship; I qualified as a Marine Engine Fitter at the age of 21. I worked for almost seven years on the engines of new ships under construction.

"You do recall that conversation when last we met, the one you recounted to Annie Hall earlier? I was 6 and could see no better prospect for my life than to follow in your footsteps and see the world. Your letters home, your stories of travel and visits to incredible places have just been such an inspiration to me. As a consequence, I am pleased to announce that I'm leaving the docks and taking up a new role for a large London-based company as a Marine Engineer but serving their operations in the Far East, particularly China and Japan".

I could not contain my excitement, what is it about us Mahers that, once we set our mind to it, we can achieve anything that we want? Joseph explained that he would not be based in London, but they wanted him to open an office in Shanghai from where he would have responsibility for the whole fleet in, or traveling through, the Far East. It was his job to organize the repair and maintenance of the ships, as they were needed.

He explained, "I have a period of paid leave and am due in Shanghai on Monday December 3rd 1906; I have lots of time to spend with you, if you would like that." Like it? I would love it! The chance to get to know my youngest brother, I could think of nothing else I would be happier to do.

We talked about the family at length. Our father Patrick had died just over 5 years earlier and I had not gone home for the funeral. Joseph was very reassuring that there was no expectation that I would make the long journey, indeed I would not have been able to arrive in time.

I had also missed the wedding of our brother Thomas William Maher on Friday April 19th 1899, that was just 10 days before our father had died. "You probably remember that Thomas wanted to join the Royal Navy. He worked with us in the dockyard for a short while before he joined up in 1891 when he was only 19 years old. Since then he has traveled extensively. His task was clerical work, the official R.N. title for his job was a "writer". He largely dealt with the payments of wages to the crews so he had an impressive service record that showed him serving on a lot of ships, when in reality he was only there for a few days before moving on".

I asked about Thomas's wife, curious to gain an appreciation of my recently acquired sister-in-law. "Oh, she's a lovely, talented and refined woman" he enthused. "Alice Maud Mary Hamilton comes from distant Irish stock not much different from us, born and brought up in Kent. Her great grandparents came from Ireland and did well when they arrived from Dublin. At that time, her parents had been able to afford a good education for Alice and she is an accomplished musician and painter". He had seen one of her most recent paintings and he described it to me; "it's of a bowl of beautifully colored pansies, it's painted in oil on alabaster". I must say it seemed to me as though Thomas had taken a step up the social ladder when he married Alice Maud Mary Hamilton.

"It was not all good news", he told me. "They have had two children and they have died in infancy. Alice May was born on December 5th

1903, but died just after Christmas on the 28th just 23 days old. Maud Alice was born on Christmas Eve a year later but died just 8 months later in August 1905". We shared our sadness at the tragic start to their married life.

The conversation turned to the prospect of two nuns in the family. "Let me start with Alice" he began. "You know that she's a teacher, well in 1903 when Alice May died, she gallantly stepped in to support Alice Maud Mary in her grief. Later on, when Maud Alice died in infancy last August, again our sister Alice stepped in and actually moved into the house for a while.

"Thomas was away for a lot of the time and so when his compassionate shore leave came to an end our sister offered to stay on for a while. They were living then at 120 Napier Road, Gillingham, Kent and, while not far from the family, they had enough space to take up this offer of direct support.

"Since then Alice seems to be moving towards becoming a nun. There is a Belgian Catholic convent in Sittingbourne, and she has been spending increasing amounts of time there. They run the school where Alice now works, but chatting with her she feels a real vocation and feels that she can make a difference if she devoted her life to Christ."

We concluded that her older sister, Mary, was a good role model for Alice. Mary had left England alone aged only 17 and had come to New York and transformed herself into a teaching nun called Sister Dorothea.

Tempted by that idea Joseph wanted to do some walking; I took him on my favourite walk and to my favourite bench overlooking the sea. We sat and took in the seascape and the tranquillity. It was he who broke the silence in a quite unexpected and profound way. "Did you leave home in Kent" he asked, "because you were trying to escape something?" The question took me really by surprise, and I had to think long and hard for an answer; no matter though because he did not jump into the void that our silence had created, but instead just waited for my reply. I tried to explain that it was not straightforward and that in some ways the answer was both 'Yes' and 'No'. No because I did not run away but had been sent away; Yes, because once I had attuned to my new circumstances, I felt a great sense of inexplicable relief and, yes, he was right, about my having escaped something.

"I didn't know the circumstances of your leaving; can you help me?" I tried to explain that when we arrived from Ireland there were just the three children, myself, James and Patrick all born in Clonmel. Over the period until her death, Mother was to give birth to eleven. He expressed surprise at this because he was not yet alive when there was more than a handful of children. After our arrival in Kent, John was born in Sheerness, as was Margaret and Mary in quick succession. Then we had lost Patrick aged only 7, which took a heavy toll on mother, and then when I was 11 Thomas William was born. It was at that stage, with 7 surviving children, thus far, and with mother pregnant again with Alice, she took the decision that I should have a new start and go into service. In that situation, she could be sure that I would be properly fed and clothed and could start learning skills; just the simple process of being in another family environment and seeing how other people lived, she thought, would be good for me. How right she was.

"Did you, in those first twelve years feel under any threat. Or that you were in some way deprived?" After some thought I responded that, at that time, I had not felt particularly deprived. At that time, in the midst of an immigrant community, everyone was in the same boat and there was no real point of comparison to indicate that your upbringing was not as generous as that enjoyed by other children. Under threat? Yes, I did but I didn't know, and wasn't aware even then, why that should have been the case. Even on my last visit to Kent when Joseph was still a small boy, I felt that dread again, and it came through contact with our father. Perhaps it was his drinking and all the time he spent at the pub; he was much like a stranger to us and the money he spent there impacted on what we could eat or wear. Yet here was a man that we were meant to look up to; I found it very hard to do that and perhaps as a consequence he seemed like a figure of dread to me; potentially violent and unpredictable.

"I was born the year you left for New York", he reminded me, "so it was different. I think father reacted differently to boys than he did to girls, and I wonder whether that is why you, Margaret and Alice all left for a more protected lifestyle?" Joseph explained that father took quite an interest in him and encouraged him into the shipyard.

By contrast, and with the benefit of hindsight, the poverty in which I lived was now very evident to me; simple things like the hunger, the threadbare clothing, mostly hand-me-downs, since I was the eldest daughter, donated by other families; clogs which seemed such a mark of poverty or shoes that had great holes in the soles and had to be bolstered with cardboard to avoid walking directly on the pavements. Poor personal hygiene was rarely commented upon and I must have looked like a Dickensian waif wandering the streets of Sheerness.

It struck me then, over the childhood of these 11 siblings, that would have spanned about 36 years, it would allow each of those children to have a different perspective on their parents. It was only natural then that Joseph, born 18 years after me, was born into a 'different' family than the one I had been part of. His childhood was just beginning as I was leaving England for the U.S.A.. He would know little of my childhood and I would have little understanding of his.

He told me that things had got worse after mother died when he was just seven years old. Only when in his teens, and when he could go out to work and earn money, did things start to improve. It was only with hindsight and the passage of time that you could really see it for what is was. "I wonder if that background that you described Annie, was in any way responsible for your need to escape?"

We pondered on such matters seemingly interminably and still I could not lay to rest the deep-seated anxiety that I harbored about those early years. As Joseph began to understand in more detail my life since coming to America perhaps he could begin to understand that, despite memories that my childhood left in me, my life-experiences since coming to work for Georgiana had been transformative.

It seemed quite natural to me to rely on this young man; even though he was almost two decades my junior, he was nonetheless kind and loving and supportive. He understood both my family origins and, increasingly my new persona, which had gone now beyond the role of a servant, and was quickly establishing me as a pillar of the Long Branch community. Joseph seemed to understand some of my anguish and torment and was generous with his time and his attentive listening. I had him at my side for many weeks and looked forward to his continuing support.

The first ordeal I would ask of him while he lived with me, was to accompany me to the reading of Georgiana's will in New York.

CHAPTER 33

Georgiana's Will

THE FACT THAT Georgiana had remembered me and Adele in her will was a real surprise even though she had talked about looking after me if anything should happen to her. At 10:30 on the morning of November 13th 1906, Adele and I, along with the long list of Georgiana's beneficiaries, had been summoned before the Surrogate of the County of New York at the County Courthouse, New York. When the summons to appear had been delivered by courier in mid-August, it gave rise to a lot of speculation and excitement in Long Branch and different parts of New York and Dover.

The impressive Notice in the New York Times didn't help to allay the growing sense of this being a significant moment. It read: "THE PEOPLE OF THE STATE OF NEW YORK, by the grace of God, free and independent" and went on to list 40 beneficiaries plus the three executors, Charles Harvey Hartman, Manuel De Forrest Bolmer and Thomas H. Bolmer.

Adele, Joseph and I had travelled up the night before and stayed with the O'Briens. Joseph was enthusiastically received by the O'Brien family, especially by the children. They were all fascinated by his stories of the ships he had helped to build and of his skills in maritime engineering. Knowing what we had to do the following day, we had an early night so as to be fresh for the morning.

That meant we were outside the courthouse in plenty of time; the subway had made travel in New York so much safer and easier. We were able to watch as people arrived, and I was surprised that I knew so many faces. I should not have been; these were all the people that Georgiana felt deeply and strongly about, most of them I had met in my years in New York. What I did find surprising, and I think that Joseph did too, was the number of people who went out of their way to come across and greet me. They were all very kind and wanted to know how I was keeping and how my new life was going. Of course, I deliberately sounded very upbeat, and made a point of introducing my brother to them, an international marine engineer, and reminded them too that Adele had worked for Georgiana for many years.

The Surrogate's Court was held in a large room with a block of fixed bench seating and individual chairs behind them. At the front were the key players; Charles Harvey Hartman, Manuel De Forrest Bolmer and Thomas H. Bolmer, as the executors, and an assemblage of lawyers. An Usher explained to us that places had been reserved on the bench seats for each of those summoned before the court; with a second seat for a guest; Joseph, Adele and I sat together towards the back. We had to show our summons and have our names ticked off on a list.

As we took our seats, De Forrest got up and walked directly to where I was sitting. "Annie" he said, "how lovely to see you again". He seemed much older than his years would tell, he was only six years my senior but at fifty-four years of age he had a real presence. He still had a good head of hair, only slightly receding, but to compensate he had grown an impressive moustache. De Forrest was not the caricature of an artist; for example, at this event, he dressed in a suit with a waistcoat and flamboyant necktie; every inch a gentleman.

"Annie, I don't have time today to spend with you, as you can imagine things are a little hectic here and I have a series of meetings after the hearing. I am often in Long Branch, and I wondered if I might visit you there again?" My response was without hesitation: "Yes of course you may, call in at any time." With a beaming smile he responded, "I'll look forward to that enormously; we have a lot to catch up on".

He took my hand and squeezed it, and then turned and walked back to his proper place.

It was a long proceeding and a key part included the first full public reading of the will. I knew that Georgiana had an original will when she was married to Richard Arnold. They had spent hours in discussion and with lawyers trying to make it clear that Georgiana was independently wealthy. She had already agreed to be cut out of Richard's will and she had made sure that Nellie when she was born was included as a main beneficiary in her will as well as Richard's. However, with the deaths of both Richard and Nellie, there had to be a new will. It must have been a trauma for her trying to come to terms with the loss of these two special people in her life, and one can understand why she hesitated or delayed. However, when she remarried in 1899, she had to make her wishes clear.

Since I had been with her during her final few days I knew already what others were to learn that morning; it was only when she was gravely ill that Georgiana thought to make her views substantive. I knew that she had anticipated dying as her final days drew on. Georgiana died on May 18th 1903, her new will was written on May 13th 1903 and a final codicil added on the day she died. People were left wondering how she coped because she had been ill since May 1st, which was a Friday, and she had got worse and worse as the weekend progressed. How did she summon the strength to meet with lawyers and write a will?

Here we were in the Surrogate's Court and about to learn of its contents: A Clerk of the Court stood to read it out: "The last will and testament of Georgiana E. Hartman".

Of course, the main bequests were to her extended family: paintings, some silver and "to Harvey Hartman all my horses and carriages, harnesses and stable equipment and all my household furniture and articles of personal use or adornment". In addition to this there was a separate one hundred and fifty thousand dollars and, as an Executor, a 4th part in the residue of her estate. Harvey Hartman would be a very wealthy clergyman.

There was a whole list of bequests to the staff who had served her so well and so faithfully for many years; largely they were modest sums, but when it got to me and Adele, the clerk read out "I give and bequeath, unto Annie E. Maher five thousand dollars and unto Adele Maria MacCullough five thousand dollars". We looked at each other in astonishment, open mouthed, but of course the proceedings required our silence. Five thousand dollars was such a lot of money; you could buy another property in Long Branch for five thousand dollars.

Manuel De Forrest Bolmer was remembered too with ten thousand dollars and, as an Executor, a 4th part in the residue of her estate. The dear Frederick Courtney, Lord Bishop of Nova Scotia was gifted five thousand dollars. One of the most touching moments was in Georgiana's bequest to the Babies Hospital of the City of New York the sum of five thousand dollars to endow a bed. The codicil made on her deathbed was not controversial but gave additional money to the children of her deceased brother, five thousand dollars each, and to her remaining two siblings ten thousand dollars to be shared between them.

Georgiana had done as she had promised me that time in the kitchen of my home; her bequest would certainly help to support my every need and would add to my growing portfolio. Secure for life; or that was how it felt.

It was on Monday November 26th 1906 that I went with my brother to New York, to wave farewell to him on his long journey to start his new life in Shanghai. It was one of the saddest moments and is imprinted upon my brain. He held me close, as we waited, in a hug that was so tight I thought I would not breathe again. "You are not to worry about me Annie, I shall be fine. My concern is for you; you have been through so much recently." I laughed and smiled.

As the days had worn on towards the point where Joseph would have to leave, we both had worked on my future safety. I was coping with yet more loss and both of us wanted to be sure that I would survive in the coming months. We ensured that I had a framework of friends around me who understood my problem and would be active in helping to support me in the hard times that would undoubtedly follow; my neighbors for example. We agreed that I would try to make friends within the local catholic community in the hope that they might watch out for me too.

As the ship pulled out of the dock, he was standing on an upper deck and waved to me and blew kisses until he was no longer in sight. What had amazed me was that this man had taken such a hold on my life. I knew very little of him when he arrived on my doorstep, and here I was weeping at his departure. He had gained my trust and my confidence almost instantaneously and was able to talk to me, and I to him, about the most personal of things, about the most troubling of things. I know that Joseph was my, much younger, brother, 18 years my junior, and yet I felt him to be at least my equal in age and in capability. The little boy who wanted to travel the world like his big sister Annie would, I felt, certainly make his mark on its landscape. When would I see him again?

CHAPTER 34

Eden by the Sea

THE SUMMER OF 1907 found me still bothered by the legacy of questions that had haunted me for years. Self-doubt and occasionally self-loathing: a sense of being abandoned: loneliness; all these feelings came tumbling in on me when I was least expecting it. I found it increasingly hard to pull myself round. Georgiana had taught me the trick of imagining all my troubles being put away, wrapped in a brown paper parcel and then consigned to a high shelf out of reach, then just returning to the routine things of life that were easily accomplished without dark shadows hovering over me; that worked sometimes.

I suppose too it was the echoes of my strict Catholic upbringing that were haunting me again and made me question why I seemed to lack the faith to just go along with the ideas that were part of my religious past. So many people in my lifetime seemed able to accept this unquestioning approach. When I thought of Georgiana and her entourage, her commitment to her Episcopalianism was unreserved. She and her husbands and even her young daughter had devoted themselves to the church and to the work of Christ.

I thought of Georgiana's work for the Babies Hospital. She had devoted hours of work to the Board, for raising money and generously gifting part of her wealth to them when a new ward or new equipment was needed. She gave endlessly and unquestioningly to this and other Christian causes. The hospital provided sanctuary to poor children and orphans of New York, understanding that living in the extremes of hot and cold caused real health problems for young New Yorkers. Those children were offered sanctuary in New Jersey in a specialist hospital far from the polluting effects of city life.

Perhaps here was the answer for me. I should find some way of helping and supporting young people in Long Branch. My answer came, as if from God, when I read in the local newspaper of the Sisters of Charity of Star of the Sea; they were appealing for help from the Long Branch community. I knew that they wanted more accommodation for their Christian Mission and School in Long Branch and now had placed an article in the "Long Branch Record".

I found myself sitting in my living room talking with three nuns. I did let it be known that I came from a very devout Catholic family and that two of my sisters, Mary, now Sister Dorothea and Alice, now Sister Ambrose, had both devoted their lives to the faith. I also, in case they were in any doubt, outlined my background since arriving from New York, and told them of my properties in Long Branch. I didn't use the phrase "capitalist" which was how I described my employment on the 1905 census return, but left the rest to their collective imagination.

I then just listened to them and their aspirations to create a larger base in Long Branch. Their needs were quite simple; they wanted a new office base, accommodation for the nuns and perhaps a property large enough to have 2 or 3 classrooms. Once they had achieved that, then they would need help with new equipment for teachers and children; if there was any way that I could help with that, they would be most grateful. We parted with a polite handshake and my promise that I would contact them again if I thought of something positive I could do to help.

The answer was not long in coming and again divine intervention seemed to be the case. I had only recently moved in to my adjacent newly-built property, vacating my original house next door: My intention had been to let the house out, either to a long-term tenant or perhaps for New York families wanting to spend a holiday in Long

Branch. With my property portfolio I had developed a skill for filling those houses with willing tenants and the income that was generated was quite considerable, adding to the coffers.

The nuns responded to my second invitation just a week later and arrived punctually and I took them into the living room where tea had been laid out on an occasional table. Annie, from next door, had agreed to help out and, once everyone was sitting, proceeded to serve them tea. Once done, she excused herself and left me with the nuns. We engaged in small talk for a while; they outlined the, limited, progress they had made in the few weeks since their newspaper coverage had appeared.

Now it was time to cut to the chase. I asked if they had noticed the house next door when they arrived. I told them that I thought it might fit their needs exactly for an office, living quarters for the nuns and a new space for the school. On the top floor was a very large single room that would make an ideal one-room schoolroom. It could easily accommodate the children they wanted to cater for.

Was that the sort of property they were looking for? "Well yes", came the unanimous answer. They had not thought of anything larger than that, but something along those lines. I went across to my desk and returned with a large envelope. I handed it to the most senior nun and she held it hesitantly in her hands. I suggested she look inside and see for herself. She opened the envelope and pulled out a large parchment.

"But you own the house?" she queried as much for her colleagues as for me. I explained that I had only very recently vacated it to live here, the new house I had built next door to my original home. I said that if they would like it I would arrange with my solicitor that the deed be transferred to "The Sisters of Charity of Star and the Sea" for the purpose of opening their school; it would be theirs, at no cost to themselves, and they would have the base they were looking for. It had been refurbished and well maintained and should involve very little additional cost for them and they could move in as early as they liked.

Now I understood the joy that Georgiana got from her generosity. These three women could not believe what had happened. They were all on their feet hugging each other in turn and hugging me too. "Miss Maher, how generous and kind, how can we accept such a gesture?" "You are not to question the 'how' of this, it is God's will that I support you and it is not for any of us to question God's mercy". Sister Dorothea would have been proud of me.

A footnote to that experience came with a knock on the screen door just two days later. It was the Long Branch Record editor, Benjamin Bolseau Bobbitt, whose newspaper had alerted me to the nuns' search for a home. I was reluctant to invite him in, so we sat side by side on the glider on the porch. He seemed genuinely intrigued and began asking some searching questions about what brought me to Long Branch. I explained that I had visited a number of times with New York families and that I was so enamored with the place that I always wanted to buy property and move here and, with the grace of God I managed to do just that. "It's like heaven here, my Eden by the sea", I eulogized.

After a while, and our conversation closed, he made some passing remarks about my remarkable generosity and stated his intention to put a piece in the following week's newspaper; "I'll send you a copy" he promised.

This was not my motivation at all; I was not looking for thanks or praise but just to experiment with Georgiana's form of generosity, simply to see what a difference it made. In fact, I promptly forgot about it.

I forgot, at least, until a clunk on the porch announced the arrival of the "Long Branch Record" the following week. The piece was prominently displayed as front-page news. It read as follows:

"Sisters Have a New Home

"Possession Taken of House in New Ocean Avenue Today

"The Sisters of Charity of Star of the Sea Academy today take possession of their house in New Ocean Avenue, presented to them by Miss Annie Elizabeth Maher, a resident of Long Branch for the past four years.

"Miss Maher has traveled extensively, but considers Long Branch an "Eden by the Sea." She is an ardent admirer of the Sisterhood, their mission appealing strongly to her. Speaking of it, she said: "It covers all the ground, from the battlefield to the college, taking under the cloak of charity all the ills that man is heir to, regardless of creed or condition."

It made me sound somewhat pompous but I cut out the article and posted it to Sister Dorothea nonetheless; my new-found generosity would, I knew, give her great pleasure.

CHAPTER 35

On the Record

I HAD NOT expected to make my mark on Long Branch. I had after all arrived at Elberon in the role of servant, housekeeper or lady's maid, whichever way you wish to describe it. To the elevated socialites, permanent and holidaying, I was of the serving class. You can imagine my surprise then when I received an invitation from the editor Benjamin Bolseau Bobbitt of our daily newspaper the "Long Branch Record", to write for him.

I was asked to see him in his rather untidy office, cluttered and dusty, and as I was ushered into an old buttoned leather chair, Mr. Bobbitt peered over his spectacles at me. He greeted me with "Miss Mayer?" not a good start. "It's Ma'her", I corrected, "It's got two syllables pronounced like Marr with a slight "her" at the end". I explained my lifelong difficulty in getting my name pronounced properly and that it was like my calling him "Mr. Bobby" continually. He apologized, but not before we had established a nickname I would use for him in later dealings: "Bobby".

He explained that after nearly four years, the pressure of producing sufficient material for a daily publication brought its own stresses. He had been looking for someone to supplement his team and to cover local stories, not working as a full-time journalist, but someone he could call upon at times when circumstances demanded. "Ideally", he explained, "it would be someone equally comfortable in the Elberon area as well as in Long Branch itself. Local knowledge and local contacts are important, but most importantly I need someone used to writing."

He explained that after we had met only a few days before, he was impressed by me and my stories of Elberon. I was flattered and surprised that I should even be considered suitable. I wasn't sure what sort of material he wanted me to write about; the bottom line was that it was anything that took my fancy. He raised the matter of payment, but I suggested that such discussions might be left until we both were clear that I was up to the task. In the end however he suggested what seemed a reasonable compromise; that I would be paid by the column inch of any material published. That worked out quite fairly I thought, it balanced any inclination I might have to extend the piece beyond what was necessary, subject to his editorial role tempered of course by his need to increase copy. We agreed that I would look for some event or situation that took my fancy and that on my next visit I would have that ready for him.

I began to realize that one of the side benefits of this opportunity was that it could supplement the income from my growing portfolio of property. I went back to him two days later with my first piece, and Bobby seemed delighted. He printed the edited version of that in the paper on August 26th 1906 under the banner, "EDITORIAL COMMENT" and it read:

"Values in Long Branch

"The real estate market in Long Branch City, which includes North Long Branch, Branchport, Long Branch, West End, Hollywood and Elberon, has been very active for the past half year, owing to the many improvements that have been made to the beach front, such as the new walk, and to the Casino, the widening of Ocean Boulevard, and the concerts now given by the Government Carlisle Indian Band: they have altogether made an increased demand for desirable property. There are not more than fifty unrented cottages in the city of Long Branch this season."

It seemed like an important step for me and gave me a new independence and role in my new home town. I had accepted that, as a matter of course, pieces were not attributed to the author. If any attribution was needed to impress the reader with the veracity of the work, then it might, as with this first piece, be printed as Editorial Comment.

In fact, my second piece of submitted material, suggested to him before I left his office at our first meeting, was a poem I had written in praise of Long Branch. Bobby agreed that it fitted the specification and asked that I send it to him, with no promise that he would print it. It appeared in the "Long Branch Daily Record" on 31th August 1906 and read:

"Long Branch, the Beautiful.

"Oft have I wandered o'er Friar's Bridge,
And on the glossy banks of the old
Thames stood.
Bound, as it were, in rapturous mood
Killarney's mountains and lakes! Ah,

They seem Devine,

And what can compare with the ancient Rhine?

Loch Lomond so serene, its black waters washing o'er

beds of Green.

Thoughts and memory linger, comparisons vast and

far in bold relief.

Yet where on earth a spot to compare with you, our

own, our Long Branch

fair?

Where woodland dell and silvery brook

Ripple and sleep, as o'er the ocean vast we look.

Ah, return again the thoughts that were dead,

Refreshed, renewed on the Eden Bed.

Oh, Eden by the Sea, afar from yonder beauteous bluff

In fancy yet I see Lake Como's placid grandeur rise,

Re-echoing my heart's desire

To Him so noble and so true,

Who love as only British do,

With heart and soul and pen.

Ah! years have passed since hand in hand we strayed

Along thy silvery strand.

Ah, now, how changed,

The sea in all its majesty rolls on.

"Yon Esplanade, "Bluff Walk," I now understand.

Ah, the Boulevard so grand, so grand,

And oh, ye divine Indian Band

Oh, Eden by the Sea, not only to Him

and me are you sublime.

Where men are brave, not the few,

And women, oh, so good and true!

Ah, yes, and beautiful my sisters, you.

What has not Heaven given

To this Eden by the Sea?

Men who are what men should be,

Protectors ever of their flag and thee.

Women beautiful and good,

Being all a wife and mother should.

Struggling on from day to day

To help, to watch, to wait, to pray.

They love, they honor and obey.

What more for this Eden by the Sea.

Endowed with health's invigorating balm

The ozone of the sea combined with woodland's sleepy

pine.

"And so for heart, and lung and head

We find as it were, in this garden bed,

The solace that comes to the brave and true,

Knowing they have done as they should do.

"And now my sister, my wish for you,

The good, the brave, the beautiful, the true,

May our Eden garden flourish on

From early morn till set of sun,

Infusing health and happiness vast as the sea

To each dear one.

Oh, proclaim ye waves, near and far

Resound ye vales!

Be as it were, our light-house star

To guide our brethren from afar

To reach this heaven this side of the bar.

ANNA ELIZABETH MAHER."

I thought it not a particularly erudite piece of poetry but Bobby's willingness to publish it in full was an important signal.

Over time the writing became something that I relished while giving me a direct interest in the goings-on in my own community. I learned, from seeing how he edited my work, that our job was not just to print news but also, by appealing to the readers' baser instincts, to encourage them to keep buying the paper, to get more. Having learned this lesson, one piece in particular went through with hardly any editorial intervention.

"Cleveland Boarding House

"A house at the corner of Troutman Avenue and Simpson Street was raided by the Monmouth County Assistant Prosecutor. He went around the local police, implying that they were corrupt. The house was called the Cleveland Boarding House and it was run by Phillip Jaresky and Joseph Davis. The house had 4 girls working there. When arrested, 3 of the girls were downstairs drinking "attired in nothing but mosquito netting. The fourth girl was found upstairs, with a male companion."

Apart from the enjoyment that I found in producing this copy, I was able to document the things that affected my houses and property. For example, to publish the decision, based on the public notice I had been sent by the City Council of Long Branch, to change the name of my street.

"AN ORDINANCE changing the name of a public street extending northerly from Sea View Avenue to North Long Branch from the names of Simpson Street and New Ocean Avenue to Ocean Avenue.

"BE IT ORDAINED by the City Council of Long Branch: that the name of the public street beginning in the northerly line of Sea View Avenue and running northerly to North Long Branch, heretofore known by the names of Simpson Street and New Ocean Avenue shall hereafter be known and designated for all legal purposes as Ocean Avenue."

One of the lessons that I had learned was the power of the press to rewrite history and the reputations of individuals. One of my favorites, given his known background in the margins of criminality, was to sanitize Con Gaskin in one piece of very local news.

"SAVED BATHER IN 20 FEET OF WATER

Capt. Conover Gaskin Rescues Woman in Trouble in Surf. Had it not been for Captain Conover Gaskin yesterday a woman boarder at the Barnwell Cottage would have drowned. As it was she had a close call.

___

"The woman, a Mrs. Booker, with a Mrs. Oliver, started to go in bathing near Captain Gaskin's fishery. The Oliver woman remained close to the shore, as the surf was threatening. Mrs. Booker, however, was more venturesome, and was soon in deep water, much to her sorrow. She was about to give up her struggle for life, as she was being carried out in deep water, when Captain Gaskin saw her peril.

"Without waiting he removed his coat and vest and was soon swimming close by the prostrate woman. He pulled her ashore, where restoratives were applied. The woman is recovering from the shock.

"The rescue took place at one o'clock yesterday afternoon."

We did laugh that evening when Con and his wife Charlotta came over to Barnwell Cottage to celebrate the events of the previous day. Of course, Mrs. Oliver and Mrs. Booker were both fine and enjoyed more of the "restoratives" in several glasses of Con's local brew. Annie and Catherine were delighted by the free advertising and reported three more bookings in just one day. As for Con, he became acknowledged wherever he went in Long Branch as "Captain", a title he had never bestowed on himself.

So here was an unexpected twist in my drive to be more generous to others with my time and money, as Georgiana had been. I was now employed as a journalist and was beginning to turn this to my advantage.

I continued to report local news for over 10 years and the demands on me were even greater during the war years when the men of New Jersey enlisted and the shortage of workers across a range of businesses became increasingly evident as women moved into those roles. Ironically, like many in my position, I was asked to resign in 1919, some months after the war, when one of those men returned, as his new-won disability did not prevent him from being a very effective reporter. But still I missed the work, missed the creativity and most importantly missed my role in the community and the people that I would routinely meet.

CHAPTER 36

The End of Art

DE FORREST BOLMER, the man nearest to my heart, seemed indestructible. He was active, creative, fit and well cared for.

The news that he had died reached me belatedly in Long Branch; he had died at home of a heart attack on June 7th 1910; he was only 58.

Of course, I was now just an unimportant and remote figure for his family members, but would have gone to the funeral had I known about it. They had no reason to know of the increasingly close relationship that had grown up between the two of us, and so had no reason to invite me personally, instead leaving it to the usual newspaper notices and word-of-mouth for the news to spread. By the time I knew, he was already in the ground.

His passing went almost unnoticed. His great contribution to the art world was largely unrecognized, just a footnote in the credits for other artists.

Georgiana would have been as devastated as I was, had she been alive. As it was I was alone with my grief.

Grief can be burdened by "what-ifs" and my loss of De Forrest was no exception. This outstanding man had made such an impression on me; he was flamboyant, yet self-contained; he was a loving, caring person and yet alluringly distant. He had a strong and sensual masculinity about him and yet that seemed unrequited. How should I have taken his hesitancy? There were moments when I felt that he would speak of feelings for me, but then remained silent and yet comfortable in my company. I would watch him as he created landscape paintings that I felt I could walk into, and yet he never took me by the hand or invited me in. My concern at the outset was that I wanted nothing to disturb my place with the Bolmer or Arnold households; no hint of scandal, no broken relationship that might call into question my place there. To that extent, I must have seemed aloof and reserved, but nothing was further from the truth in terms of my growing feelings for this man.

No matter how I tried and how successful I was in my work for, and with, his sister Georgiana, I may have been, in his eyes, nothing more than a servant. There were countless examples of gentlemen taking advantage of servants, both male and female, working out their sexual gratification on them. Dominant in the household hierarchy, there was rarely complaint about this abuse of power, unless of course that contact led to unwelcome consequences in terms of pregnancy and disease. In such cases the objects of those advances were quietly removed from sight and from service and the cycle of inappropriate behavior started all over again.

De Forrest Bolmer was not guilty of anything of the sort, and that partly explained his distance from me. He was a principled man and would not take advantage of his power or position in such a way, perhaps leaving the sense that he was holding back.

If I was correct in my reading, that the two of us enjoyed a real affinity, why did I not choose to make the first move? To make some sign in word or gesture or touch, that I wanted to be more than good company. What if I had done so, how might it have changed both of our lives? What if we had found a way to commit to each other and to make our lives together? What if?

All of that was in the past now; I would never truly know what De Forrest Bolmer thought of me and how he might have reacted to the proposition that we make a life together. Instead, I was to face the rest of my life without him, never again to have the opportunity to express these feelings I harbored but had never given expression to.

In all of my time in this great country, I had a small group of people to thank for making me what I was, who had been very kind to me and brought me opportunities beyond my wildest imaginings. Richard had recognized what I brought to Georgiana's life and had helped me in the execution of that role; but then Richard had died. Dear sweet Nellie had been the focus of our lives since Richard's death before being so cruelly snatched from us. Then Georgiana, my dear Georgiana, who was such a key person in my life in America, who had trained and tutored me to be able to accomplish the challenges she gave me, then to be lost to me for ever. Now, the only man I thought I loved, De Forrest Bolmer, snatched from me before we were able to express any feelings that we might have had for each other.

With De Forrest's death, it brought home to me just how lonely and unhappy I was.

I recaptured part of him when I saw an advertizement in the January 30th 1911 edition of the "New York Sun". There buried away on page 12 was an advertizement for an exhibition and sale at Clarke's Art Rooms. The same advert ran in the New York Times the following day buried on page 19. On offer for sale were over 300 landscape and marine paintings that had been removed from his studio at The Beaux Arts. The sale had been ordered by De Forrest's brother, Thomas, who was executor of his will.

I was there on both days of the sale on West 44th Street New York on Thursday 2nd and Friday 3rd February 1911. The sale evenings did not begin until 8:15 p.m. and the light snow that fell on Thursday became heavy and persistent on the second day of the sale. Despite the conditions, I made certain that I was waiting at the doors of Clarke's when they opened at 7:30 each evening.

Perhaps as a consequence of the weather, the sale was not well attended and that kept prices low. I recognized in the catalogue many of the pictures for sale and several of them had particular meaning for me. They were not all landscapes, though that was his forte, and I chose two city panoramas, one of Paris from Sacré-Cœur and another of the Trevi Fountain in Rome, just a stone's throw from the delightful Caffè Greco where we spent many happy hours in the company of artists and poets. The area around the fountain was so busy and congested, I had arranged for him to use the balcony of a home overlooking the fountain. The elderly Italian lady who lived there was only too pleased to help and refused all offers of payment. As a gesture, on the second morning I took along a box of pastries that were the speciality of our Caffè Greco. They had presented them for me in a white box tied with a beautiful ribbon. She was delighted and insisted that I sit with her in her kitchen and drink strong coffee and eat cake; at least it gave De Forrest some peace and quiet to complete the painting.

Another painting that jumped out at me was a seascape. This was of the foreshore at Long Branch and had clearly been painted recently. Hanging on my wall at home, these pictures would remind me of him and our times together. I purchased these three paintings and a further three landscapes that I recognized from our European trip and arranged for Clarke's to ship them to me in Long Branch.

I had dressed very modestly for the event and was muffled up in hat, scarf and heavy top-coat against the snow and the cold, but partly too to protect my anonymity. While I recognized a lot of the people at the sale, and in particular Thomas Bolmer, I did not wish anyone to share in my recapturing of De Forrest or of the secret passion I held for him, and I am sure he for me.

When the delivery arrived, I had decided where I wanted to hang each piece; they were to form a small exhibition of his work with the pyramids at Giza at the center, and featured prominently on a wall in the entrance hall where I would pass them many times each day.

CHAPTER 37

Teaching and the Older Man

ADELE HAD COME a long way since that waif I had interviewed as a potential Nanny for Nellie.

After Nellie's death, Adele was assigned the alternative role as Secretary for Georgiana. She had begun to accumulate skills and to develop a presence that belied her chaotic origins in Ohio. The death of Georgiana meant that, like me, Adele had to invent a new persona and a new way of life. Her savings were not going to sustain her for ever; she needed employment.

By 1904 Adele was working as a private tutor to children from a number of local Long Branch families. She worked at her James Street house. Broadly speaking this was helping young people with basic literacy and numeracy.

One of her early students was Ivy Troutman and the task she was assigned, by Ivy's father John, was to help build Ivy's communication and social skills. Ivy was 21 and had a strong ambition to be an actress, but she lacked the refinement needed to carry off some roles. Adele gave her a good grounding in grammar, elocution and deportment. They formed a strong bond despite the 12-year age gap between them.

While her parents were not the most highly regarded in Long Branch, Ivy had aspirations. She already had some parts in local shows but her ambition was to hit the big time. She needed support in the very areas where Adele had thrived; her basic education was lacking and her reading skills challenged; she had to read scripts. Most importantly it was her need to transform from the small-town girl-next-door and to learn to characterize ladies of refinement with the appropriate accent and deportment. Adele was in her element and brought to bear all the lessons and learning she had acquired in New York.

The Troutman family owned a small hotel just on the other side of the tracks from Ocean View, called Troutman's Cottage, which they advertized in the New York press:

"Long Branch – Troutman's Cottage, Long Branch
Avenue, short distance from cars and beach. Sea view

from every window. Table first class. Apply at once at

73 West Twenty Third Street".

What they had not included was the horse racing season when a large group of well-to-do New Yorkers would arrive in town whenever there were race days. They had made a thriving little business out of their guest house.

Ivy was to make her New York professional stage debut in Wallack's Theater on 30th Street and Broadway in "The Last Appeal" in 1902. Adele had a crucial part to play too as Ivy's coach and mentor. Adele moved into Ivy's family home at 114 Long Branch Avenue, during the intensive period of rehearsal, and undoubtedly contributed to her success.

Her performance was warmly acclaimed and that led to an offer for her to join the Theatrical Company run by Miss Amelia Bingham. The success of her troupe allowed Amelia to surround herself with acclaimed performers: Harry Woodruff, Creston Clarke, J. H. Gilmour, Frank Lander, Myron Calice, and Louise Galloway. Now Ivy Troutman was to be included among this array of glittering stars.

Adele returned to her teaching in James Street having helped Ivy launch herself into her chosen career. If anything, this helped to widen

Adele's range of tutees as she gained a reputation for her skills as a teacher. She continued her contact with the Troutmans and had taken on the tutelage of Ivy's younger sister, Myrtle Diamond Troutman.

Adele was emerging into quite a local celebrity and she and her tutees would sometimes drop in for afternoon tea with "Auntie Annie". One such, Viola Lorenson, was a regular visitor to my house and it was a great joy seeing Adele idolized by the young people she worked with.

I suppose that I should not have been surprised when Adele disclosed to me her new status in the Troutman family; she was to be "Resident Tutor" and to live at the Troutmans' house full time.

I did tackle her about it and questioned the wisdom of a step that might damage her reputation. Lydia Troutman, John Troutman's wife, had died in 1893 and as a widower with three children he was particularly vulnerable to gossip and innuendo.

Adele was not for persuading. She explained to me what she thought Georgiana's approach to life had been; "find an older, rich husband" she explained. I protested that this was not what Georgiana had thought or done. Richard was wealthy, but not as wealthy as Georgiana and her family. When in 1899 Georgiana had married Mr. Hartman, he was Rector of St. John's Episcopal Church in Dover. Georgiana's will after her death in 1903 showed how extensive her wealth was; she had remembered me and Adele in the most generous way and had assured our future lives.

Was Adele really thinking of a life with John Troutman as a means to wealth and security? She had shared no details of intimacy or affection between them. But what was most difficult for me in the conversations we had about her possible new life was her leaving me, though of course I never expressed it in those terms. We had been together, been through things together, grown together in moments of grief, happiness and in feminine intimacy.

Looking back, I had been assaulted by a range of losses and now my loss of Adele was to be just another? When my brothers Patrick and James both died I was a youngster but, from my 20th year, the pace of loss had been escalating: siblings William, John and Margaret, my mother Alice and most recently my father Patrick, all dead. And then my lovely people in the U.S.A., Richard Arnold at 56, then Nellie, my beloved Nellie. I shared in Georgiana's other tragedies too, her mother and father within 3 years of each other, and between them her sister Gertrude, then her half sibling William Brevoort Bolmer, each one adding to the cumulative burden.

But my greatest loss of all, beyond that of siblings or parents, was the loss of my darling Georgiana aged only 46. I had known Georgiana since I was barely 18 and had imagined growing old in her service. She nurtured me under her constant guardianship and taught me the ways of the world that I could only have imagined. She introduced me to people I would never have met, and to places I might only have dreamed of.

When I thought back to my Irish and then my English heritage I sometimes wondered what might have become of me if I had given in to the pressures of working-class conformity, scraping together a meager existence; would there have been a man and a marriage? Children? The thought of sacrificing myself to a dockyard laborer with my intellectual stimulation limited to cooking and cleaning was a step too far.

Adele did her best to reassure me that she would not be far away and that our friendship would never be in doubt, no matter what the circumstances. That would undoubtedly prove to be a hollow promise.

In the Fall of 1904 Adele did move permanently to join the Troutman family and then, in December 1911, she married John Jay Troutman. Adele was 40 years old. I did receive an invitation to the wedding, but I did not go. John Troutman died in October 1912 when he was

64 years old. Their daughter Katherine was born during 1912 further leading to gossip and speculation about Adele's role in the household and about the unexpected wedding, after all these years.

She and the family did continue to run Troutman's Cottage as the Willow Grove Boarding House until about 1914. That was when Adele Troutman moved to Vineland, New Jersey to live on Brewster Street. Whether the move was her trying to protect Katherine from continuing comment, she never disclosed. She got herself a teaching post and continued her teaching career that had started in Long Branch.

As for Willow Grove, it was left empty until the weather rendered it derelict. It was a well-known spot for local vagrants and drug addicts and eventually burned to the ground.

One legacy that Adele had left me was her introducing me to Catherine and Annie; they were good neighbors and friends and helped me to recover my sensibilities.

CHAPTER 38

Catherine's Death

IT WAS IN December 1913, after a particularly long evening on the Sunday night, that Catherine failed to appear. Annie found her in the morning, prostrate and dead on the bathroom floor. She was 65 years old and a local paper, "The Asbury Park Press", kindly said that she had "died of paralysis". Annie and I and the local brew knew what kind of paralysis that had been.

Dear Annie Hall; she had continued to cope, because she had to. She and Catherine had been the same age and had shared their lives running Barnwell Cottage together for over thirty years. She was devastated by this loss, having committed her life and her love to this woman and to their joint enterprise. Annie continued to do this, partly out of her devotion to Catherine.

Catherine, in her last will and testament, had left her entire estate including the house to Annie S. Hall. This was common knowledge locally having been reported in the local paper, "Catherine E. Barnwell of Long Branch in her will, dated May 7th, 1910 appointed Annie S. Hall, executrix of her estate and bequeathed her all her property of every description. The subscribing witnesses were Adele M. MacCullough and Meredith Saunders."

For me it was another death of someone special to me.

Several months passed in which I supported Annie as well as I could. In the light of the nature of Catherine's demise, Annie had promised to limit her drinking; that was a particularly difficult promise to make and to keep, given the amount that Annie and Catherine had drunk, and that their guests and visitors to Barnwell Cottage expected. Catherine's death served only to increase the amount that Annie drank.

Con was still her supplier and I saw him going in and out of Barnwell Cottage carrying flagons of hooch. Annie Hall needed it, her customers expected it and, as long as the local police were otherwise occupied, it was a trade; everything proceeded very efficiently and very calmly. One morning there was a knock on my door and Con stood on the threshold in an agitated state.

"Have you got a key for Barnwell Cottage" he asked breathlessly. "Yes, I have; why?" "I was taking some hooch across to Annie this morning, but could get no answer; the curtains are still closed and I can see no signs of life". I got the key from the hook in the kitchen and we hurried next door.

"Annie? Annie?" I called as we tentatively opened the door and went in. It was hard to see but, as my eyes became accustomed to the dark, I could clearly see a figure lying prostrate on the couch. I opened all the curtains to shed some light on the situation. Con was already there, he lifted Annie's head and, with a finger of the other hand, was trying to clear regurgitated food from her throat.

There was a sudden coughing and spluttering and Annie's eyes opened as if on organ stops; she panicked to find herself in the arms of this big burly man. I went to the other side of the couch and reached for her with my hand, stroking her face reassuringly; "you're O.K. this is Annie from next door and Con from across the street. We were worried about you. You've been a bit poorly; no, don't try to move just rest there until you feel a little better."

Con went into the kitchen and returned with a glass of clear liquid. "Here, take a sip or two of this" he encouraged. I raised an eyebrow at him. "Hair of the dog", he explained, "she's had a skinful last night and we need to top her up a little so that she can come down more gently." Annie spluttered as the liquid hit her throat, then was regurgitated and flowed down her chin onto her clothing. "And another sip," encouraged Con. Miraculously she seemed almost instantly more alert.

"I'll go home and get Charlotta to come and help". His wife arrived back, by herself, in what seemed a very short period of time. Between us we helped Annie up and took her to the bathroom. We stripped her of her soiled clothes and sponged her. When she was clean and slightly sweeter-smelling, we sat her on her bed and put clean underwear on her and then her nightgown. We laid her back on her pillows and immediately she started groaning and lifted her arm to her face. "Spinning ..." she said. Charlotta collected the glass and encouraged her to have a further drink. After a short while Annie was on her back snoring loudly. "I'll stay with her Charlotta" I reassured and shortly Annie and I were alone together, she snoring and me wondering what would be the next knock on the door. Such things always come in threes.

CHAPTER 39

The War to End All Wars

THOSE OF US with family in England learned of the onset of the war in Europe in 1914 with some alarm. The president, Woodrow Wilson, was keen for the United States to be neutral in such affairs; this view was clearly supported by the majority of U.S. citizens, even though there was no great affection for Germany and the Germans. However, as events started to unfold, especially stories of the atrocities in Belgium, opinions began to harden. Belgium had been a neutral country since 1839, however the German army needed access to the eastern regions of France where the French Army were concentrating. It was not just that the Germans violated its neutrality, but the atrocities carried out at the time of the invasion and during the period of occupation against the Belgian population were deeply shocking to Americans, not least because they understood the flimsiness of the neutrality of nations in times of war.

There were then acts of war taken against shipping that cost American lives. The British had imposed a sea blockade on Germany and so, from a German perspective, boats flying the British flag, whether naval or civilian, were a legitimate target. However, when a Cunard Ocean Liner R.M.S. Lusitania was torpedoed and sunk in only a few minutes on May 7th 1915, just off the southern coast of Ireland, killing well over half of the 1959 passengers and crew, some of them American, public opinion swung decisively in favor of American engagement. Controversy still rages about whether the Lusitania was an innocent passenger liner or whether it was also carrying equipment to support the British war effort.

There was a particular Irish catholic attitude to American engagement; we had been struggling for independence from the British for generations, and at last there was the Government Act of Ireland which allowed for Home Rule. It was only passed in 1914 but was then suspended for the duration of the war. It led many Irishmen and their descendants to believe that the most effective route to self-government was victory for the Germans. You can imagine the controversy and argument that this caused within the multi-national communities in Long Branch. Later in 1916 the "Easter Uprising" in Ireland, which was put down brutally by the British and the leaders of the uprising executed, created outrage among many Irish immigrants. However, it did not sway the belief of the general public that the U.S.A. should join the war on the side of the British.

In January 1917 the Germans resumed their sinking of shipping and a number of American ships were included in those lost. Eventually on April 6th 1917 the U.S.A. declared war on Germany and only months later declared war on the Austro-Hungarian Empire.

Three days later, "The New York Times" devoted the whole of its page 3 to reports of the American decision being enthusiastically supported back in England; for the first time the American Stars and Stripes were hung on the Houses of Parliament in tribute. The plans of the War Department to prepare for war were also included in the reports. From our perspective in New Jersey there was to be training for men and officers; of the 14 training camps set up initially, one at Fort Myer in Virginia was meant to be a staging area with men from New Jersey, Delaware, Maryland and Virginia. With French help and with French Officers, a trench system was built with the French training the Americans about trench warfare.

Enlisted men and reserves were initially limited by age between 21 and 44. The conscription to the armed forces was, over the space of the following many months, to decimate communities by tearing out their men, many of whom would never return. The social impact of this was to throw women into a more central role in the workforce. My humble task of reporting the news and issues in Long Branch seemed, in this light, not to be so outrageous.

For my own part, I wrote a piece for "The Long Branch Record" that was published on April 9th 1917 about the reactions in England to the U.S.A.'s entry into the war. I titled it, "Stars and Stripes Float from Windows in London". Mary Stevens from New York, now Lady Arthur Paget, had raised $1.2m dollars for the allies during the war. Together with descriptions of rallies and large numbers of Americans already fighting as part of allied troops, it created a nice rounded story. To top it off, or rather as a footnote, the editor had added a map of the globe and a table of figures showing that more than two-thirds of the world's population was involved in the conflict: 1,144,400,000 out of a total of 1,691,751,000.

There were some interesting impacts of the war. As the number of camps grew, one near Long Branch was Camp Vail. I wrote a piece about the number of marriages there had been between local girls and members of the forces based there. On Monday February 18th 1918, my piece was titled, "Soldiers of 55th Battalion, Camp Alfred Vail, Wed Red Bank and Elberon Girls." I then proceeded to give the accounts of two weddings and another planned. It brought a little humor to an otherwise bleak period and painted some positive messages about the unexpected benefits of being at war.

By November 12th 1918, The Record reported extensively on the end of the war, initially cautiously; "Must Await Final Peace" was one headline. Even so we were able to bring positive good news, for example, "All Draft Calls Halted by Peace: "Honorable Discharge" for those still waiting".

Slowly over the months, Long Branch was able to revert to something like pre-war normality; except of course nothing would be normal again for those lost or injured in battle, those bereaved parents of soldiers killed and the wives with the new title "widow". The senselessness of war seemed so evident, particularly as in the President's own words, "This is the war to end all wars".

CHAPTER 40

Last Gasp in Long Branch

IN THE DAYS and months that followed, Annie Hall and I spent more time together.

Annie could not give up drink and so, almost inevitably, hers was a slow and gentle decline; she drank more and more often, going to the seafront to seek the company of others who drank and, generally, rather lowered her standards of decorum.

From my perspective, I feared that my end was in sight too. I was increasingly depressed and quite convinced that I would not live out the decade. That having been said, 1920 seemed a long way away; it was not.

There were times when I tried to pull myself together; I tried to keep in touch at the church, but found it difficult. I knew I was losing when The Sisters of Charity of Star of the Sea gave me back the house next door that I had gifted to them to set up a school. I don't know if retribution was in their minds, but it must have been somewhat of a disadvantage to have your benefactor living next door who seemed to be slipping from being a pillar of the local community to be associating with less than wholesome characters.

Annie Hall and I did increasingly get ourselves into trouble, sometimes even with the police. We were often out socializing, trying to laugh off our tragic histories; Annie Hall would sometimes be a little drunk and we were often noisy, sometimes rather boisterous; people started to complain about our behavior. We were never arrested, but we were occasionally escorted home by the local police; I suppose you would say we were "known".

On New Year as we saw in the new decade, 1920, we had cause for a great celebration. I had not thought that I would live so long and, though my days were certainly numbered, this seemed a particular landmark to celebrate. We did so down at the beach where many hundreds of people gathered to see in the New Year. When the moment came, there was laughter and cheering, people kissing and hugging each other. In one silent, stolen moment Annie Hall and I just hugged and hugged each other, more in relief than anything. The embrace went on and on until all the noise had died away and we were left, clutching each other like two lost souls.

What did we do after that? We went home and got more drunk.

CHAPTER 41

Prohibition Years

A CONCERN ABOUT the abuse of alcohol was becoming a real issue as the new decade began. To understand it you have to consider its origins. The drive for temperance started as a women's movement based on some real need. In the mid-19th Century a woman was completely subservient to her husband and he could beat her and neglect her and his kids and she had no recourse at all; the Temperance Movement began with this in mind.

The culmination of the efforts of the Temperance Movement was Prohibition which was made the law of the land in January 1920. New Jersey was one of the last states to ratify Prohibition because they were so set against it. Even though the law was ratified in 1920, it was not enforced in New Jersey for quite a while.

The Prohibition issue was highly divisive and split into competing factions:

"The Drys" were those who wanted Prohibition. They tended to be Protestant people whose families had been in the U.S. for a while. They found the incoming hordes of Italians, Catholics, Jews, Poles, the "new immigrants", threatening and they saw Prohibition as something that would set them apart as "real Americans".

"The Wets" on the other hand were those who did not support Prohibition and tended to be more liberal about the incoming people and didn't believe Prohibition was good for the country because it could cause outlaws to take up the distribution of liquor. They proved to be right; because New Jersey was on the coast and close to New York, the Mob came to New Jersey and started importing liquor by boat up and down the coast.

There was a more troubling aspect to Prohibition; in the 1920s, the Temperance Movement was hijacked by American xenophobes who were in fear of losing their way of life because of industrialization and immigration. This way of thinking fitted in with the dogma of the Ku Klux Klan and the Prohibition debate revitalized the organization. One of the largest rallies they ever held was in Long Branch in 1924.

Politicians further used xenophobia to argue that the grains used to brew beer (by Germans) could be used to make bread.

For Annie Hall, life became very difficult and more unsettling. As constraints began to bite on what alcohol could be sold and where, it became more and more difficult to obtain booze legally and it put pressure on small businesses, like Annie's at Barnwell Cottage that had relied on offering customers a bar service.

Most people in New Jersey purchased a lot of liquor before the law went into effect. If they already owned it, it wasn't illegal to drink it. Annie had a good-sized house and a basement and outbuilding to store things. Thanks to Con, there was a supply to last for quite a while. However, by 1923 or 1924 most of those stockpiles were running out, and people turned to illegal liquor; they didn't agree with Prohibition and so there was widespread flaunting of the law.

It was Annie Hall who sourced a batch of illicit alcohol. I think it had been Con who was the provider and he had grown increasingly desperate to find new sources of his raw materials. On this occasion, apparently, barrels had washed up on the foreshore just in front of the fishing ground. They were quickly spirited away to Con's storage before anyone was much the wiser. He used this for a further stage of distillation producing a high-alcohol content and it emerged from his processing some weeks later and was a much sought-after commodity.

Of course, Annie had her regular demand to meet from her guests and so was first on Con's list, and numerous flagons were secreted away in the cellar of Barnwell Cottage.

The effects of this brew amongst the regular drinkers were not immediately apparent. There were, however, growing rumors that it was a "bad batch".

One evening I had gone to see Annie just to check that she was alright. She was actually on the porch, glass in hand and a bottle of hooch on a table. "Will you keep me company?" she asked, gesturing towards a second, empty glass; she poured me a shot. Very quickly I felt extremely unsteady after finishing the glass; my head was spinning and I was feeling as though I had drunk the whole bottle! It took only a few more minutes before Annie started to show an increased concern for me. The next thing I was aware of was when Con and Charlotta were kneeling at my side and trying to speak with me.

I was not able to respond properly and, with one of them on each side of me, they helped me back to my house. There we went upstairs and they lay me on my bed. I was out cold as though completely intoxicated. In fact, I had lost those minutes since first taking a drink; they had been completely erased from my memory.

I learned later that I was unconscious for almost 18 hours and that Charlotta had stayed with me for much of that time until she felt she was happy with me and thought that I could be left to sleep it off.

CHAPTER 42

Joseph Revisited

IN FACT, SHE was not at all happy with me and I learned she had immediately made contact with Sister Dorothea in New York to explain a developing problem. Sister Dorothea, my Sister Mary in her guise as a nun, in turn contacted Joseph by cablegram to his Far Eastern office in Shanghai. The first I knew of all this was when Joseph stood on my doorstep.

If I was confused before, I certainly was confused now. "Are you not going to invite me in?" asked Joseph. My uncertainty must have been quite evident and I rather bluntly asked him what he was doing there. He explained the concern expressed by my neighbors to Sister Dorothea and it was that which had prompted his visit.

As I sat at the kitchen table, he made me tea while he talked. "What I hope that you will agree to, is to allow me to help. I am here for as long as you need me and would be happy to devote as much time as it takes to support you and to fathom what is wrong with you." "And how do you suggest we do that?" I demanded.

"First I want to get a consultation with a brilliant local doctor who is developing some interesting theories and strategies for people with problems akin to yours. He is keen to stress that it is not something in your mind that is the fault; you are not crazy or drinking to excess. Instead he is looking at clinical and bacteriological explanations. I met him on the ship on the way to New York when I first came over; he was just finishing a lecture tour of Europe. He is highly regarded and when I contacted him last week he agreed to see you, just to make an assessment and propose a possible course of action for us to follow in coming weeks; his name is Dr. Henry Cotton." Before I knew what was happening, I had agreed to a consultation, with the only condition I insisted upon being that Joseph accompany me.

Dr. Cotton had recently been appointed to Trenton Asylum but had a private practice nearby where he saw his wealthier clients. It was to this practice that my brother Joseph brought me. We drove in my car to Trenton; though I felt nervous about driving myself, Joseph was perfectly competent to do that.

Joseph had done a lot of reading and research and had talked me through Dr. Cotton's education and experience. As I sat in a small waiting room I re-read the notes Joseph had given me. Even so I had no real idea what to expect, but when I met Dr. Cotton I was surprised by the personable character that I was to confront for the first time.

He was 46 years old and his C.V. read very well. He was born in Norfolk, Virginia and attended public schools in Baltimore and then John Hopkins University. He graduated from there and worked in hospitals in Maryland, Baltimore and Massachusetts. His teacher and mentor was Dr. Adolf Meyer and he worked closely with Drs. Berkley, Stewart and Hurd. He had a 3-year period of postgraduate study in Munich, Germany where, amongst others, he had been studying under Professor Alois Alzheimer. On Friday November 15th 1907, he was appointed as Medical Director of the New Jersey State Hospital for the Insane.

He ushered us into his consulting room where Joseph and I sat in two deep leather chairs in front of an expansive desk. To one side of the room was a table, clearly designed so that patients in a prone position could be examined by him; it was covered in a white cotton sheet a pillow at one end. Near it was another large leather-bound chair but it had a higher seat and worryingly it had a headrest, arms and feet that had leather restraints which could be used to immobilize patients.

He must have seen my face as I looked at that chair. "Oh, don't worry about that, it is a relic used by my predecessor here. I don't believe that restraining patients is appropriate and I would never do that; it's just one of the barbaric hangovers of a previous, less-enlightened age in medicine." He had put me a little at my ease and now began to talk about the consultation. "What I propose to do is to take down some factual information. Then carry out a short, non-invasive examination. Having done that I think I will be in a position to propose a course of action for us to follow.

"Firstly, the presenting problem is your confusion after consumption of alcohol; can you give me your thoughts on what, how much and why you drink?" I was very self-conscious; my brother sat on my left and this man peered down at me from his office chair across a huge mahogany desk; it was very intimidating. I started hesitantly, "For most of my life I have not drunk. I have held a number of roles in my working life when the expectations of me were high, but there was no room for confused thinking. It is only since 1900 when I bought a home in Long Branch that drink entered the equation at all".

This was really hard but I persisted if for no other reason than people would not be able to say that I had not done my best. I had been through a series of tragic events with the death and loss of family, friends and loved ones; I suppose I was feeling very low. I tried to avoid the temptation of drink, partly because that was what everybody else did and I lived in a location where access to cheap sources of alcohol was easy. I did not always succeed.

The problem with my current confusion really started when Annie, a neighbor, and I drank some locally-distilled spirit. I explained that drinking per se was not a problem; I was firmly in control of my drinking. This seemed to have been the effects of just one bad batch. With that off my chest I felt I could sit back and relax a little.

"Thank you", said Dr. Cotton. "That was a very clear and insightful explanation; you clearly are a very intelligent woman. Can I now turn to other areas of your general health? How have you been feeling in yourself? Any coughs or colds, aches and pains, toothache, sore throats? Everything on track with your woman's monthly cycle?"

"Well" I started, "I think I am in generally good health. I have had a few sore throats and the odd toothache or two, but nothing that I could not cope with and resolve with a good gargle. Nothing else at all with the specifics you mention." Dr. Cotton rose from his desk chair, "Would you mind if I took a look at your teeth and tonsils?" he enquired, "Come and sit over here on my torture chair, in the light where I can see better." His use of the words 'torture chair', that's what it looked like and that's how it felt as I sat with my head tilted back onto the headrest, was deeply unsettling.

He prodded and poked in my mouth and apologized when a small groan escaped as he inspected one particularly troublesome tooth. He felt under my chin and down the length of my neck. He looked deep in my throat as I said, 'Aaaah' at his command. When he was finished, he was all softness and thoughtful; "That will do very nicely Miss Maher" he said. "Come and sit down again next to your brother and we can then consider what might be wrong and how we might set about to resolve your situation".

He seemed deep in thought for a long period of time, making notes and behaving as though we were not there. Eventually he looked up and said, "I am going to give you a brief explanation of my conclusions and then propose a course of treatment, if that is acceptable to you". Of course, it was; that was why we were here after all. We said nothing.

"Firstly, let me say that your drinking of this illegal alcohol is a very serious problem for you and one that you should give the highest attention to. I understand when you say that you think you have your consumption of alcohol under control, but believe me when I say this self-deception is common amongst heavy drinkers; I don't think your drinking is under control at all. You are just inured to its effects and are increasingly able to function apparently quite normally while being seriously intoxicated. This is common with alcohol-dependent individuals."

I began to protest, expressing my innocence of any tendency to heavy drinking. He spoke over me.

"You should not feel that drinking is 'your fault' and that you are to blame in any way; circumstances have conspired to bring you to this point where you have come from a successful career to this lesser state of affairs where your body craves alcohol.

"What I think is going on here is caused by infection; I have come to term it 'focal infection'. In your case, and we would need to undertake further more detailed tests and examinations, I believe that the root of the problem is an infection focused on your teeth and possibly your tonsils as well. You know how tender your teeth are and how painful at times; this signals to me a serious infection that has spread through the blood stream and has started to impact on your brain function. This focal infection means that your brain has started to react unusually and that this causes the aberrations in behavior you have described to me."

"Are you suggesting" Joseph asked, "that you believe that my sister's drinking has been brought on by toothache?" He felt there was a certain logic in what had been offered, but it seemed a long way to him between toothache and taking to the hooch. "Yes, I am", Dr. Cotton replied "I understand how this suggestion might come as a shock to you, it is new medical thinking that has emerged from a recent sea-change in our understanding of perturbations of the brain. If you think for a moment how we have conventionally treated patients exhibiting these sorts of symptoms, we have locked them up, often using restraints, and thrown away the key. How different our institutions would be if we understood that we needed to effect a cure of the patient's focal infections in order to cure them and release them to return to their normal life."

My brother, who had been taking extensive notes throughout the interview interjected again. "Can I ask how you would cure the infection in Annie's tooth?" he asked. "Well there is only one sure way", explained Dr. Cotton, "we would remove the infected teeth". Now it was my turn, "Teeth?" I exclaimed, "I thought you said there was an infection in one tooth". "We have no way of knowing until we begin the treatment", he said, "in some cases the removal of a single tooth might be sufficient, but what we are trying to achieve here is a return to the steady state. If we remove a single tooth and the infection reoccurs elsewhere in the gums, then we will have squandered an opportunity. To avoid any reocurrence and to give you peace of mind about the future, I would suggest that we remove all of your teeth."

I sat back shocked and exhausted by his explanation. Again, it was my brother who intervened: "How do you go about the task of extracting all of someone's teeth?" "In my experience, though in the short term it might seem painful, the most effective way is to remove all the teeth in one sitting. Of course, there would be proper medical and nursing care during the procedure and, after any short-term pain, within a week the gums will begin to heal and leave a mouth clear of any current or recurrent focal infection. Your sister's problems, after a short period perhaps of 3 months, will have been resolved. I predict that her drinking problems will go away and that she may find it easy to give up alcohol altogether.

"If she's had all her teeth taken out, how does she eat?" asked Joseph quizzing Cotton again. "In the short term that is difficult and basically, after a few days of diet, Miss Maher would be able to take in food that had been pulped so that no chewing was necessary. Once the gums had completely healed one option would be to have a set of dentures, that is false teeth, made and fitted. They are advancing all the time in this type of restorative dentistry, and after only a relatively brief period Miss Maher would be looking like her old self".

"Can you give an absolute guarantee of success? Joseph asked. "Well there are no 'absolutes' in medical treatments" he said, "for example the focal infection might have spread further and affected the tonsils and adenoids; you heard your sister's complaints of a recurring sore throat." Joseph, asking the question close to my lips, "And what would you suggest if the infection had spread in this way?" After a brief pause for thought, "Well, again, like the teeth there is only one way to fully resolve the problem and that is through surgical intervention; the extraction of tonsils and adenoids.

A silence settled over the room like a storm cloud.

Now it was my turn; I stood and held out my hand to him, "May I thank you Dr. Cotton for such an interesting and thought-provoking consultation. I think the matter needs further consideration, so my brother and I will take our leave of you, and we will discuss with you later as to how we think we should proceed." Joseph too now rose to his feet, shook hands and we left.

We had been with Dr. Cotton for almost an hour; we paid for his time when he presented us with his invoice before we got to the front door. Neither of us could face the journey back to Long Branch and so we found a hotel in Trenton that was happy to serve us some refreshments in their comfortable lounge so that we could chat. Neither of us, at that point, had given any clue as to our reaction to the consultation.

As our order was taken and we were left alone I did say to Joseph, "Tea is fine for me but, do you know, I feel as though a very stiff drink is what I really need." We laughed out loud, and Joseph retorted, "Shhh, Dr. Cotton may be listening!" More laughter.

After our tea had been delivered and we were alone again, I asked Joseph directly what he thought. There was a long pause for consideration. "My answer might differ if I felt there was any indication that Dr. Cotton's treatment would lead to a good result, with you feeling better in yourself and losing your current state of confusion. I was shocked at his radical proposal and felt his methods were bordering on the barbaric."

I was so delighted at his response which mirrored mine entirely, I leaned across and hugged him in my arms and found myself gently weeping on his shoulder.

We decided that it would be appropriate that my brother write to Dr. Cotton to tell him our decision about treatment under his care; it was, after all, my brother's acquaintance with Dr. Cotton that had given rise to the consultation. He wrote to Dr. Cotton that evening.

"Long Branch, New Jersey

Monday November 6th 1922

Dear Dr. Cotton,

I write first to thank you for seeing us both today. I greatly appreciate your time and effort in conducting the consultation so thoroughly.

"My sister and I have spoken at length about her condition and it seems to me that the acceptance that there is a problem is the first step towards a remedy. We have, and will continue to seek, methods and support for her while she recovers.

"Your proposition of a focal infection lying at the heart of her problems was an interesting one. We shall certainly follow closely the development of those ideas.

"However, surgery, perhaps even radical surgery as you have described to us, seems to offer the prospect of a cure but needs to be set against the painful, disfiguring remedy that you propose.

"With this in mind, I should like to politely refuse your offer of treatment for my sister and wish you well in the future.

"Yours faithfully
Joseph P. Maher"

Joseph stayed with me at Long Branch for a further two weeks and we were able to catch up. In the time he was with me he insisted that I should rest and allow him to look after me. I lay in bed for the first few mornings and was brought breakfast on a tray. Each day when I emerged at about noon, he had already cleaned and tidied the house. When I expressed surprise at his diligence he explained that it was a habit he had learned while working with mariners. "You don't have much space in crew's quarters on board, so it's a function of necessity and you just get into the habit".

Joseph had remained single all this time and was now 44 years old. He had however met what he called a very nice girl, Mary Catherine

Hyland, in Shanghai. She was originally from Dublin but went out with her parents when her father found employment there. Mary was a teacher; there was now a very large population of foreign workers who had flooded into the city as the Far Eastern trade links built up. English-speaking schools, modeled on the English curriculum, were favored by these usually affluent families. Joseph Paul Maher would go on to marry Mary Catherine Hyland on March 26th, 1927, when he was 49 years old.

CHAPTER 43

When You Need Family

IT HAD BEEN an ominously quiet period since Joseph had gone.

Letters were infrequent and it was thus a great surprise for me to receive an envelope. It was from my sister Mary, now a teaching nun in Ohio, and was reminiscent of the first letter I had from her almost 36 years previously, telling me she was coming to the U.S.A. from Kent. She was now Sister Dorothea, though in some settings it was permissible to use her family name as well, so my sister Mary Maher had transformed into Sister Dorothea (Maher).

She explained that her Mother House was in Ohio, but that she had been teaching most recently in their school in New York. As a consequence, she had kept in touch with the New York O'Briens and was a regular visitor to the O'Brien household. Further, she was in regular correspondence with the family in Kent and kept everyone there up to date with the lives of the U.S.A. family members.

What she proposed was that she and our two cousins from the O'Brien family, Josephine and Margaret, might come to Long Branch for a weekend so that we could spend time together. They had each visited separately but this time was the first where they were to come in numbers. I dreaded the prospect; not only was I out of the habit of entertaining but I felt anxious about their seeing the changes in me.

They traveled from New York by train and I had told them that, as the station was just at the back of the house, I would be waiting for them on the porch when they walked up the pathway. The greeting was warm and tactile. We spent a long time chatting and catching up.

Margaret was now married and as Mrs. George Higgins had 4 children. Her younger sister Josephine O'Brien had married William Cox and so far she was childless. Sister Dorothea had done well as a teaching nun and found great joy and fulfilment in caring for young people. In turn, children seemed to embrace her and took great delight in her company.

I had changed the linen on three beds and had shown them to their rooms; they seemed quite content with their accommodation. Sister

Dorothea had asked for some quiet, private time and had stopped in her room, while Josephine and Margaret joined me downstairs.

Annie from next door had, as suggested, waited a decent interval before she came in through the kitchen entrance and joined us in the lounge. When we talked it through, we were concerned that I might need rescuing from my relatives by then. However, Margaret and Josephine seemed to have warmed to Annie, as I had on our very first meeting.

They were intrigued by stories of Con Gaskin. We explained that our neighbor was one of the most adept suppliers of illegal booze. Attempts had been made to drive out the demon-drink, through stiff regulation and taxation while calls for Prohibition were growing louder. Where there was a thirsty market, ways could be found to provide the illicit alcohol. Con's favored method was to go into the distilling business.

Alcohol sale was now prohibited with increasing enforcement of Prohibition by the police. However, there was money to be made from such ventures and criminal gangs often sought to profit from the trade.

Con had his own recipe, for what he called "Distilled Wisdom", and he would sell it in flagons to a select market of locals. Annie Hall was part of Con's marketplace and she would take regular deliveries that she would store, hidden in the cellar.

Sister Dorothea joined us and after introductions she said to me, "Annie, I wanted to go for a walk by the sea; can you come with me and show me the sights?" This figure, dressed head to toe in black, this rather serious and austere person who generated a deferential response in me and, I suspect in all of us present, was my younger sister, almost 10 years my junior. Yet she spoke with such authority and determination that it didn't occur to me to do other than meet her request with enthusiasm.

We walked out onto Ocean Avenue and turned left and along to Sea View Avenue, then right and thus down towards the water's edge; less than 500 yards from my front door. The Grand View Hotel was at the end of Sea View Avenue on the ocean; it was visible from my house, and represented the fading glory that was this part of Long Branch. The boardwalk extended south from the hotel and we turned onto it south along the shoreline. It was such a great way to see the ocean and feel the cool breezes.

I explained about the vulnerability of the coastline to storms and even hurricanes that annually moved northward from the Caribbean Sea.

One recent storm had washed away 200 feet of sand in front of the Grand View Hotel.

My sister was calm and encouraged me to talk. We found a wooden bench to sit on quietly from which to watch the sea and the waves; it was the same bench that Joseph and I had sat upon only a short while ago. There was virtually nobody else around and at that time we were content with the companionable silence interrupted only by the sights and sounds of the waves and gulls. The tranquility brought back strong memories of the peaceful Fall break that I took in Long Branch at Wright's Cottage, with Georgiana, Nellie, De Forrest and Adele.

Prompted by her I found myself disclosing details of my lifetime that I had never shared with anyone. About the fun and the sadness in my time with Georgiana and her family, and with Adele. I spoke in detail about the travel arrangements I had made and the places we had visited in Europe and Africa and then across the U.S.A. and Canada. She remembered my portrait photograph that I had professionally taken in Halifax, Nova Scotia, and then posted back to the family in Kent. She wistfully remembered how father had made a wooden frame for it and that it sat on the high mantelpiece in the living room, like an icon. She also revealed how that picture had inspired her to think further afield when considering her lifetime's future, rather than to confine herself to local interests; in that, we were not that much different, Mary and I, though a decade apart.

She asked me "How are you feeling, coping after the death of Georgiana and the departure of Adele?" I tried to explain that I had managed by withdrawing into myself a little. About how trusted and trusting was my relationship with my neighbor Annie Hall but that I was basically doing fine.

"No" she said, "I mean how are you really feeling?" I just stared at her in disbelief for a while; then uncontrollable tears; tears that flowed down my cheeks and dripped onto the boardwalk. I could not speak, there were just tears at first. Then slowly began the convulsions of my sadness, eventually my whole upper body shook and I was crouched over almost in a fetal position with my head and shaking shoulders tucked onto my knees, and endless tears.

Sister Dorothea reached for me with both hands. She took me and drew me to her, with my head on her shoulder and my grasp around her back. We were like that for what seemed an eternity, perhaps an hour or more. No words, just the tears and the comforting embrace. When it was over and my tears and shivering had subsided, I felt tired and drained; but very fragile as if the simplest touch would push me over the edge again. Not what I wanted; I had been to the edge of that particular precipice and the endless depths, I did not want to go there again. We sat and looked into each other's faces, again for a very long time. Sister Dorothea's smile had broken out and it warmed me back towards reality.

"We must talk about your other problem" she softly inserted. I found it so hard to do that, but reassured by Sister Dorothea's calm matter-of-factness, I was able to own up to the confusion that I now felt. I explained that the effects seemed to be an intermittent problem, like today and my perfect recall of facts.

"Joseph wrote to me after his last visit", she explained, "he was worried about you". From somewhere out of nothing something snapped in me; was it a sense that Joseph had betrayed my trust? I stood suddenly and then stalked off back home.

When I slammed in through the screen door, the background noise of voices was suddenly still and as I walked into the living room, my cousins, and Annie Hall were gaping at me. I slammed the door as I left the room and made my way upstairs just as Sister Dorothea got back; I went into my room and I slammed the door again, leaning against it for support and breathless from the exertion and the emotional energy.

It was then that it struck me how uncharacteristic my behavior had been; I had been known for my calmness under pressure and was credited with a serenity that was absent now. Slamming doors? I can't remember, in the whole of my life, doing such a thing. And even though she was my sister, shouting at Sister Dorothea? I could not believe myself and what could have prompted such an outburst.

I crossed my room and threw myself face down on the bed; no tears now, just exhaustion. I don't remember the act of falling asleep at all but, as I stirred, dusk was falling and in the semi-darkness the sound of the ocean seemed to be the only noise. If there is true isolation and loneliness, then I felt it there and then.

When eventually I made my way back down the stairs, the house was silent and empty. Again, the feelings of abandonment flooded over me. I wandered outside onto the veranda and there, the shadowy figure of Sister Dorothea was rocking gently on the glider. "Why don't you come and sit by me?" she suggested, tapping on the empty space to her left. I walked across and settled down onto the cushion. It was quiet, save for the distant sound of seagulls and a dog barking nearby.

"Your neighbor has gone home," she explained "and our cousins have gone up to bed. They could see that you needed space, but send you their love and say how lovely your Long Branch home is and they look forward to seeing you in the morning." I didn't reply.

It was growing chilly, and we went inside. "Should we have some tea?" she asked. I dutifully made a typical pot of English tea, warming the pot, three teaspoonsful of tea leaves, left it to stand while the tea brewed, and then poured out two cups, just as we would have done in Kent.

As we sat at the kitchen table, we found a way to talk openly again. Sister Dorothea's kindness shone from her and she was clearly used to leading a life where the needs of others came first. She didn't admonish, but instead asked questions. These were the questions I had to face up to and attempt to answer.

I took time to apologize to her for my earlier behavior. "How could I have been so spiteful, truculent, rude to you, and so inhospitable to my New York cousins? I am so very sorry." "You are not to worry my dear", she responded in her soft voice. "It never happened."

In those first exchanges, we shared memories of Kent and the family. Of the heartache and the loss as we were growing up. Sister Dorothea was surprised that I still had memories of Ireland, leaving there at just 4 years of age. Clonmel was a memorable place with its walled and fortified town, I remembered the Drugstore, also run by Mahers, in the center of the high street and the toy shop; here I would stand fascinated and just look. There were displays of doll's houses, dolls and prams, glass marbles and jacks. I would look, but not ask of course.

We came inevitably to the matter of religion and faith. In answer to her question I explained that I had observed so much tragedy and hardship in my life to date, witnessed the insufferable things that one human being was able to inflict on another, that I could not imagine how any God would allow it. I noted Dorothea's life of abstinence and celibacy; I told her that I too in my way had taken similar vows early on.

I had never found a man, perhaps with the exception of De Forrest Bolmer, for whom I felt any physical attraction. In a way, De Forrest's gentle manner had the same attractive qualities that I found so endearing about Georgiana and Adele. Together, as we had been at Wright's Cottage, for example, we were like a close-knit group of kindred spirits; gender did not enter into it and the strong sense of mutual attraction worked on a number of levels.

She talked for the first time of her life in the convent; there was a single-mindedness within the group and a dedication to Christ and to the lives of the young people He had put in their hands. She conceded too that she was part of a strong bond that existed between the Sisters. They would do anything for each other and would support each other during moments of crisis. It was certainly something of the sort that bound my troupe of friends together though the background motivations were very different.

We came back to the question of my health. "I don't have a drink problem" I explained again; "I hardly drank at all when I was working". I had to admit that since moving to Long Branch, surrounded by people who did drink, it would have been very easy to succumb; Catherine Barnwell and Annie Hall, the Gaskin family, (the provider of much of our illicit stocks), the fishermen at the shore would spend a lot of their time with the bottle; but I had not given myself up to that life.

It had been one occasion, just one glass of some illicit spirit that seemed to have affected me so badly. I owned up to periods of confusion, of lost periods of time that I just couldn't account for, and fluctuations of temperament, as earlier that day when I had seemed to lose control. I was glad now to be able to talk openly about it.

My visitors were due to return to New York the following day, but not before we had shared breakfast together. I was much more relaxed and was able to concentrate on Margaret's and Josephine's stories of their lives and of their families.

We were on the platform of Long Branch just before mid-day; we embraced as the train pulled to a halt. One last hug from Sister Dorothea; "God bless you my dear; may His love go with you." "And with you" I replied. The train pulled away and my feelings were very much like how I had felt at the station at Sheerness in Kent, when I had left my former life behind me. I wondered now what this new life would look like and for how long. As Sister Dorothea, Margaret and Josephine pulled away from Long Branch station on their return to New York, I did not know then what a pivotal role all three of them would play in my life over the next decade.

CHAPTER 44

The Arrest

I WAS APPARENTLY found lying at the side of the road in Long Branch late in the evening on March 18th 1924. Two patrol officers took me back to the sheriff's office.

I may have been semiconscious and my invective incomprehensible but I managed to put up a brave attempt to fight them off. They carried and pulled me into one of the open cells, bare except for a narrow wooden bed and a chair; a chamber pot sat beneath the chair for the convenience of residents.

I fell to the floor, groaning as the door of the cell was closed and locked by my captors and they left me alone. Using the bars on the doors I hauled myself to my feet and screamed so loudly it echoed around the whole building. When no answer came, I picked up the wooden chair and smashed it against the bars sending wooden splinters scattering across the floor of the cell and the anteroom.

I collapsed back onto the floor and my whole world went dark, and then black.

As I came to, much later, my head was spinning and the room would not stay still. I was conscious suddenly of another person in the room, sitting on the edge of the bed, watching me try to restore some sense of decorum.

"Well, Miss Maher", came the disembodied voice, "we meet again". As I stared up at the face before me, and tried to focus, there was a growing familiarity in the features I saw.

"You remember me? It's Dr. Cotton".

My sharp intake of breath came with the realization of who this man was and what that might mean for me. I screamed again as loudly as I could muster, "No! No!" The two patrol officers rushed in half-expecting to see Dr. Cotton under attack. Instead he sat impassively on the bed just observing.

"There's a straightjacket in the bag, if you would be kind enough to get it out for me" he said. "We are going to need to restrain her in order to get her to Trenton." I heard those dreaded words and began screaming again and fighting with all my might as they tried to get the restraining garment on. My arms seemed twice the length with the spare sleeve-material extending towards the floor, then each arm was dragged across my body and the end of the sleeves tied behind my back rendering me completely defenseless.

"You had better sit her down on the floor for her own safety" Dr. Cotton instructed. He left the cell to talk to Sheriff George Roberts. They were in the next room, but the door was open and I could hear every lie and distortion. "Yes, she is known to me, and she is a lunatic who is a danger to herself and others". How could he lie like this about me? "I will instruct two of my staff, Dr. John C. Clayton and Dr. Harvey S. Brown, to attend here in the next few hours to make a formal assessment for the record. First thing in the morning, even if you have to wake him, get the Judge to swear an order for committal to Trenton on the grounds of lunacy. When that's done bring her up to the hospital and I will take over from there. In the meantime, she is restrained and you will find she quietens down and will be more easily managed.

Rather than being easy to manage, I spent the next several hours protesting loudly. On the arrival of the two doctors, I would not allow them near me and, even though restrained, I could still kick out and head-butt anyone who came within my range.

I was admitted to a mental institution on March 19th 1924; the State Hospital, Trenton. My Committal Hearing was before Rulif V. Lawrence, the Judge of the Common Pleas Court, and I was shipped there to attend the hearing. The Judge barely acknowledged my presence, but he noted that the institution "had been directed to enquire as to the sanity of the said Annie Maher". In the interim I was to be held temporarily at the State Hospital.

The judge concluded, "And it appears to me from the certificates aforesaid, and from the testimony of the witness aforesaid, that the said Annie Maher is insane and that she be committed and confined in the New Jersey State Hospital permanently or until restored to her right mind or until further order of a court of competent jurisdiction".

I returned to my senses slowly, and as my sensibilities returned I realized what had happened in the last 24 hours. I had had one of those missing periods in my memory. I do not know how or why Dr. Cotton had been asked to attend, but he seemed to be intent on proving my incapacity. Was this all because of Joseph and my rejection of his proposed treatment of my problem in that letter of November 6th? Surely not, it made no sense.

Here I was though, with the Court's permission, confined to Trenton Asylum, to be assessed by Dr. Cotton and his associates as to my sanity.

CHAPTER 45

Committal June 1924

I AWOKE ON June 21st in a strange new world, in a small room, lying on a bed, the cream-painted walls rising high above me. On the end wall, the bars on the window could not keep out the bright sunlight that poured through the glass. No restraints, no straightjacket, the door was slightly ajar.

Dr. Cotton entered the room and pulled up a chair next to my bed. I was apoplectic; all I could remember were his statements about the treatments he had described to Joseph and me, so indelibly had they been seared into my memory: "Remove the teeth and tonsils and any other part where infection might lurk".

I felt my only recourse now was to shout and scream in the hope that he might be deterred. I shouted all the names of people who had cared for me and who had loved me, the living and the dead, and pleaded to them to help me. I thought it had the desired effect as, and without a word, Dr. Cotton got up and left.

I took myself, unsteadily, to crouch near the corner of the room furthest from the door. Two orderlies entered and came across towards me. They tried to raise me to my feet at which point I punched, bit and shouted with all my might. A heavy fist struck me across the face and I sank into unconsciousness. When I woke, I felt dreadful, in a dreamlike state without really understanding where I was or what had happened. I instinctively put my hand to my face and felt the swelling and bruising around my right eye socket. My eye was almost closed and what vision I enjoyed was blurred.

What had roused me was the arrival of the same two orderlies. When they lifted me this time I was unable to resist. I was pulled out of the room and along the corridor, with my feet dragging along the floor behind me. I was roughly dragged into another room where I was dumped unceremoniously into a chair to sit on the opposite side of the desk to Dr. Cotton. The two orderlies stood guard, one on either side of the doorway, as if to prevent me from escaping; not that I was capable of doing that.

It was Dr. Cotton who began; "Annie Maher, it is some time since you and your brother visited me isn't it?" I could only groan in response. This then was about his ego, and taking revenge for having his ideas, about how he might treat me, firmly rejected. 'Well then, I am commissioned by the court to make an assessment of your state and propose a course of treatment".

"No! No!!" I screamed again as I tried to stand; I fell headlong across the floor. The two orderlies intervened hoisting me to my feet again; I struggled again to no avail. "Take her back" was Dr. Cotton's instruction and I was removed equally unceremoniously, though not without resistance, to my room where I was flung on the bed. I hit my head on the wall on the far side of the bed as I went down, and again slipped into unconsciousness.

I woke, though I could not tell how long I had been like that. I now suspected that in my unconscious state, at least on two occasions, I had been drugged. I could see needle marks on my left arm and that confirmed for me what had been happening. I became aware that I had been put into some sort of utilitarian hospital gown, open all the way down the rear.

Suddenly I became aware of figures in the doorway. Two, different, orderlies were looking down at me. "Time for some treatment for you Annie" one of them threatened. My practiced response was immediate; I screamed and shouted and as they approached me I hit out as best I could, biting and scratching whatever flesh I could reach. They had brought reinforcements this time and two women in nurse's uniform came to their aid and they had me prone and laid out as they grabbed a limb each. They carried me like that down the length of two long corridors; all that time I screamed and shouted, twisting my body violently trying to escape their grip.

I became aware of a sympathetic wailing from other rooms along our route. It seemed in response to the noise I was making, but it built into a cacophony of sound that bounced off the walls of the corridors. Was this Hell?

Large double doors opened in front of us to reveal a treatment room. In the center of that room was a large leather-bound chair with a high seat and it had a headrest, arms and footrest, all with restraints. I feared what was coming and made one last great effort to avoid it. I writhed and screamed but to no avail. They forced me into the chair and secured a wide leather belt around my middle that fixed behind the chair. Then in turn each wrist was strapped to the armrest and then each ankle to the legs of the chair. I was now almost totally immobilized, only my head free to move. Then they lowered from above a skull-cap like contraption made of brass, onto my head to prevent that final movement. The headrest was leaned back sharply so that my throat was pulled tight and my mouth partially open; it was excruciatingly uncomfortable. The final indignity came with the wodge of material they stuffed into my mouth to stifle any further noise I might want to make.

It all became quiet, as if waiting for something; that transpired to be Dr. Cotton who walked into the room wearing a cavernous green gown and a red rubber apron that covered him from neck to ankles. The two nurses stepped forward and produced a trolley with a tray of implements. "Now Annie, I know this is not what you want, and it may be painful, but it is for your long-term good and it will, I am sure, make you better."

The material in my mouth was removed and before I could react it was replaced with a rubber wedge that was placed so as to force my mouth wide open. Dr. Cotton approached with what looked like pliers. He started with my upper jaw, and I felt the cold tool as it closed and fixed on one of my front teeth. With an upward pushing and twisting motion he tore the tooth from my gum with an accompanying pain that made my heart rate increase and my screams gurgle from my throat.

I felt liquid running down my chin and down my throat. Dr. Cotton worked quickly and efficiently around my mouth removing each tooth one by one. The pain became too much and I drifted in and out of consciousness. Even in this state of semi-consciousness I was vaguely aware of the manipulation of my head, mouth and jaw. Jets of water washed away the blood and debris and after 30 minutes of unbelievable pain, physical and emotional trauma, he was finished.

I felt the restraints being removed and, as with my arrival, my limbs were used to carry me back along the corridor.

From 1924 to 1926, I was subjected to Dr. Cotton's Assessment of my Insanity. My transformation from being occasionally confused to being classed as incompetent and insane had been swift, unexpected and unjustified.

Those two years were to include further surgical procedures and invasive investigations that stripped me of all dignity.

On June 14th 1926, just over two years after being incarcerated, a medical history Affidavit by Dr. Henry A. Cotton, Superintendent of the New Jersey State Hospital for the Insane at Trenton, New Jersey read as follows:

"Henry A. Cotton, of full age, being duly sworn according to law, on his oath deposes and says that he is the superintendent of the New Jersey State Hospital for the Insane at Trenton, New Jersey and, acting in such capacity, he is charged with the care of all patients in said asylum; that one Annie Maher is an inmate of said asylum having been admitted on the on March 21st 1924 upon the certificates of John C. Clayton and Harvey S. Brown, two reputable physicians residing in this state, and has since been continuously confined therein as an insane patient.

"Deponent further says that Annie Maher is insane and by reason thereof the said Annie Maher is in no way capable of governing herself or her estate; that the following is a full medical history of the said Annie Maher while confined in the state asylum.

"Patient admitted to hospital March 21st 1924, giving a history of being mentally incompetent for the past seven or eight years, during which time she had indulged in alcohol to excess. In order to procure alcohol would sell furniture, and she also had hallucinations of sight, saying that a bad man and woman removed these household articles. Three months prior to admission, she had been using alcohol continuously. At the time of this examination there is no change in her mental condition. Provisional diagnosis, "Chronic Alcoholic Intoxication"."

This was such a perversion of the facts that it would hardly withstand scrutiny. Yet where was the corroboration of the truth to be found? I had, for those two years, been refused access to family or friends, and had no access to writing materials so I could not communicate with the outside world.

It was on the basis of these factually inaccurate and incorrect reports that on June 28th 1926 Judge V. Lawrence made an "Order of Commitment of Annie E. Maher to be held as a lunatic at the State Hospital at Trenton".

CHAPTER 46

The Caretakers

I LIVED, AS if in a nightmare. This place, Trenton Hospital for the Insane, was my new home, but for how long? I was in the grip of a system that would not willingly let me go.

The medical staff were focused on Dr. Cotton's brutal procedures; I heard the screams of other in-patients who were dragged from their cells to the operating theaters; these routine noises were heart-rending. Patients knew what surgery meant; the use of ether, or at times no attempt to anaesthetize the patient. The extraction of all my teeth had been undertaken with no anesthetic at all. I had been strapped to a chair, my head restrained and my mouth wedged open so that Dr. Cotton could access my teeth with his pliers.

My strategy was clear; I would deter the medical staff from considering doing procedures on me by screaming, shouting, scratching anyone in a white coat who came near me. This proved to be quite effective and after a while they seemed to give up on me. They had removed my teeth and removed my tonsils, and I was determined that they would have no more of me.

Eventually I was moved from the medical wing and put into a ward with a total of about 30 other patients. We were a sorry sight and some of the poor souls here had been incarcerated for 10 or 20 years. We had in common the sunken sallow faces of patients whose teeth had been extracted. We were the lucky ones; invasive surgery on some patients had left them terminally injured and they never escaped to the relative peace of this place. Most on the ward allowed themselves to be victims of the institution and had given up hope of ever recovering from the traumas that they had been subjected to, or of being released.

All of my affairs were now to be dealt with through the Monmouth County Orphans' Court, and the Courts required that I be served with all papers relating to my case, and so I was able to follow proceedings though it would prove very difficult to challenge any of the outcomes of those deliberations.

Subsequently a search was made for my next of kin and three names were put forward. My sister, Sister Dorothea, residing at St. Mark's Convent Sheepshead Bay, New York. Then from my maternal family, the O'Briens: my second cousins, Margaret Higgins (nee O'Brien) of 582 East 4th Street, Brooklyn in the City of New York and Josephine Cox (nee O'Brien) 8203 6th Avenue, Brooklyn, New York. The three of them had previously made that trip to Long Branch to see me and to see if help was needed.

By the time of the court case, Josephine and Sister Dorothea renounced their right of my guardianship in preference to Margaret. They all agreed that Sister Dorothea could not devote the necessary time to the task and that, of the two cousins, Margaret was the older, more practically minded and used to such legal dealings; they requested of the court that Margaret be appointed as my Guardian. On September 2nd 1926, Judge Jacob Steinbach Jnr. "ordered that guardianship of said Annie Maher be committed to the said Margaret Higgins".

Her main task was to represent me in the courts and to manage my homes, property and money. On that date in 1926, the courts had assessed my total wealth, including all my real-estate, as being valued at $24,800. I had no idea where that figure came from and it was undoubtedly too low. Either they had just got their sums wrong, or someone had stolen from me. I was not in a position to challenge their conclusions, not least because during "my period of assessment", which had gone on for over two years, I was denied any access to my family or friends.

"The letters of guardianship to be issued accordingly upon which the said Margaret Higgins shall enter into bond to the Ordinary in the sum of Twenty-four thousand eight hundred dollars ($24,800) conditioned for the faithful execution of her office according to law, which bond shall be first approved by this court."

Apparently, Margaret failed to act as the courts required; she did not submit accounts to the court on time, or at all. It was telling that during the whole of her period as "Guardian" she did not visit me at all, neither did her sister Josephine. Only my own sister Mary, Sister Dorothea, made efforts to help me.

While I was in that state of limbo, subject to Dr. Cotton's assessment over two years, and unable to have any communication with my family, it was Sister Dorothea who tried to find out about me and to get reports on my condition. It was from newspaper reports that she learned of another Doctor who had been sent in to Trenton to assess the claims made for the success of Dr. Cotton's treatments. Reading between the lines, Sister Dorothea concluded that Dr. Greenacre was skeptical about what had been going on at Trenton and resolved to make contact with her and ask for her help.

In fact, the responsible body was The Columbia Casualty Company, a corporation of the State of New York, duly authorized and licensed to transact business in the State of New Jersey; it was they who would monitor Margaret Higgin's enactment of her obligations as Guardian of Annie Maher. Margaret held these responsibilities, rather incompetently, for 11 years before eventually being relieved of her Guardianship by the courts on June 21st 1935.

The role of Guardian was then assigned to Harry Truax of Elberon on June 22nd 1935. He retained this role and, except for a brief period, remained my guardian to the point when I was finally adjudged to be profoundly insane, and the money ran out.

CHAPTER 47

Doctor Greenacre

AFTER THE COMMITTAL hearing, I was permitted to receive visits from Sister Dorothea, and it was she who told me about Dr. Greenacre. Even before the embargo on family visits was lifted, Sister Dorothea learned that Doctor Greenacre arrived at Trenton just months after I had been confined there. She determined to try to elicit some detail about my condition and care from Dr. Greenacre, rather than from the Trenton administration who had provided only bland, noncommittal responses to her many enquiries.

Greenacre and Cotton had studied under Meyer. A strange chemistry existed, and was to persist, between the esteemed Prof. Adolf Meyer, Dr. Henry Cotton and Dr. Phyllis Greenacre. Adolf Meyer supported and promoted Cotton and his working practices throughout, even though the evidence presented by Cotton became increasingly suspect.

Greenacre on the other hand was hugely skeptical and wanted the opportunity to assess the extraordinary claims of success made by Dr. Cotton and the Board of Trenton.

In his period at the Trenton Asylum, Dr. Cotton had made great claims for his work there. Based on the idea that he outlined to Joseph and me, that of Focal Infection affecting different organs in the body and thence moving on to infect the brain, his thesis that surgical intervention to remove those organs that harbored the infections seemed eminently logical. When he was able to provide statistical evidence showing that his recovery rates in dealing with patients in this way were hugely better than conventional methodologies, he became a celebrity within his field. Adolf Meyer rarely questioned Dr. Cotton's work or published results; only Phyllis Greenacre chose to investigate and then challenge his claims, but then she was only a woman!

Adolph Mayer's approach to Dr. Greenacre was dramatically different from the way he dealt with Dr. Cotton, and he seemed to frustrate her at every turn. His only gesture towards her, perhaps from a feeling of guilt, was to help her secure a post at the Cornell Medical Center in New York.

His greatest sin was, later, to suppress Dr. Greencare's critical work on Cotton's procedures at Trenton, for had he not done so he might have saved many lives. He did however facilitate Greenacre's "academic study" at Trenton and, very reluctantly, Dr. Cotton agreed to it.

That's why in the Fall of 1924, after a short delay since her arrival in July, Phyllis Greenacre began her work studying the record of Dr. Cotton. This was a very sensitive issue, and she had to maintain a professional relationship with Dr. Cotton. However, her three-part study was bound to throw into the spotlight the claims made by Dr. Cotton and the realities in the institution.

In desperation for news of me, Sister Dorothea wrote to Dr. Greenacre in September 1926, to ask if her sister had been one of those she had studied.

Her reply was very kind and helpful, though not at all reassuring; my sister shared her letter with me on one of her visits.

Trenton

Monday 6th September 1926

Dear Sister Dorothea,

As you may know, I am a researcher working as part of Dr. Meyer's team and have been asked to evaluate the extraordinary results emerging from Dr. Cotton's work at Trenton.

The group that I have studied were admitted before your sister, Annie Elizabeth Maher, became a patient at Trenton so she is not included in any of my research work.

However, your enquiry did prompt me to seek her out and to make an assessment of her condition for you. However, this report must remain confidential between the two of us and has no standing in the treatment, or the recording, of your sister's case at Trenton. It will not be lodged at Trenton as an official assessment of Annie Maher's condition.

I will first describe her physical condition.

Annie Elizabeth Maher is in a poor physical condition; I am told that some of this injury to her person was caused prior to her arrest in 1924. She has been crippled by an injury to her right knee which appears to have suffered some trauma. The joint is clearly painful and movement in it restricted. This makes walking difficult and her gait awkward.

I noted swelling to the right eye socket, cuts and abrasions to her arms and body, which are healing slowly. There appear to have been different sequences of injuries over time, since the rates of healing are different across the range of injuries I saw. I am told that Annie has periods of extreme violence including self-harm and attacks on other patients and staff members. In these fits of violence and the attempts to restrain her, I am told that she has accrued this series of injuries.

As part of her treatment during the assessment and in an attempt to cure her, several operations have been carried out. Firstly, since the clinical assessment seemed to identify the teeth as the site of focal infection, all of her teeth were removed. The gums have healed but, of course, her facial shape has changed due to the loss of teeth and her diet has been modified because of the difficulty she now finds in eating solids. As a result, she has experienced considerable weight loss. Following the teeth removal and with no significant improvement in her condition, an operation was performed to remove her tonsils; after the two operations to remove teeth and to remove her tonsils vaccine was also administered. These vaccines, made by a local pharmaceutical firm, "Squibb's Laboratories", are used to boost the immune system and help the body to fight infection.

Since then, and with still no clear improvement in her condition, two other possibilities have been considered. A cervical infection had been diagnosed and the enucleation of the cervix is being actively considered. There is also a concern for a different focal infection in the bowel and consideration is being given to possible surgical intervention to remove the source of that problem.

Annie Maher's mental and emotional condition:

When I visited, her she was initially curled on her bed, rocking and groaning quietly. She became much more agitated when she realized I was there, screamed and lashed out, and seemed fearful. I spoke with her quietly, asking after her wellbeing; her responses were largely inaudible though she used the same words and phrases repeatedly. From what I could gather she seemed to be saying, "Star of the Sea" and "They have all my money". She repeated names too saying, "George Yana", "Joseph" and "Manuel"; however, there must be serious doubt about her mental capability and concerns for some form of dementia.

You will be pleased to learn that when I mentioned your name, "Sister Dorothea" it did provoke a response from her. Her face lit up and she seemed to repeat, "Mary-Alice" which I guess might mean something to you.

That is all I can report at the moment, but when I am at Trenton I will look in on her and report any significant developments to you.

I understand that, now the court has adjudicated on her condition and the period of assessment is complete, you will be able to visit her at the hospital and I suggest that you contact the hospital administration to arrange for such a visit.

With every good wish,
Phyllis Greenacre.

Sister Dorothea told me later that she was left worried and fearful for the future. It seemed to her, she said, "that a light was fading and that the world would be a darker place when it was eventually extinguished".

There were no mirrors in Trenton and, while vanity was not one of my weaknesses, I had always dressed in a conservative fashion and avoided the use of any makeup to my face, except for a little powder perhaps. However, it was not unusual to catch sight of a person in a mirror or in a shop-front window and recognize who that person was; a sense of physical self-image was important.

With Sister Dorothea's description offered her by Dr. Greenacre, I became suddenly aware that I was no longer that person I recognized before. Of course, I was aware as I looked down at my body, I could see my sore and swollen knee, I could see my thinness and my loss of weight, but I had lost that overall three-dimensional subconscious image of myself.

I had though discovered one mirror. In the crafts room, where inmates were allowed to go to experience the therapeutic benefits of practicing needlecraft and painting, there stood a small office in one corner of the space. It was a bare room except for a small desk and chair where records were kept up to date, but inside that room was a full-length mirror. I had seen it used when the orderly helping with a piece of work, perhaps dress making, would allow them to try on their new garment and then go into the office to have a full-length view of the garment being worn.

I went to that room in the evening after Sister Dorothea had regaled me with Dr. Greenacre's observations of my physical condition. It was close to the ward where I slept and so aroused no suspicion when I left and went down the corridor a short way. The door was rarely locked and I slipped in, pressing my back against it as I closed it behind me. The evenings were light and so I could see around me perfectly well. The door of the office was unlocked too and I went inside.

I had looked down at the floor as I presented myself in front of that full-length mirror, then closed my eyes. As I looked up and stared at this being who was looking back at me, the shock was profound. This was not a person or a body I recognized. The hair was unkempt and straggly, the body slouched and bent forward, it was so thin that the inmate's uniform hung from the skeleton like a shroud.

I just stared for a long while. Then I undid the buttons at the front of the uniform and allowed the garment to slip to the floor. And stepped out of my underwear; I was naked. The sense of shock multiplied in me. My skeleton was clearly visible and my flesh hung from it like old discarded rags. My hip and knee had been so damaged that the whole side of my body seemed foreshortened and bent.

For the first time in years I was able to look at my face directly and saw just this distorted mask, a sallow complexion, the jawline and cheek bones standing in stark relief, the mouth shrunken and pursed without teeth to give them shape, eyes sunken within sockets that seemed like a bottomless pit, with barely any flesh to bring relief to this skull.

As I watched this other person stooped in front of me, I could feel the tears begin to run down my face. I stood and I cried in the deep solitude I felt, knowing that I was unrecognizable to anyone from my former life, as Annie Elizabeth Maher.

CHAPTER 48

Continuing to Fight

NOTWITHSTANDING SISTER DOROTHEA'S concerns for my future, I was beginning to settle into a way of living that was tolerable. My motivation was, not least, because I wanted the courts to reconsider my case and have me released.

I had deliberately feigned my own insanity for periods when I was aware that the medical staff had designs on my body. They had wanted to experiment with further surgical procedures, and I was committed to not allowing this to happen. I had tried to reason with medical staff, but there seemed no way of overcoming Dr. Cotton's influence and dogma.

My strategy was simple: to behave in such an aggressive and difficult way that they would understand any attempt to operate on me again would be fraught with difficulty. Now that family visits had been allowed, I gambled that they would not risk any further possible injury to me; I already had injuries to my hip and knee that made walking difficult and bruises and abrasions all over my body. However, I did not underestimate the force of their explanation, that had been used frequently about patients like me: "Well of course they are insane and these wounds are self-inflicted".

My strategy worked easily; whenever I was approached by any member of the medical team, I would become very noisy and behave erratically, implying violent outbursts. At other times, when I was with fellow inmates and ward orderlies, I was able to relax and even enjoy some of the pastimes offered to inmates. The sewing group was the first that I joined and I soon recalled all of the skills that my mother had taught me and that I had learned over the years in working on my and Georgiana's clothes. It was so gratifying to be able to work with people and to help people again.

The orderly who organized this therapeutic activity for the group was called Alice; she seemed grateful for my help in managing and supporting the work of the patients. We would sit together and chat between sessions and I must declare that it was so good to have intelligent conversation once again.

After a little persuasion, Alice agreed to do one more service for me even at the risk to her own employment. She would act as mail clerk and smuggle letters in and out for me. That meant my giving her home address in Trenton for replies to my correspondence; she would then bring any incoming mail to me when next she was on duty. I shared with Alice Joseph's joke; "Shhh ... Dr. Cotton may be listening": We laughed.

I cannot begin to describe what a profound impact this had on me and my sense of wellbeing. For the first time in four years I found myself able to smile; the intrigue and the tension that it introduced for Alice and me generated part of the excitement; it was a sense of "beating the system".

Of course, I wrote first to Sister Dorothea. It was a short letter, just to make that initial contact and invite her to write back to me at Alice's address. I needed some funds too, so that Alice did not bear any of the cost in serving as my postal service.

I heard back from her in just 10 days. Alice brought the handwritten envelope in to work and slipped it to me when nobody was watching. I excused myself to visit the bathroom and sat there in a cubicle fumbling to open the letter. Sister Dorothea had gone further than I had anticipated and had written to other members of the family and to some friends to tell them of my new communication arrangements. Within a few months I had letters from Joseph, from my other sibling-nun, Sister Ambrose, in Kent and from Annie Hall my neighbor in Long Branch.

Now I knew that the subterfuge worked I took one final step in my bid to question the practices at Trenton; I wrote to my old friend Benjamin Bolseau Bobbitt (Bobby). It was a hard letter to write. The last that Bobby had heard of me was when I had been arrested and incarcerated as a lunatic at Trenton. My introduction had to be very slow and detailed so that he could grasp the enormity of the injustice done to me. I left it at that so that I could await his reply and judge his reaction before proposing what, together, we might do about it.

It was some weeks before his reply came through on Alice's secret delivery service. Bobby, from his reaction, was clearly a bit taken aback by the claims I made in my letter to him. He started by quoting from the materials readily available and published elsewhere about Dr. Cotton's work and the accolades awarded him both at home and overseas. He didn't at any stage in his letter say that he didn't believe me, but asked if I had more detail.

In my reply, mailed by Alice only 2 days later, I avoided any comment about my position but instead pointed him in the direction of other similar situations where Dr. Cotton, Trenton and/or members of the medical staff were being questioned on their practices. Those examples were not too hard to find. The cases of Howard Pierce, Lyndon P. Smith, James A. Hendrickson, Mrs. Frank W. French and then the case of the distinguished lawyer and politician Dr. James R. Nugent.

In all of these cases patients were claiming malpractice against the hospital or Dr. Cotton. In some cases, they claimed that this was perpetrated with the active collusion of some of their family members.

Bobby did not publish any of this, as far as I could tell, however the scrutiny of what was going on at Trenton became more intense with each passing month.

CHAPTER 49

Look on the Bright Side

DR. COTTON'S REFERENCE to the Bright Committee "framing him", related to another body of complaint that had emerged from a very early point in Dr. Cotton's stewardship of Trenton. As the months and years rolled by, these complaints grew into a cacophony of sound that was too difficult to ignore.

As early as February 1915, the "Asbury Park Press" in New Jersey reported the case of Howard Pearce who, Dr. Cotton told his father in a letter, was seriously ill and confined to bed. It was later revealed that Howard had died three or four weeks before the letter was written.

Then there was Lyndon P. Smith of Princeton who on August 20th 1918 set out a Bill of Complaint filed at the Mercer County Branch of the Supreme Court and sought to recover $10,000 in damages against

Dr. Cotton and members of the medical staff. Smith alleged that "his detention at the hospital damaged his health, credit and standing in his own community and that he was detained against his will". The response of the clinicians named, Dr. H. Cotton, Dr. Edward Funkhauser, Dr. R. Grant Barry, James T. Blake, a supervisor, and Harry Garra, Thomas Deaton and Thomas B. Taylor, attendants at the hospital, was that Smith was insane.

"Smith was committed to the hospital on the initiative of his wife and that he was subject to no force except what his mental condition demanded to restrain him. An examination of the patient showed that Smith was insane and not entitled to his liberty."

"The patient is mad" was to prove an almost incontrovertible defense when the complainant had previously been categorized as insane.

In 1921, a case was brought by James A. Hendrickson who was suing his brother for conspiracy to have him illegally confined to Trenton Hospital. Hendrickson, a graduate of Princeton University and Columbia Law School and the son of the Supreme Court Justice Charles E. Hendrickson, alleged that a skin disease was the cause of his mental problems. Dr. Cotton was credited with curing the insanity ordering that Hendrickson should have several teeth extracted (due to focal infection); Dr. Cotton had diagnosed the case and said that the condition of his teeth (not the skin disease) was responsible for his state.

Dr. Cotton found himself again the subject of court action in January 1924. One of his patients, Mrs. French, with the assistance of a sympathetic nurse, had escaped from Trenton Hospital by making a rope from her bed-sheets, and escaping down it through a second-floor window. Mrs. French then claimed that her mother, Dr. Cotton and W. W. Stephenson, the controller of the Mutual Life Insurance Company, were part of a conspiracy to illegally detain her after submitting her to morphine injections without her consent. In echoes of my case, her mother told the press her daughter's trouble was liquor, "you know the sort of liquor we are getting nowadays".

Here was the conundrum for the authorities; Dr. Cotton was able to produce the evidence that surgical intervention in the treatment of the insane produced some astounding results. The contemporary methods of restraining patients, locking them up from society and thus isolating them, with little hope of release, was hugely expensive and saw thousands of Americans in worse than jail-like conditions in what seemed to be an escalating crisis. Dr. Cotton was the new messiah in the treatment of the mentally ill; his reputation across the country was outstandingly regarded and his reputation internationally even better. After his lecture tours of Europe, for example, mental hospital clinicians were so impressed with his results that they too adopted his surgical approach. For example, in Birmingham, U.K. surgical intervention was adopted and set the scene for decades of such treatments. Dr. Thomas Chivers Graves, in charge of both Rubery Hill Mental Hospital and the nearby Hollymoor Hospital, took Cotton's theory and methodology even further arguing that he had introduced the latest scientific advances, namely Dr. Cotton's scientific advances, into the treatment of mental disorders.

Cotton had the support of his Board and of some of the most significant academic experts in the field, especially Adolf Meyer.

Senator William Bright, leader of the Republican majority in the New Jersey legislature, formed a committee to investigate waste and fraud in the state government. After a few months, their attention was drawn to the Commission for Institutions and Agencies that ran both prisons and mental hospitals. Burdette Lewis, the Commissioner, had doubled his department's budget in six years and therefore was a prime target for the Bright Committee.

This led to an investigation into how hospitals were funded and in a very short period of time began to take what turned into an avalanche of complaints about Trenton Hospital in general and Dr. Cotton's methodology in particular.

Dr. Cotton was called to appear before the committee to face some of these allegations. One of the most telling was of Mrs. Quackenbush, an elderly woman who had been released from Trenton only a few days before taking an axe to her feeble-minded daughter. What followed was an increasingly focused investigation of the whole Trenton culture. The committee had not yet questioned the new surgical approach and indeed criticized Cotton for not having removed Mrs. Quackenbush's teeth and tonsils before releasing her, assuming that this action would necessarily have effected a cure.

The committee continued to take evidence from former patients, from staff and former employees. Over one particular weekend two female patients were found dead, their bodies suffering a mass of contusions. This prompted an outcry and calls for an investigation into brutality at the hospital. This was not helped when, before the Bright Committee the following Wednesday, Cotton stalked out of the room apparently in a deranged state. He had suffered a breakdown. The Board came to his rescue and secreted him away from Trenton in an attempt to ride out the storm. Then they decided to respond to the allegations made by and to the Bright Committee in a robust rebuttal. This had the impact of splitting the committee, leading to argument and disagreement; and progressively the committee descended into chaos until they turned their focus upon other issues. Dr. Cotton had survived the scrutiny and the criticism.

Dr. Meyer had tried to engage Mrs. Cotton on the topic of Dr. Greenacre's report; since she was so close to Dr. Cotton's thinking and understood his devotion to his work, he felt she might be able to help. Mrs. Cotton responded to his letter to her on January 2nd, 1926.

Trenton, New Jersey.

Dear Dr. Meyer,

Thank you for your very kind letter. I appreciate it.

I am afraid you misunderstood our not accepting your and Mrs. Meyer's most friendly and kind invitation to stay with you. So, I shall have to be frank. Not for many years have I allowed myself the pleasure of staying overnight in the home of a friend where there were small children. Possibly I would now be justified in breaking that rule – but I have not yet done so. Added to this was the feeling on Dr. Cotton's part that were we with you we would be taking too much of your time, at a time when you were particularly busy. These were our feelings and it is unfortunate that we may have seemed unfriendly when we meant only to be friendly in the truest sense.

In regard to the work of going over the report – I believe that would have progressed and something good would have been accomplished had the conferences been alone between you and my husband. It was the presence of a third person (Dr. Greenacre) that made the situation what it was, I think.

After his years of experience and tremendous labors, you could not expect him to be told by a young woman of limited experience that his work was all wrong – and that he did the patients more harm than good – without developing on his part an attitude of defense.

You – by yourself – would never have made such a statement.

We came home – not with any idea on Dr. Cotton's part of being unwilling to go farther or of closing the matter but because he thought he would like to talk it over with Dr. Raycroft and I thought a little recess would be for the best. I do not feel in a hurry and time does so much – bit-by-bit progress may be made.

Dr. Cotton's work is the most important thing in life to him. Who knows that as well as I? It is his <u>misfortune</u> that it has been so.

Looking over it all and knowing the price paid – it has been a big price in more ways than one –still, I see the gain to the cause.

On many sides and from many sources one sees that the physical care of the patient is being given more attention and whether he ever gets the credit for it or not – that has been brought about by his work.

Credit is relatively a small thing.

Though I and he differ many times as to ways and means – even to the point of bitterness – I do believe in the value to the patient of detoxification. I cannot help believing – having followed every step of the way and having seen in myself – my children and my friends – aside from patients – the happy results.

In regards to the colon removals – you know that this was long a source of great distress to me and a topic on which my husband and I finally were unable to speak.

But I respected his attitude and lived in hope and now my hopes have been rewarded and I see him learning new methods and ways of treating the colon by physiotherapy etc. so that only in extreme cases will he in future resort to its removal. His eagerness to go always on and try new ways wins my admiration.

For this reason, it seems to me any report made could not be final – there is still so much to be done!

As to statistics – the discrepancy it seems was due to the fact that these were not made by the same method and therefore should not be compared.

He would be perfectly willing to accept the figures obtained by your method provided they were compared with figures computed on the same basis.

Since coming home, he has had a statistician from the State House go over the hundred cases in 1922 and the result was thirty-two recoveries.

Also Dr. Cotton has talked with Dean Eisenhart, assistant head of the Mathematics department at Princeton.

Dr. Cotton will himself write you of all this – I only speak of it to show you that he also desires facts.

I am sure you will be willing for future talks, and things do work out.

With warm regards from us both to you and Mrs. Meyer.

Sincerely,

Della R. Cotton.

Dr. Cotton did, in a way, achieve some credit, even though he never returned to his role as Director. Instead the Board made him Medical Director Emeritus and appointed him Director of research work, but never again was he to step into the patients' living quarters.

Dr. Cotton died suddenly on May 8th and it was reported widely in the press: "The Salt Lake Tribune", "The Princeton Daily Clarion" and the "Courier-News" in Bridgewater New Jersey which devoted a whole column to his death and his career. The detail offered by some was that he had complained of feeling unwell shortly after luncheon at his club and had gone to the pantry to prepare a remedy for himself and that he dropped dead there of heart failure.

CHAPTER 50

Follow the Money

I HAD ACCUMULATED considerable wealth while working in New York, and had bought property and land in Long Branch. These generated an income over a long period of time to add to the generous bequest from Georgiana in her will.

During my committal hearing an assessment was made of my assets. It was one of the responsibilities of my Guardians that income and expenditure that changed those assets should be recorded and a regular statement of accounts should be presented to the Court.

As the initial Guardian appointed by the Court, Margaret Higgins did find the problem of having systems in place that could record that income and expenditure difficult to manage. As a result, income and expenditure were not recorded effectively, reports were not made to the Court and she was eventually relieved of her duties.

The role was then taken on by Harry Truax, who had legal and accountancy skills and was much more able to manage the whole process.

On December 5th 1926, in Margaret Higgin's petition for Letters of Guardianship, she states that "Annie Maher has personal property to the value of $12,400 which consists of money deposited in a saving account in the Long Branch Trust Company amounting to approximately $11,000; money due from an endowment policy in the New York Life Insurance Company which has a matured value of $900, and furniture in her home worth approximately $500".

I found this was markedly less than I might have thought given that, in 1903, my wealth and assets were quite considerable; I tended not to squander or to spend and I had a good eye for property, land and other investments. I had considerable savings, insurances and pension. That meant that I had a continuing income; my interest payments alone in 1928/29 amounted to $1,289. There were outgoings of course; in that same period charges were made against the income of $654.88.

By 1934, Margaret was clearly having problems keeping up with the requirement, as Guardian, to keep on top of the flow of my money.

In July of that year she asked the Court for a delay in the deadline for making a submission. She asked for a delay until September 7th but in fact was granted a delay until October 25th 1934. Margaret failed to meet that deadline too and the Court Order that followed read, "Your petitioner therefore prays that this Court may revoke the letters of guardianship heretofore granted to the said Margaret Higgins, as aforesaid, and remove her from said office: and for such other relief as may seem meet and just in the premises."

In fact, she had submitted a full set of accounts dated October 16th though they were not entered into the Court records until January 24th 1935. By February 21st Margaret was served with an Order to give a new surety required if her Guardianship was not to be revoked; she failed to comply. Margaret was ordered to attend before the Court on April 18th 1935 at 10 o'clock in the morning. There it was "Ordered that the letters of Guardianship granted to the said Margaret Higgins be and the same are hereby revoked and the said Margaret Higgins is hereby removed from her office as such guardian."

Harry Truax was ordered to replace her. And in his first report on the accounts on June 22nd 1935, he exonerated Margaret from any wrongdoing.

"Error in accounting of former Guardian, wherein the principal of the Fagan mortgage was given as $1,700 when in reality it is $1,600. This error was carried through previous accounts and shows a shortage of substantially the same amount in the account of May 1930 and the account of October 1934.

"It is difficult to make the former accounts balance with the known facts. A thorough investigation convinces this accountant that errors which appear in the former accounts were not errors of willful misrepresentation, but errors of failure to keep a good system of records."

Harry Truax diligently kept the accounts, sent reports to the Court on time and reported in a very detailed way.

CHAPTER 51

Twelve Good and Lawful Men

ON DECEMBER 15TH 1936, Harry Truax applied to the courts for a "commission in the nature of a writ de lunatico inquirendo may issue out of this court to inquire of the lunacy of the said Annie Maher." This was another opportunity for me to try to overturn the ruling that I was "insane"; if this failed, I did not know what I would do.

As a matter of routine, I and my nearest relatives, Sister Dorothea and our two cousins, Margaret and Josephine were routinely copied in to all these proceedings. This was to be a very significant event in my tragic life at Trenton and so the three of them said that they would attend the Hearing; only Sister Dorothea came.

This was to be a lengthy process and involved reviewing all the historic and current information as to my state of mind, and then this was presented to a Jury for consideration after which the Judge would rule.

I could not believe what I was reading as I pored over the documentation. It seemed to me that they were presenting the case in such a way that it would go unchallenged in the Court.

The Court took evidence from a number of key people, and what is of particular note here is the very strong similarity between these witness statements. It is possible that they were using a specific template provided for such purposes, or that there was a high degree of collusion between the people involved.

To give just one example, an Affidavit was submitted on September 24th 1936 by Dr. Robert G. Stone who had taken over as Medical Director from Dr. Cotton:

"1. I am a practicing physician licensed to practice in the state of New Jersey. 'I have been practicing for 30 years. I am now and have been for 6 years now past, Medical Director of the New Jersey State Hospital at Trenton, New Jersey and as such have had under my observation and care Annie Maher in a petition for commission of lunacy named.

"2. I have been one of the attending physicians to the said Annie Maher and have been well acquainted with her and have frequently discoursed with her and observed her behavior, words and actions, from time to time.

"3. According to the records of the New Jersey State Hospital, the said Annie Maher was committed to this institution by the Honorable Rulif V. Lawrence, then Judge of the Monmouth County Pleas Court on May 28th 1924.

"4. On September 15th 1936, I examined her and found her in an exceedingly nervous and excitable condition. Her physical condition is poor and she is subject to the possibility of a paralytic stroke. She is depressed and there is a senile change. Her ideas are of religion and she claims that some church has all her money. She is unable to care for herself, etc.

"5. As a result of my examination and of the statements made by the said Annie Maher, I concluded that she is suffering from a senile dementia and is deprived of her reason and understanding to a very great degree, and I believe the said Annie Maher is in no way capable of governing herself or her estate."

There were similar statements from Dr. John and Dr. M. Mras,

Dr. Clayton at least recorded the injuries I had suffered in Trenton; he included: "Her physical condition poor: crippled; injured to hip and knee; She was depressed and undergoing a senile change."

An Affidavit signed on November 9th 1936, by Dr. Harvey S. Brown, was identical in wording to those of Dr. John and Dr. M. Mras.

The final blow for me was on reading the last Affidavit signed on November 20th 1936, by Margaret Higgins, my cousin. Sister Dorothea said that Margaret seemed surprised, though I know not why, that her statement was read in open court; I think she felt guilty being portrayed as the person damning her cousin, and this is certainly how it felt. She explained to Dorothea that the proceedings had been initiated by Harry Truax and that he had just sent her the papers to have signed and witnessed; she had not really bothered to read them in detail, so familiar were the facts. Nonetheless, she would be the one to go down in history as finally signaling the approaching end of any hope of my release.

Her statement included, almost word for word, what had been said in the doctors' submissions: "Annie Maher is now and for the space of twelve years last past and upwards has been so deprived of her reason and understanding that she is rendered altogether unfit and unable to govern herself or to manage her affairs".

The petition was duly granted on December 15th 1936, and so it was to go to court, in front of a Jury of twelve good men, to reach a final determination as to my sanity.

"We have to say something", Sister Dorothea pleaded with me. "if the jury are presented with that level of evidence against you, then they will reach a wrong decision. We have to do something to present a counter argument".

There were three judges jointly appointed to manage the hearing, so that if one was absent the proceedings could continue. They were: "Henry D. Brinley Esquire, a Master in Chancery of New Jersey, Dr. Frank G. Strahan, a practicing physician of over 15 years last past, and Joseph J. Kiernan, Esquire, all of the city of Long Branch, County of Monmouth".

Just over a month later, the jurors had been identified by Sheriff George H. Roberts and summoned to appear at Freehold Courthouse, in the County of Monmouth and State of New Jersey at 10 a.m. on Monday January 18th 1937. The determination of my sanity would rely on the judgment of these twelve men: C. H. Roberson, Kenneth Cooper, Jamie McMahan, John Von Bargen, Samuel Rosengasten,

Joseph Du Bois, Thomas Moher, Daniel Shock, William Colton, Joseph Levy, Max Helman and John Ratti.

In the Courthouse the Jurors stood and the oath was read to them.

After our conversation, Sister Dorothea had met with Harry Truax, as my legal Guardian, to argue that a great injustice would be done if the 'witness' statements were not challenged in front of the Jury.

With Truax's support and having checked all of the wording with me, Sister Dorothea's evidence written to the Court was ready. We worked on it for a long time to try to get the tone absolutely right. At least someone from my family was speaking up for me. Her statement read out to the Court was as follows:

"Sister Dorothea (Mary Maher), ordained on May 29th 1888 in Zanesville Ohio in the Order of St. Dominic at St Mary's of the Springs, of full age, being fully sworn according to law, upon her oath deposes and says:

1. I am the sister of the aforesaid Annie Elizabeth Maher named in the foregoing petition. I have heard the same and know the contents thereof, and the matters and things therein set forth are not true.

2. The said Annie Maher is in my mind not a lunatic, or suffering some form of dementia. She is able to converse in a restrained and coherent fashion and seems well able to account for and to manage her own affairs. To illustrate this, we have corresponded at length during the period of her incarceration and I have this available should the Court wish to peruse it.

3. Annie Elizabeth Maher, having been arrested for allegedly being drunk and disorderly, was summarily committed to Trenton Asylum, with no efforts made to analyze the cause of her symptoms and behavior.

4. She has been traumatized by the treatment given to her there including the brutal extraction of her teeth and tonsils and physical assault resulting in actual and serious injury to her person.

5. She has subsequently been fearful for her life at the hands of the medical staff at the Asylum. This has been most apparent in her aggressive behavior when approached by members of that medical staff which has been wrongly interpreted as a manifestation of mental illness and dementia.

6. In other situations, with other patients, some nurses and orderlies, and with other of her friends with whom she has corresponded, she has shown herself to be quite capable.

The jury pondered for only a brief time before re-emerging to give their verdict on my sanity. I must say that their summary of my mental state was not a surprise to me given the weight of medical and other evidence that had been put before them.

They concluded that:

> "The said Annie Maher, at the time of taking this inquisition is a lunatic and of unsound mind, and does not enjoy lucid intervals, so that she is not capable of governing herself, her lands and tenements, goods and chattels, and that she has been in the sure state of lunacy for the space of twelve years last past and upwards, and the Jurors aforesaid upon their respective or affirmations aforesaid."

I was to be cast into Trenton's embrace for the rest of my life.

After the verdict, the family were able to visit but only Sister Dorothea came to see me; I think Margaret in particular, but also Josephine, just found it too hard. Dorothea tried to ensure that I had everything physical that I needed and any extraneous medical expenses covered and she would buy me clothing for example. But in the end those visits stopped.

In a letter, written to me by Dorothea's Reverend Mother, she explained, in the gentlest and most reassuring of terms, that my sister had suffered a stroke and, in the short term, until she was sufficiently recovered, she would be unable to write or visit me.

One classic moment that will remain with me forever, and was the last time that I saw Sister Dorothea, she was sitting by my bedside while I dozed gently; a nurse, not one I had seen before, came in to attend to me. Seeing Sister Dorothea, she began, as if she needed it, to offer an explanation of my condition; Sister Dorothea did not have the heart to stop her. She explained about my insanity and dementia and that I would not understand anything that was said to me, because my brain was irrevocably damaged. When she had concluded, and seemed to be awaiting some sort of response from Sister Dorothea, I sat bolt upright, looked at the nurse squarely in the face and said clearly and loudly: "There's nothing wrong with me!"

Dorothea and I looked at each other and smiled.

EPILOGUE

MARCH 12TH 2019, less than 4 weeks short of the 70th anniversary of Annie's death, at a cemetery in Trenton, I stand at an unmarked grave; the plot is known simply as Section O, Avenue G, Grave 51. Since I opened this story, I have traveled a long way with my Great Aunt, Annie Elizabeth Maher, who is buried here. Clearly, I have learned a lot, perhaps as much about me as her. We coincided on this earth for less than two years and I never met her but somehow, now, I feel very close to her; I think I feel her hand on my shoulder.

When I first went to Freehold New Jersey to the county archive to enquire about the woman mentioned in that passenger manifest, I was met by a bemused clerk. Seemingly reluctant she went off to look in the records and, on her return, even more reluctantly suggested "we do have only one Annie Elizabeth Maher; but she is only yours if she was a lunatic".

Like me you will have heard her voice leaping out at you from the events and stories told here since that prologue. Perhaps she and her story have touched you too.

I was only 23 months old when Annie died here in America. It has taken 70 years for any member of her family to visit her and all I can do is to bring a simple bunch of spring flowers and stoop to lay them on her grave.

As the story unfolded I was reminded of the telling sentence in Terry Pratchett's book, "Going Postal". *"Do you not know that a woman is not dead while her name is still spoken?"*

Now though I can speak softly to her knowing that she will hear. It will be the first time in many years that anyone has stood here and spoken her name. "Annie, Annie. There there, at peace now. You have not been forgotten. The sadness of your passing, the pain and torment that you suffered, is shared now, and you can rest easy. And your life Annie; your life is inspirational. Your strength and your courage and your resilience a credit to you and a credit to our family.

"There will be people of my generation and of my children's generation, and their children, who will be inspired by the example you have set, who will take strength in knowing that, whatever the circumstances and the background, they can make a good life for themselves, grow as a person and bring light to the world, as you did. All they need is to be strong and resolute, determined, hardworking, loyal, and that will lead to untold rewards. Your name, Annie Elizabeth Maher, will go on being spoken as your story is told and retold; you are alive and with us always."

I stand and stare at that bare patch of earth, now adorned with simple flowers and I ponder about a gravestone. But a marble stone would seem so out of place in the starkness of this grid of otherwise unmarked burial plots. Instead, these lines stand as the monument to the extraordinary life of a remarkable woman: Annie Elizabeth Maher.

As I step away to join the kind people who had helped me in my search for Annie, I do not try to wipe away the tears that flow down my face.

FOOTNOTES TO HISTORY

Dr. Phyllis Greenacre's Report

Though Dr. Phyllis Greenacre's report had concluded that, "There is practically no evidence of positive results obtained by detoxification methods", contrary to all of Dr. Cotton's assertions, her report had been well and truly suppressed until rediscovered in a locked cupboard in Trenton by Professor Gilbert Honigfeld.

Harry Truax

The role of Guardian was assigned to Harry Truax of Elberon on June 22nd 1935. He retained that role and, except for a brief period, remained Annie's Guardian to the point when she was finally adjudged to be profoundly insane.

Annie's money eventually ran out and remaining assets were given away to debtors in part payment of residual debts. That having been completed, Harry Truax was eventually discharged from all further duties on May 15th 1941.

Sister Dorothea

Sister Dorothea Maher had a distinguished career as a nun and as a teacher. Following her stroke, she spent her last 10 years being confined and cared for in Mohun Hall, at Mother House in Columbus where she died on February 4th 1962 aged 93. She was the last of that generation of the Maher family.

Annie Elizabeth Maher

Annie died in Burlington, New Jersey, U.S.A. when she was 89 years old. She was an inmate of the N.J. State Hospital at Trenton for 25 years. She died of stomach cancer.

Annie is buried in St. Mary's Cemetery in Trenton. It is located at 1200 Cedar Avenue in Hamilton, N.J. zip 08610. The plot is Section O, Avenue G, Grave 51.

REFERENCES

- Cotton, Dr. Henry A: "The Defective Delinquent and Insane; the relation of focal infections to their causation, treatment and prevention" ISBN 9787-0-260-38268-9. Reprinted and copyright by F.B.&C. Ltd. in 2017 from the original text published by Princeton University Press in 1921

- Scull, Prof. Andrew: "Madhouse: A Tragic Tale of Megalomania and Modern Medicine" ISBN 978-0-300-12670-9 first published in 2005 Yale University Press

- Honigfeld, Prof. Gilbert. "Dead End: The Lives of Henry Cotton". Seattle W. A., Amazon Books, 2009 ISBN: 978-1442106857

Research Bibliography

- Robinson, Scribner & Brights, Attorneys for the Petitioner, The Broadway Surface Railroad Company (Ed.). (1885). *New York Supreme Court, General Term - First Department* (Vol. 1). New York, N.Y.: Douglas Taylor, Law Printer. Doi:

- "The Season: an Annual Record of Society in New York, Brooklyn and Vicinity" Edited by Charles H. Crandall: White, Stokes & Allen 1883 New York

- "Confessions of a Social Secretary (Classic Reprint)" By Corinne Lowe Publishers: Harper Brothers Corinne Martin Lowe, Forgotten Books Copyright 1916

- "The Gilded Age in New York, 1870-1910" Esther Crain: Publishers: Black Dog & Leventhal. ISBN: 13 9780316353663

- "Season of Splendor: The Court of Mrs. Astor in Gilded Age New York" Copyright Greg King Published John Wiley and Sons ISBN-10: 0470185694

- "Long Branch People and Places" Gabrielan, Randall. Published: Arcadia Publishing **ISBN**: 0946538204

- "Entertaining a Nation, The Career of Long Branch" by Federal Writers' Project of the Works Progress Administration of the State of New Jersey; Federal Writers' Project Long Branch, N.J. 1940

Photo References

- Alice Austen House Aliceausten.org

- "Through the Years, 1825 – 1950: One Hundred and Twenty Fifth Anniversary" Author: Arnold, Constable & Co. New York 1950. New York Public Library

- "Prohibition on the North Jersey Shore" Matthew R. Linderoth The History Press Charleston SC 29403, 2010

- "American Art Directory, Volume 9" Contributor American Federation of Arts Publisher R R Bowker 1911 ISBN 10: 1357166501

- Letters to and from Edward Gay Gay family papers B-G circa 1865-1920, Box 1 Folder 11 Digitized

ANNIE ELIZABETH MAHER FAMILY TREE

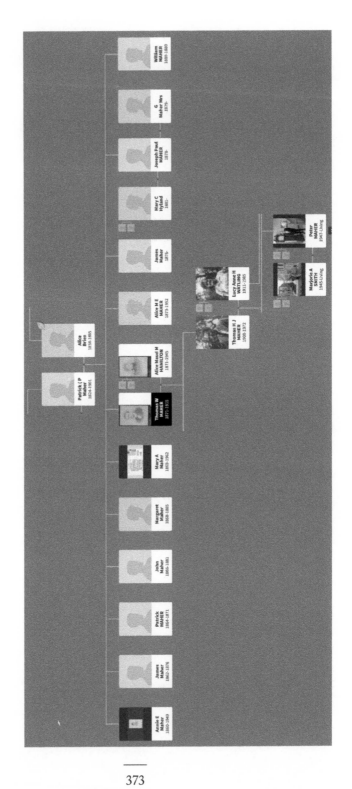

Portrait of Annie Elizabeth Maher